"Are you accusing me of being a lecher?"

Chase complained good-naturedly.

"I haven't met a fly-boy yet who wasn't, Captain," she returned evenly. "Even when they're wounded and just coming out of anesthesia, they're reaching for you."

A chuckle rumbled through Chase's chest. "Can't blame the guys. You're a beautiful, desirable lady."

Rachel colored fiercely. Ordinarily, she could handle a compliment, but when it came from Chase, her womanly instincts responded differently, scaring her, yet beckoning her at the same time. "You're probably the worst of them all," she muttered.

He smiled at her but said nothing as he slid his hand along her shoulder.

Heat spread through Rachel, and she began drowning in his very male smile. Suddenly, Chase seemed dangerous—almost more dangerous than the enemy they were trying to evade.

Dear Reader,

With all due fanfare, this month Silhouette *Special Edition* is pleased to bring you *Dawn of Valor*, Lindsay McKenna's latest and long-awaited *LOVE AND GLORY* novel. We trust that the unique flavor of this landmark volume—the dramatic saga of cocky fly-boy Chase Trayhern and feisty army nurse Rachel McKenzie surviving love and enemy fire in the Korean War—will prove well worth your wait.

Joining Lindsay McKenna in this exceptional, action-packed month are five more sensational authors: Barbara Faith, with an evocative, emotional adoption story, *Echoes of Summer*; Natalie Bishop, with the delightful, damned-if-you-do, damned-if-you-don't (fall in love, that is) *Downright Dangerous*; Marie Ferrarella, with a fast-talking blonde and a sly, sexy cynic on a goofily glittering treasure hunt in *A Girl's Best Friend*; Lisa Jackson, with a steamy, provocative case of "mistaken" identity in *Mystery Man*; and Kayla Daniels, with a twisty, tantalizing tale of duplicity and desire in *Hot Prospect*.

All six novels are bona fide page-turners, featuring a compelling cast of characters in a marvelous array of adventures of the heart. We hope you'll agree that each and every one of them is a stimulating, sensitive edition worthy of the label *special*.

From all the authors and editors of Silhouette *Special Edition*,

Best wishes.

LINDSAY McKENNA
Dawn of Valor

Silhouette Special Edition

Published by Silhouette Books New York

America's Publisher of Contemporary Romance

To the brave women and men
who sacrificed in Korea
And to Gene and Marcia Margolis, longtime friends.

SILHOUETTE BOOKS
300 East 42nd St., New York, N.Y. 10017

DAWN OF VALOR

ISBN: 0-373-09649-6

First Silhouette Books printing February 1991

Printed in the U.S.A.

Books by Lindsay McKenna

Silhouette Special Edition

Captive of Fate #82
*Heart of the Eagle #338
*A Measure of Love #377
*Solitaire #397
Heart of the Tiger #434
+ A Question of Honor #529
+ No Surrender #535
+ Return of a Hero #541
Come Gentle the Dawn #568
+ Dawn of Valor #649

*Kincaid trilogy
+ LOVE AND GLORY series

Silhouette Intimate Moments

Love Me Before Dawn #44

Silhouette Desire

Chase the Clouds #75
Wilderness Passion #134
Too Near the Fire #165
Texas Wildcat #184
Red Tail #298

Silhouette Books

Silhouette Christmas Stories 1990
"Always and Forever"

LINDSAY McKENNA

spent three years serving her country as a meteorologist in the U.S. Navy, so much of her knowledge about the military people and practices featured in her novels comes from direct experience. In addition, she spends a great deal of time researching each book, whether it be at the Pentagon or at military bases, extensively interviewing key personnel. She views the military as her second family and hopes that her novels will help dispel the "unfeeling-machine" image that haunts it, allowing readers glimpses of the flesh-and-blood people who comprise the services.

Lindsay is also a pilot. She and her husband of fifteen years, both avid "rock hounds" and hikers, live in Ohio.

LOVE AND GLORY: BOOK IV

The Trayherns

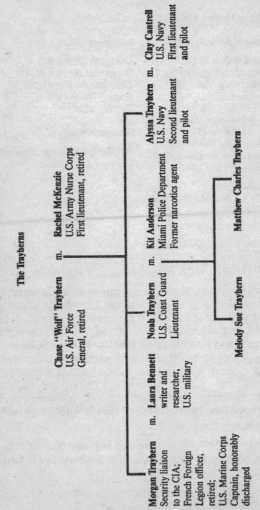

Chase "Wolf" Trayhern
U.S. Air Force
General, retired

m.

Rachel McKenzie
U.S. Army Nurse Corps
First lieutenant, retired

Morgan Trayhern
Security liaison
to the CIA;
French Foreign
Legion officer,
retired;
U.S. Marine Corps
Captain, honorably
discharged

m.

Laura Bennett
writer and
researcher,
U.S. military

Noah Trayhern
U.S. Coast Guard
Lieutenant

m.

Kit Anderson
Miami Police Department
Former narcotics agent

Alyssa Trayhern
U.S. Navy
Second lieutenant
and pilot

m.

Clay Cantrell
U.S. Navy
First lieutenant
and pilot

Melody Sue Trayhern

Matthew Charles Trayhern

Prologue

"Merry Christmas!" Standing in the living room doorway, Rachel Trayhern captured the attention of her three grown children and their respective spouses. Two large, flat packages wrapped in holly-patterned paper and garlanded with shiny ribbons balanced precariously in her arms. Her husband, Chase, came up behind her, bearing a third package.

Seated on the sofa, Aly, their youngest child and only daughter, laughed and clapped her hands, her short red hair glinting copper mischief beneath a gaily decorated lamp. "Mom, Dad, you really outdid yourselves this time! Look at the size of those gifts, gang. We're gonna make out like fat rats this Christmas!"

Clay Cantrell, Aly's husband, grinned and shook his head. "You're such a kid, Aly."

Aly stood to relieve her mother of the bulky parcels. "And you love it, Cantrell. If it weren't for me, you'd get serious about life."

"Thanks, Aly. Put them on the coffee table, would you?" Rachel instructed as she took a place on the couch and smoothed her dark green slacks. Chase joined her, draping a proprietary arm around her shoulders.

Chase's dark hair was liberally sprinkled with silver, yet the lighter strands made his deeply bronzed features more handsome than ever, Rachel thought. Years as a general in the air force had kept his posture straight and proud, his frame as lean as when she'd met him in Korea in 1951. Memories of their war-torn first encounters washed over her, and she gave her husband a secret look, filled with love for him alone, before she addressed the assembled family.

"Your father and I felt that we should all get together for at least one Christmas." Rachel's gaze moved to her left, where Noah, her younger son, sat with his wife, red-haired Kit, and their two young children. "We're so happy you could all make it. We of all people know how hard it is for military folks to coordinate a trip like this. Thank you for coming," she said, her voice suddenly husky with emotion.

Signaling both his presence and his support, Chase squeezed Rachel's shoulder. In his eyes, his wife was beautiful, hardly showing her age. Her hair was still a sleek black cap, cut short to enhance the natural loveliness of her features. Just that morning he'd complained that he had enough gray hair for both of them—and for once she'd agreed with something he'd said, without an argument.

Now he looked at Morgan, their oldest son, and his demure wife, Laura. "For some years now," he began, "our entire family has undergone a trial by fire that your mother and I never could have envisioned." His throat constricted with feeling as he saw Morgan's harsh features tauten.

No, the memories would never go away entirely. The shadow of suspected treason had nearly ruined Morgan's life—had, in fact, hung dark and heavy over all the Trayherns, nearly blotting out a two-hundred-year family tradition of pride and patriotism. Chase and Rachel's firstborn had finally been exonerated of all charges relating to his devastating experience in Vietnam, but the emotional price he'd paid—in lost years of youth and innocence, years spent in doubt and dishonor—had been steep. Now he ran a security firm in Washington, D.C., and worked with the C.I.A. and other branches of the government concerned with national security. He'd gotten an honorable discharge and, with his back pay, was able to start his own firm.

"Getting all of you together means more than we could ever tell you. Because of what happened to Morgan, Aly and Noah suffered much tougher going than they would have otherwise." He gazed at the other children. They, too, had paid a price as they attempted to hold their heads high, face down prejudice and continue the Trayhern tradition of military service to their country. "Fortunately, in running this gauntlet, you each found a partner you could love, one who believed in you more than in the so-called truth the press and Pentagon were spreading about Trayherns."

Rachel nodded in tacit agreement on what was most important in life—values she and Chase had attempted to instill in all three of their children. She thought she saw tears form in Morgan's eyes and watched as blond, petite Laura reached over, her slender fingers covering Morgan's large, dark hand, sunburned from years spent overseas. Thank God Laura had come into her son's life. Without her, Morgan might still be lost to them, might never have come home.

She felt Chase gently stroke her shoulder, and she returned to the present, to the family gathering. "Since Morgan's ordeal has finally ended," she said, "we wanted to celebrate the family. A sort of victory celebration, if you will," she added quietly. She pointed to the three large packages in gay Christmas paper. "Over the past year, your father and I went through the boxes of photographs we've taken since the time you were born." She smiled gamely, tears once more threatening. "You're all so wonderful, and you've made us so proud."

Chase gallantly took over Rachel's explanation. "Your mother and I sorted the photos, put them in order, noted names and dates and places, and made copies of them for all of you. We thought you might want to share them with your own families now—your children . . . and their children."

Recovering her composure, Rachel winked at Chase. "We even found some photographs of the two of us when we met in Korea during the war. I don't think any of you ever saw them."

"Wonderful!" Aly clapped her hands again.

"That's great, Mom," Noah added eagerly, taking his two-year-old son from Kit.

"Yeah," Morgan said with a twinkle in his eye, all traces of sadness gone now. "We never did get the *full* story on how you two met."

"*Collided* would be a more appropriate word," Chase said wryly, sharing another secret smile with Rachel.

Rachel rose, moving to the table. She picked up one of the wrapped photo albums. "Well, let me get these distributed first. Fair enough?"

An enthusiastic chorus of voices met her ears.

Approaching Noah, she handed him the package. His military-short black hair and large, intelligent gray eyes made him a heart stopper in Rachel's opinion. Women had always been drawn to his handsomeness, and later to his crisp Coast Guard uniform; she was glad that Kit valued Noah's sensitivity even more. It was an essential, if rare, trait in a man—one she'd had to coax out of Chase over the years.

She smiled at her younger son, who held the package as if it were a fragile, priceless gift. "Thanks, Mom," he whispered.

Rachel gave the second package to Aly, who immediately began to rip off the wrapping. Clay rolled his eyes, and Rachel ruffled the short red hair her daughter wore in a becoming pixie style just as she had as a child.

The last package was for Morgan. "Last, but not least, to our firstborn son . . ." She kissed his recently shaven cheek.

Murmuring his thanks, Morgan gently placed the gift in Laura's lap. "Go ahead," he encouraged his wife, "you open it."

"But it's your album," Laura protested softly.

"Ours," he corrected, sliding his arm around her to give her a hug.

Chase's gaze never left Rachel as she distributed the gifts. When she returned to the couch and sat down, his arm automatically, possessively, went around her.

Chase, Rachel thought, was her bulwark of strength, allowing her to reach out to their children, to give them the love and support they'd needed to grow, to grow up, and to struggle through so much hardship. As cries of joy and surprise rang through the living room, Rachel leaned against Chase, enjoying their children's responses to the albums. A fierce love for her husband welled up within her, and she leaned to kiss him quickly but warmly. His eyes sparkled with surprise—and a decidedly masculine promise of things to come.

"Mom," Aly broke in breathlessly, jabbing her finger at a photo, "this is you in Korea as an army nurse! Wow, I never saw these before! Please tell us how you and Dad got together." Glancing at her two brothers, she added slyly, "The three of us know bits and pieces, but not the *whole* story."

Chase chuckled, his arm still around Rachel. "I think I'll let your mother begin."

As if he always deferred to her. Ha! Rachel thought, not without fondness.

"Honey?" he prompted innocently.

The room quieted, and, suddenly nervous, Rachel clasped her hands in her lap. "Well," she began softly, a little bemused, "it was the worst day of my life, if you want to know the truth. I'd finished nurses' training, joined the army and was promptly sent over to a MASH unit in Korea. I thought I'd be tending patients, nothing more. Was I ever wrong...."

Chapter One

Yongchong, Pusan, South Korea
August 1, 1951

"Rachel, get the hell out of here! The enemy's broken through our lines!"

Rachel whirled around, her green eyes widening. *Get ahold of yourself, Rachel McKenzie. Don't you dare panic! You've got one more patient to get aboard that helicopter.* She saw the fear in Dr. Bob Short's face as he stood tensely at the other end of the tent. Their mobile army surgical hospital unit was caught in the middle of a major attack by North Korean soldiers who had broken through the U.N. lines.

"Did you hear me?" he thundered over the noise of the helicopters landing and taking off outside the MASH unit. "You be on that next chopper!"

"All right" she yelled back. The rattle of gunfire was growing closer. And so was the constant thump of mortars exploding all around them. "I've got one more patient to get aboard, and then I'll leave."

"The rest of the nurses gone?"

She nodded. "Annie went on the last flight. I'm the only one left besides you three doctors."

"We haven't got much time," Dr. Short warned. "The Australian commander whose company tried to stop the charge radioed. He says the enemy will be here in fifteen minutes."

Licking her dry lips, Rachel moved quickly to the end of the large canvas tent known as "recovery." Pvt. Larry Constant smiled weakly up at her. He was still in critical condition from receiving a bullet wound in his chest two days ago. His young face was pale, bathed in sweat.

"Last but not least, Larry," she joked, meeting his concerned face with a smile.

His mouth stretched into what was supposed to be a returned smile but pulled into a line of agony. His brown eyes were dark with panic. The drugs weren't halting the massive pain he endured. "Look, Miss McKenzie, forget about me," he managed to say. "You'd better hop that chopper yourself. The North Koreans—they'll torture you—"

"Hush," Rachel whispered, efficiently tucking the blankets beneath the thin mattress of the cot. Any moment now, the last two orderlies would carry Larry to the safety of the helo waiting on the landing pad just outside the MASH unit. "Wounded first." She managed a brave smile, although her stomach was a hard knot of fear. "And I'm not wounded, young man. You are." Quickly her experienced hands adjusted the IV, getting ready to carry it above Larry's head when the orderlies took the cot. Rachel noted that her hand was shaking, and she wondered if the private saw her obvious fear.

Just as the two enlisted men slipped inside the wooden door of the huge rectangular tent, an explosion rocked the area. Rachel bit back a cry, shielding Constant by leaning across the cot. Dirt and rock pelted the tent savagely, making the structure shake and groan.

"Get him out of here!" Rachel croaked. A quick look confirmed that shrapnel had made several rips in the fabric above their heads.

"But—" Larry cried, protesting as the orderlies lifted his cot.

"But nothing," Rachel said tartly, walking quickly beside him, holding the IV high. "You're going home, soldier, where you belong. Now stop your chatter. That's an order." Her cool efficiency affected the men dramatically. They steadied the cot, making each movement count, and the private shut his eyes and surrendered to her order.

The lantern light within the tent faded into the gray, brackish dawn as they wove their way between the empty tents. Rachel tried to stabilize her breathing, her heart banging away in her chest as they assaulted the rocky path leading upward to the landing pad. Her MASH unit was the farthest forward in Korea, always the first to take casualties from the constantly shifting front. They had saved hundreds of young men barely out of their teens from dying because of their proximity to enemy lines. Larry Constant was yet another living testament to the importance of the unit being so close to the fighting, in spite of the risk. Despite the valiant effort of Republic of Korea troops, known as ROKs, to halt the surge of North Koreans, the line had broken, and the enemy was now funneling through the break like an out-of-control juggernaut. Rachel knew that her MASH unit stood in their path, unarmed and undefended. It was up to the nurses and doctors to evacuate their patients to safety.

More mortars landed, spreading eerie yellow and orange tentacles of flames outward. Rachel winced, instinctively moving closer to her patient to protect him. The gunfire was oppressive. Her mind raced. Ten other nurses had made it safely aboard the helos that were now bearing their patients back to MASH units far removed from the front.

Wind from the whirling blades of the helo that sat on the smooth dirt landing pad buffeted them as they climbed onto the flat surface. Rachel saw the pilot frantically waving his arm out the window, the gesture sharp and obvious. Not wanting to be a stationary target, he urged them to hurry. The orderlies quickly attached the cot to the specially designed runner on the side of the helo that would carry the patient outside the aircraft.

Rachel realized with a sinking feeling that the helo was already packed with personnel and patients.

"Two more," the pilot yelled out the window above the roar. "I can only take two more people."

Once Larry was strapped in, Rachel grabbed both orderlies. "John, Pete, get on board."

"But, Miss McKenzie, what about you?" Pete asked, his young face covered with grime and sweat.

"There's one more chopper coming. I'll get on board with the doctors."

Another mortar went off, this time within thirty yards of the landing pad. The enemy was close enough to try to destroy the aircraft. Giving Pete a shove,

Rachel watched the orderlies reluctantly climb on board.

"Get out of here!" she shrieked at the pilot. "Lift off, lift off!"

Rachel ducked low, running from beneath the rotor blades that whipped faster and faster. Dust kicked up in huge, rolling clouds, making her eyes water. Her shoulder-length black hair swirled around her face, and she pulled strands of it away from her eyes. The helo was loaded to its maximum weight, floundering off the pad and fighting to gain altitude. She hurried back down the rocky path toward the tents. Now all she had to do was find the three doctors so they could wait by the pad for the last helicopter to arrive.

Dr. Steve Hall found Rachel first as she ran between the recovery and surgery tent. He was a colonel and head surgeon of the MASH unit, a man of fifty-five, tall and robust. Gripping her arm, he frowned.

"Why weren't you on that last helo, Rachel?"

They both stood, panting hard, having used the past few hours to remove all their patients from the approaching enemy. "It was full. I'll be flying out with you guys."

Hall nodded grimly. "Stay with me. We need to round up Bob and Joe."

Tiredness swept through Rachel. She was stumbling every few steps now, the toes of her heavy black GI boots digging into the freshly churned South Korean soil. The grayness of dawn lay on the horizon like a warning. Following Colonel Hall, weaving between the now empty battle-scarred tents, new emotions that had been held at bay began to filter through Rachel.

Fear had never entered her mind in her concern for the safety of her patients, who were more like hurt and defenseless children in her eyes. Fierce and protective mothering instincts had made her and the rest of the nurses work tirelessly to evacuate their fifty patients. Thinking back, Rachel realized the enormity of what they had done and suddenly felt more weary than she ever had in her life.

The mortar attacks stepped up, the sharp bark of rifle fire testing the limits of her coolness. Throughout the evacuation Rachel had maintained her composure for the good of the younger nurses. Her patients, who had already faced the war and been severely wounded, were even more frightened. The only gunfire Rachel had been around was when her father had taken her hunting in the Catskill Mountains of New York State. The sound always hurt her ears. And she really didn't believe in killing anything.

So what was she doing here in Korea at a forward MASH unit? Blinking back tears caused by the dust in her eyes, Rachel trotted beside Hall, who was quickening his stride in an effort to locate the surgeons. She wanted to press her hands against her ears. The heavy helmet on her head was creating an ache at the base of her neck.

There was no time to ponder or answer her own question. They found Lt. Joe Pensky and Capt. Bob Short at the administration tent, destroying the last of sensitive material, preventing it from falling into enemy hands.

"Leave it," Hall ordered, making a curt gesture for them to follow him. "That last chopper said it will be here in ten minutes. Let's get up to that pad. *Now.*"

Bob Short stared at Rachel after throwing the last of the files into a fifty-gallon drum they had used to destroy the documents. Flames licked above the rim, highlighting their sweaty, dirty faces.

"I thought you'd already left, Rachel."

"The last chopper was at its weight limit."

Short cursed, something he didn't do often. "Dammit, Rachel—"

"Stow it, Bob," Hall growled.

Rachel fell in alongside Hall as he trotted out of the tent and down a well-worn path between several tents. The past two months of her twenty-three years of life had been spent in Korea. She had come to love the peasant families who lived nearby. And more than anything, she loved her job as a surgery nurse. Emotion welled up in Rachel, and she fought back the tears and memories.

A mortar exploded fifty yards away. Rocks and dirt spewed through the dawn, pelting them. Hall lengthened his stride. Rachel stretched her long legs more fully. In an effort to control her panic, she recalled a strong childhood memory. When she was nine years old, she'd shot up like a bean sprout, taller than any girl in her class. She'd been thin and gangly, standing out like a sore thumb among her classmates. The girls called her a freak. The boys were afraid of her. Now, her five feet seven inches of height gave her longer than average legs for a woman, and she was able to keep up with the three men as they sprinted for the pad.

"I hear it!" Dr. Pensky yelled, jabbing a finger toward the gray and red sky. "The chopper! It's coming!"

Rachel struggled to stay at Hall's heels as they climbed the hill to the pad. Yes! She could hear the thick chop, chop, chop of the rotors beating against the heavy humid morning air. Jerking a look over her shoulder, she could see the North Korean infantry coming quickly behind their T-34 tanks. The clanking of the steel-treaded monsters dominated the air, sending a chill up her spine.

The group came to a halt, gasping for breath. The doctors hovered protectively around Rachel, shielding her from possible shrapnel or bullets. The warmth she felt toward the three men was like that of a sister for her big brothers. Rachel lifted her square chin skyward. There, in the distance, was their rescue helicopter. It was coming in low, in a twisting, turning pattern in order to present a tough target.

"Five more minutes and we'll be out of this hell," Pensky gasped, casting a wary glance toward the empty MASH unit.

"In ten minutes, the enemy's gonna be here," Short huffed.

"Come on, come on," Joe muttered to the approaching helicopter.

All eyes trained on the U.S. Army aircraft. Rachel was still gasping for breath from the long, tortuous run. Suddenly, from behind them, the T-34 tanks started blasting away, their muzzles lifted skyward. The whistle of the shells shrieked across the hilly countryside. Rachel felt the concussions, automatically cringing, covering her head with her hands.

"Oh, my God!" Pensky shrieked.

A cry escaped Rachel as the helicopter was hit by a tank shell, becoming a blazing orange ball against the turgid crimson dawn. It tumbled wildly from the sky, crashing into the earth.

Hall cursed roundly. Rachel was pushed to the ground by Pensky. The next thing she heard was the sharp sting of North Korean orders being issued. Rachel's eyes rounded. She looked up and saw her first North Korean—a lean man, barely her height, his pistol leveled at their little group. Dressed in a tan uniform edged in red piping, he gave them a triumphant look. His black eyes glittered with amusement as the rest of his platoon surrounded them.

"You are our prisoners," he told them in halting, broken English.

Shock numbed Rachel. She shakily rose to her feet, gripping Pensky's arm, staying hidden behind him. Several of the enemy soldiers rushed forward, separating them, roughly frisking them for weapons. One soldier shoved Rachel into the open. He reached out to frisk her.

"Don't you dare touch me!" Rachel rasped, and smacked the man's hand, leaping back to avoid contact.

The violence of her feelings surprised her. Rachel stood tensely and lifted her chin at a defiant angle. A plan began to form in her mind. Just as soon as possible, she would speak to the three doctors about an escape attempt. Rachel wasn't about to turn into a whimpering little girl begging for mercy. No, all they needed was a diversion of some kind in order to distract the enemy's attention. Then they could make a bid for freedom.

"Hey, Chase, get your butt out of bed! Hit the flight line! We've got a scramble," Buddy Dawson said, shaking his friend and squadron leader.

Capt. Chase Trayhern sat bolt upright in his creaky cot. *Scramble!* He heard the thin, high wail of the siren drifting across the makeshift air base at Taegu, screaming out to all pilots on duty to hit the deck running for their aircraft. Dawson, his wingman, was already pulling on his flight boots. They slept in their tan one-piece flight suits. Chase blinked, trying to shake off badly needed sleep.

Grunting, Chase threw his legs across the cot, automatically shoving his feet into his boots and lacing them with expert ease. "What have we got?"

"Dunno." Dawson shoved off his cot, his red hair uncombed, and peered out the tent flap. It was still dark, but dawn was crawling up the horizon like a gray slug.

This was what Chase lived for. His squadron was the last to use propeller-driven P-51s, an exceptional fighter from World War II. His commander kept telling him that soon the squadron would be pulled off the line to receive jet training stateside. Diving for their tent opening, both men emerged and jogged down the dusty path, passing rows of tents that served as home for everyone based at Taegu.

Entering the operations tent, Chase squinted, the glare of light momentarily hurting his eyes. Lt. Col. Jake Hobson was grim. As a matter of fact, Chase thought, Hob looked as if he'd been up all night, something that happened frequently around Taegu.

"What's happening, Hob?" Chase demanded, moving over to the map of the Pusan area.

"We've got big problems, Chase. A MASH unit near Yongchong just got captured. The Eighth ROK division plus an Australian battalion had their line broken. We've got North Koreans funneling into the area like fleas on a dog." Hob jabbed his stubby index finger at the map of the Yongchong area. "Weather's good. I want your squadron off the ground pronto. We believe three American doctors and a nurse have been captured.''

Eyes narrowing, Chase muttered in disbelief, ''A woman?''

''Yes. The ROKs are telling us she's Lieutenant Rachel McKenzie.'' Hob's jowly face became harsh. ''You know what the enemy does to our men. I don't even want to think what they might do to her.''

''War's for men, not women,'' Chase snorted. ''I've always said we had no business bringing women into this war. I don't care whether they're nurses or not.''

Dawson came forward, putting a hand on Trayhern's broad shoulder. ''Take it easy, Chase. Hob, what do you want us to do?''

''The ROK division is in total disarray. They're trying to regroup. I want your squadron to fly in to strafe and bomb a truck convoy of North Koreans heading back north. The ROKs believe they have the American prisoners. Maybe, with some low and slow fancy flying, you can give these people a chance to escape.'' Hob's gray eyes grew dark as he held Trayhern's hard gaze. ''Create a diversion for them, Chase. Create havoc. Maybe those Americans will understand what we're trying to do and make a break for freedom.''

Nodding, Chase wrote down the pertinent information. He'd been in Korea since the beginning of the war and knew the Pohang area by heart. ''We'll give it our best shot, Hob. What if they do escape? Do we have any marines in the area?''

''If they can break free, they're still on their own. The U.N. troops are rallying and trying to stop the influx. The closest force is Australian. There's no white knight on any horse coming to rescue them.''

"You'd better hope they know which way is south, then," Chase griped. A woman! Of all things! He started to say it, but let it go. Time was of the essence.

Hob nodded wearily. Beneath the naked lightbulb, his thinning steel-gray hair took on a silvery cast, almost halolike. "They'd better be made out of tough stuff," he agreed. "Get going, and good luck."

"Yes, sir." Chase turned and Dawson followed him out of the tent. The air reeked of cattle dung and aviation fuel. Down the flight line, the elegant Mustangs stood silhouetted against the reddish-gray dawn. Further down, a squadron of blunt-nosed F-80 jets lined up.

"What do you think?" asked Dawson, jogging easily at Chase's side.

"About what?"

"That woman."

Snorting, Chase saw his flight mechanic, Sergeant Owens, waiting for him beside his plane. "She's in a lot of trouble—and causing *us* trouble. If only the three docs had been captured, I don't think Hob would have been ordered to strike that convoy."

Dawson shook his red head. "To think a woman's been captured. Man, that's gonna make headlines back in the hometown newspaper."

"The *wrong* kind for the military," Chase amended, throwing a salute to his sergeant. "That's why we're getting this mission." He saw his other two pilots already on the line, and he threw them a thumbs-up. "Just keep close, Buddy. The small-arms fire could be heavy when we go in."

"Or flak."

Chase agreed with a nod. He stepped up to the sergeant who cared for the plane as carefully as if it were his child. Nodding to his crew chief, Chase climbed up onto the wing and then into the cockpit.

Owens helped him strap in, then gave him a final pat on the shoulder before leaving the wing of the plane. As Chase ran rapidly through the preflight checklist after pulling on his helmet, he found himself wondering about the woman. Rachel McKenzie. *Pretty name.* McKenzie sounded like a fighter's name. He gave Owens a final thumbs-up before starting the powerful engine on the Mustang. *She'd better be a fighter.*

Swiveling his head, he saw the other three P-51s starting up, the throaty roar of engines filling the dawn air. The planking of the airstrip popped and cracked as Chase trundled the P-51 at a high taxi speed toward the end of the runway. Even in the grayness of the dawn, he could see people stirring around the rows of olive-green tents in the distance. Taegu was a main center of men and materials, as well as a forward air base.

At the end of the airstrip was "Mount Bust-your-ass." On a clear day, it was no problem missing the mountain. In fog or rain, the rocky pinnacle could be a pilot's demise. You had to shove full throttle to gain enough momentum and then, at the end of the runway, pull up at a high angle of ascent to miss the mountain. Otherwise, it did just as its name implied.

Sliding the canopy shut, Chase flicked switches and turned dials. Behind him, all in a neat, orderly row, were his three other squadron mates in their respective Mustangs.

All dials and indicators showed the engine in good working condition. Releasing the brakes, Chase steered as the P-51 howled, hurling itself down the runway. His attention was drawn back to the mission—and the woman. What a hell of a fix she was in. Chase felt his stomach tighten painfully in an uncharacteristic expression of fear—for her.

As Chase eased the stick back, the P-51 lifted off, nosing confidently into the crimson and gray sky. Moving the stick to the right and applying a bit of right rudder, Chase saw each of his men take off without incident.

"Well, Rachel McKenzie, hope you've got what it takes to escape." As the fighter gained altitude, heading toward Yongchong, Chase wondered what she looked like. What kind of a woman volunteered to come over to get shot at, bombed and mortared, much less captured? What kind?

Chapter Two

Rachel stood huddled with the doctors next to a tan transport truck. Her hands were tied in front of her with a thin leather thong that was cutting off her circulation, making her fingers numb. As a group, they'd been herded by soldiers to one side of the truck. Two soldiers scurried to change a flat tire on the lead truck, receiving a blistering tongue-lashing from the angry officer. For three hours they had sped north, deep into North Korean territory before the vehicle had an unexpected blowout.

Rachel discreetly looked around for possible escape routes, peeking from between the doctors. The convoy consisted of fifteen other trucks carrying mostly cargo and few troops. A number of tan-clad soldiers milled around, smoking and talking in low voices, waiting impatiently for the truck to be repaired. To be stalled on a road in the open was inviting attack, and the soldiers were nervous, constantly watching the sky for American jet fighters. The road was narrow and deeply rutted. It was impossible to pass the injured vehicle because the rocky hills rose steeply on either side.

Colonel Hall was looking around, too, and Rachel felt an eerie premonition crawl up the back of her neck. She sensed danger. Huge groves of trees dotted the steep hillsides, a perfect place to run for cover and hide. She saw the same thoughts flicker over Hall's sober features.

Sudden Korean shouts jerked Rachel's attention back to the convoy. The officer standing at the front of the broken truck screeched orders to his men, pointing angrily at the sky. Her gaze followed his gestures.

"Look!" she whispered excitedly to the doctors. "Planes!"

"Our planes," Hall croaked in disbelief.

"Mustangs. Prop-driven Mustangs," Short added unhappily. "Couldn't they have sent jets?"

"At least they came," Rachel whispered tautly. The military must know of their capture. Rachel's heart lifted with inexplicable joy. They were coming to the rescue! She just knew it!

Hall nodded, watching the soldiers scurrying in all directions, setting up their weapons to fire at the oncoming planes. "They're going to strafe. All right, all of you get ready. They aren't watching us that closely. They want those planes. Run. Run in four different directions. Try to escape! Understand?"

Her heart pounding, Rachel nodded. Nervously she licked her lips. The droning sound of the Mustangs drew closer. Their captors ignored them, getting ready to fire at the fighters. Shouts from various officers filled the air. The sky was blindingly bright blue, the summer sun bearing down on them.

Twisting the leather bonds, Rachel worked them frantically, trying to force them to stretch. The gesture was futile. Within seconds, the Mustangs would begin their low-level attack. Her throat ached with tension as she stood stiffly against the truck, waiting. In moments, she could be dead. Or she might get a second chance and live long enough to escape.

As she stood, watching the first sleek silver fighter plane line up to begin its attack, Rachel had one regret. She had never fallen in love. If it was her time to die, she would never know the man who could make her heart swell with unaccountable joy and love. It was a bittersweet thought that left a chasm of sadness within her as she got ready to make a dash for the grove to the right of the trucks.

"Beginning strafing run," Chase ordered his squadron over the radio. He kicked left rudder, sending the Mustang down on the deck. The altimeter unwound rapidly until he leveled off at two hundred feet. The throbbing growl of the engine deepened as he pulled back on the throttle, popping the air brakes. The fighter slowed considerably, and Chase aimed the nose down, lining up on the road. The stalled convoy appeared in the gun-sight mechanism.

"Okay, Rachel McKenzie, get your sweet rear out of there," he muttered, thumbing the trigger located on the stick. The fighter shook, the roar of the fifty-caliber guns vibrating through the fuselage.

Geysers of debris exploded in a sewing-machine-like pattern through the center of each truck on the long, snaking dirt road. Chase felt satisfaction as one truck after another caught fire. Hundreds of troops were running and diving for cover. He saw the blinking of small arms and rifle fire up at him. The "thunk, thunk, thunk" of bullets striking the fuselage peppered his awareness. Yanking back on the stick at the end of the convoy, Chase nosed the fighter around for another run. Below him, the other three fighters were making their runs, tearing up the trucks, creating absolute havoc. Where were the Americans? Had they managed to flee?

"Run!" Hall cried. The first fighter roared over, shaking the ground beneath its path.

Rachel gulped back a cry, crawling beneath the truck and appearing on the other side of it. She paid no attention to the scrapes on her elbows or knees as she leaped upright, sprinting for the cover of the trees that stood fifty feet away.

Fifty feet. It was a lifetime to Rachel. Bullets chewed up the soil all around her; the cry of angry enemy soldiers filled the air, along with the shriek of the fighters swooping over her. Gasping, she slipped, her bound hands making her less balanced on the steep slope. *Get up! Get up!* Digging the toes of her boots into the rocky, dry soil, Rachel ran blindly toward the grove. Only twenty-five feet to go!

Rachel heard sharpened cries in Korean aimed in her direction. Risking a look across her shoulder, she saw the commanding officer gesturing wildly at her, bellowing orders. He aimed his pistol. Adrenaline surged through Rachel and she lunged forward, falling into a thick wall of scratchy brush. Flailing wildly, she tore through the brush to the other side. Pieces of tree bark splintered and flew all around her. Landing hard on her hands and knees, Rachel lurched to her feet, keeping low. The officer was trying to kill her!

Sweat trickled into her eyes, her black hair matted against her brow as she struggled to her feet and ran harder than ever. Weaving between the bushes within the grove, Rachel worked her way toward the top of the hill, half a mile away. If she could just make it over that crest, maybe she could lose them and regain her freedom. Below, she heard the American fighters roaring over again in a second attack. If they could keep the enemy engaged, she could escape!

Keep moving, keep moving, Rachel McKenzie! Don't you dare slow down! Her lungs felt as if they were on fire, each breath torn from her mouth in a ragged gulp. Tripping, falling, getting back to her feet, Rachel weaved drunkenly through the grove. The rocky hill sported parched strands of yellowed grass, mute testament to the lack of water. Her thighs were cramping from the sheer exertion of her efforts. It didn't matter. Rachel crouched instinctively when one of the fighters roared only feet overhead.

Her eyes widening, Rachel saw greasy black smoke trailing the Mustang as it sank below the hill, obviously in trouble. She could hear the engine sputtering and coughing. *Oh, no!* One of the Americans had been hit trying to help them! Tears jammed into her eyes. She scrambled up the hill, the rocks cutting viciously at her palms and fingers.

The crown of the hill became Rachel's goal. Within minutes, she'd crested it and was running in long, uneven strides down the other side. Above her, she saw the silver Mustang struggling to gain some altitude, more black smoke pouring from the engine and tongues of fire spurting from beneath the cowling.

Everywhere Rachel looked, thick groves of trees dotted the rocky hills. Gasps of air exploded from her mouth as she forced herself to continue to run down the hill, heading toward the valley below lined with trees and heavy brush. At any moment that officer could be sending out a patrol to track her down. She owed these brave pilots more than that.

New determination flowed into Rachel as she slipped into the grove of trees at the bottom of the valley. Looking back, she saw no one following her. Not yet. Lifting her eyes skyward, she saw that the fighter definitely was in trouble, and so was the pilot. Halting, her legs shaking with weariness, Rachel leaned heavily against a tree, watching the drama unfold before her eyes.

The fighter was barely maintaining five thousand feet. Suddenly the engine quit. Rachel drew a sharp breath, stifling a cry. She saw the canopy pop open and tumble off. The pilot leaped from the plane. Her bound hands flew to her mouth. Just as he made his jump, the fighter rolled in the same direction, out of control. The pilot's helmeted head smashed into the tail section of the plane and his body went limp just as the parachute opened.

"My God," Rachel muttered, already beginning a slow trot in the direction of where the pilot would land. Even from this distance, she could see he was a big man, his arms and legs hanging lifeless, silhouetted against the brilliant blue of the sky.

Her legs were rubbery from exertion, but Rachel doggedly trotted down into the valley, always keeping an eye on the white parachute swinging lazily from side to side in the afternoon breeze. The North Koreans had probably seen the plane go down. Were they aware that the pilot ejected?

Rachel leaped across a dry streambed. She spotted a thin outcrop of rock near the bank. By this time, the pilot and parachute had come down somewhere beyond the grove of trees. She knew the approximate area where he'd landed, about a mile ahead of her. Bending down, Rachel placed her leather bound wrists against the rock, rubbing them back and forth.

After several minutes, the rock sliced through the leather, freeing her hands. Rubbing her numb bluish wrists, Rachel forced herself to stand. Her legs were beginning to cramp again. Disregarding the pain, she trotted along the creek bed. The pilot was down. Was he dead? If he had survived the terrible collision with his aircraft, he'd be badly injured. Her mind racing, Rachel felt helpless. Even if he had survived, she had no medical supplies to help him.

"One thing at a time," she ordered herself sternly, her breath coming in heaving gasps. The pilot had risked his life to save hers. Any effort she could expend would never make up for what he'd done. Her focus must be limited to reaching the American before the enemy could capture him.

The valley narrowed, the grove thinning. Huge rocks and boulders seemed like gray and black guardians dotting the slope. A veelike entrance to the valley was bordered by steep cliffs that towered hundreds of feet into the air.

Rachel's heart pounded in her chest, but now, as she spotted the pilot lying unconscious on the hillside, his chute still partially billowing in the breeze, the beat increased markedly. Weaving between boulders and dodging smaller rocks, she cautiously surveyed the area. The pilot was in the open, visible to enemy eyes. A patrol on one of those hilltops could spot him with binoculars. Time was of the essence.

Rachel's gaze swung from the hills to the pilot's face as she cautiously approached him. Blood was leaking from beneath his helmet, covering half his waxen face. "Please, don't let him be dead. . . ." she whispered, kneeling down and reaching out with shaking fingers, pressing them against the carotid artery on the side of his neck.

Rachel felt a bounding pulse beneath her fingertips. Good, he was alive, and if she was any judge of the situation, not in too deep shock—not yet. His face was square, with a prominent nose, thick brown eyebrows and a generous mouth. Rachel marveled at the length and thickness of his eyelashes, thinking how they softened the hardness of his high-cheekboned features, as she fumbled with the parachute straps across his chest.

He was a big man, large boned and in good shape. His chest was well shaped and massive. Dragging the harness off one arm, Rachel noticed the shape of his hand. Despite his size, he had long, almost artistic-looking fingers. They were large knuckled with plentiful hair across the tops of them. Male. He was definitely male in every sense of the word.

Pulling the rest of the chute harness off him, Rachel hurriedly gathered up the silk, jamming it between two large rocks. Hurrying back to the pilot, she began to assess the extent of his injuries. His white helmet was cracked on the right side, where he'd tangled with the tail of his fighter. She had no doubt that he was suffering from a concussion.

Gently squeezing his arms and legs, Rachel ascertained he had no broken bones. Placing several rocks beneath his heels, she elevated his legs in an effort to combat the shock symptoms. The sun was burning down, and she saw the flies starting to gather around the pilot's head. Shooing them away, Rachel shakily unstrapped the helmet. It would have to come off in order for her to evaluate the true extent of his injury.

Carefully Rachel eased the helmet off his head. The sunlight struck his short brown hair, highlighting the gold strands woven with the darker walnut-colored ones. Just as she placed the helmet aside, the pilot groaned. Joy raced through Rachel and she placed a hand on his shoulder, gripping it firmly to give him a toehold on reality. Her heart picked up in beat as his lashes fluttered. What color were his eyes? Rachel could tell so much by looking deeply into someone's eyes. For her, they truly were a mirror to the soul.

Unconsciously she held her breath. Then, as if the pilot realized she was kneeling at his right side, he rolled his head in that direction. As his lashes lifted, they revealed cobalt-blue eyes with huge black pupils. He reminded her of an eagle, his eyes large with hard intelligence.

"Don't move," she told him in a hushed voice. "I'm Lieutenant Rachel McKenzie. You injured yourself when you bailed out."

Chase blinked once. *Angel...* The word drifted across his clouded vision along with waves of throbbing pain. *What a beautiful woman.* He must have died.... A silly smile pulled at the corners of Chase's mouth. Closing his eyes, her image hovered sweetly before him. Yeah, she was heaven, all right. She was talking again, but he didn't understand her, the words garbling inside his head. It didn't matter.

"Can you hear me, Captain? What's your name?" Rachel placed her hand against his cheek, cradling his head. "Open your eyes," she commanded firmly. Her hands were sweaty, and it wasn't from physical exertion, it was because of *him*. A semblance of a smile tugged momentarily at one corner of his mouth. What was funny? If Rachel hadn't been so concerned about his condition and their dangerous situation, she would have smiled in return. Since when had any man made her feel giddy and nervous like this?

Angel Eyes. Yeah, that was a good name for her, Chase decided. Sweet face, stubborn chin and glorious evergreen eyes fraught with such concern over him. Those thick black lashes were like soft frames, emphasizing their beauty, Chase thought disjointedly. And those lips. He groaned, thinking about how they would feel against his mouth. This was one special angel. *What a way to die.*

"Captain," Rachel repeated anxiously, leaning down, her lips very close to his ear. "Can you understand me?"

Her moist breath fanned his ear and neck. Chase could swear she was real. She couldn't be. He was dead. The moment her fingers caressed his cheek, he realized differently. The words impinged upon his spinning state, and he worked at lifting his heavily weighted lids. Did she realize how much effort it took to simply open his eyes?

A tremulous smile pulled at Rachel's lips as the pilot barely opened those heart-stopping blue eyes once again. "You're doing fine, Captain, just fine," she whispered, her voice husky with feeling. To examine his heavily bleeding wound, Rachel carefully moved several strands of his hair aside.

"What's your name? Can you remember?"

Chase groaned as she touched his scalp. Damn, he felt like a mule had kicked him. *Name.* Sure, he had a name. He opened his mouth, his mind drifting again.

The wound was long and clean. Rachel breathed a sigh of relief, assured his skull hadn't been broken. The gash needed to be sewn shut, but that was out of the question right now. She returned her attention to him, drowning in the darkness of his blue eyes. He was looking at her in confusion. Again Rachel repeated her name and the fact she was a nurse.

"Angel?"

She smiled and shook her head. "I'm afraid not, Captain. My name is Rachel. What's yours?"

Taking in a deep, unsteady breath, Chase tried to remember. All he could see was her beautiful face dancing like a mirage in front of him, her husky voice washing across him like a warm waterfall. Her hair was black, a reddish cast to it, and fell into a semblance of a page boy, barely brushing her slender, proud shoulders. Well, she might call herself Rachel, but secretly, she'd always be his angel. Gathering his limited focus, he forced the words out.

"Chase . . . Tray—Trayhern."

"You're doing fine, Chase," Rachel soothed, delighted at his progress. "Come on, I have to get you hidden or we could be spotted by the enemy." Placing her arm beneath his shoulders, she helped him into a sitting position. He leaned heavily against her, completely disoriented by the movement.

Rachel wasn't prepared for his bulk or weakness. He was like a newborn foal—completely uncoordinated. Wrestling to maintain his balance in a kneeling position, Rachel brought his arm around her shoulders. "Chase, you've got to help me. We have to move. Now! Push up with your legs."

Her words kept fading then coming back into clarity, but Chase responded to the desperation in her voice. He shoved himself into a standing position. Despite her size, she held him steady. Chase was amazed because he towered over her.

Rachel gritted her teeth, taking the pilot's full weight. "Dammit, help me!" she groaned. "I can't hold you!"

Stung by her plea, Chase rallied. He'd been too long without the firm warmth and softness of a woman in his arms. She felt utterly delightful, and he wasn't apologetic about leaning on her or pressing his face against her ebony hair. Rachel smelled musky and feminine at the same time, his limited senses noted. Burying his face in the silky strands, he felt each jolting step they took down the hillside. And each jarring movement created more pain in his head.

The short walk to the grove of trees took a toll on Rachel. The pilot was semiconscious when she eased him to the ground. Gasping for breath, her shoulders aching from the bulk of his weight, Rachel elevated his feet again. His eyes were closed, his flesh colorless from the exertion. Leaning over, she pressed her fingertips to the side of his neck. Good, his pulse was steady and full.

Rising, Rachel trotted back to where the chute was stashed. Taking a sharp rock, she ripped several large gashes into the silk and tore out wide strips of the material for makeshift bandages and dressings. If only there was water nearby! Searching, eyes narrowed,

Rachel spotted a small area of green grass about a quarter of a mile away. Green grass meant water. Returning to Chase, she made sure he was as comfortable as possible, then headed for the grass in the distance.

Occasionally Rachel would stop within the grove and study the hills intently, looking for patrols. Her mind revolved back to the three doctors as she continued her trek. Had they made good their escape? If all four of them made it to safety, the officer in charge of the convoy would be torn about which way to send patrols to hunt them down. Hall's decision to split up had been a good one.

Green grass surrounded the water in the creek. Luckily it was situated at the edge of the tree grove so she didn't have to fully expose herself to possible enemy eyes. Bending down, she dipped some of the chute silk into the clear pool. Rachel spotted a tin can nearby. Washing out whatever contents had been in it, she filled it, walking quickly back to where Chase lay unconscious.

Some of Rachel's panic was receding. So far, there was no sign of an enemy patrol. As she kneeled down to clean away the blood around Chase's head wound, Rachel took a good look at the pilot for the first time.

He was solidly built, reminding her of a powerful warrior from a bygone era, she decided, gently sponging the blood from his slack face. How he fitted into the narrow cockpit of a fighter stymied Rachel. Usually pilots were shorter and leaner. Each time she touched him, a ribbon of pleasure moved through Rachel, confusing her. No man had ever provoked that reaction.

Rachel sat back on her heels, hands resting on her thighs, and studied Chase's features. He wasn't handsome. At least, not in her opinion. Then what was it that drew her so powerfully to him? Was it his mouth? Despite the cragginess of his features, his mouth was gentle, she decided. The lower lip was full, the upper well shaped, with corners turned up. Chase laughed a lot. That was proven by the crow's feet at the corners of his eyes.

The thought made Rachel feel better about Chase. Never had she met a man who seemed so overwhelmingly male. As she cleaned and wrapped his head wound, a warmth grew within her. There was something vulnerable about Chase in his unconscious state. It felt good to be the strong member of their team in the dangerous circumstances. It was her brains and efforts that had thus far saved them from capture.

Thirst drove Rachel back to the small pool of water. She was careful not to walk in the open, always hugging the tree line or moving cautiously from one huge rock to another. The humidity was rising, and the armpits of her fatigues darkened with splotches of sweat. Rachel wondered if she should risk a quick spit bath. She could smell the fear on herself from her capture earlier that day.

Perhaps later, something cautioned her. She checked the ridge of the hills around them. Seeing no one, she slipped out to the pool, dipping the can into the water and drinking her fill. Trickles of water slid down from the corners of her mouth, flowing the length of her throat and soaking into the fabric of her collar. After consuming two more cans of water, she moved back beneath the trees. Her father had always said she had the instincts of a good hunter even though she never wanted to be one. Now, Rachel thought as she hurried back to Chase, those instincts would be put to the test in saving their lives. The pilot was in no condition to lead. But he would have to be ready to walk very soon. To stay here would be foolhardy. Even deadly.

Chase felt coolness against his sweaty face. Cold against heat. He hated the hot, humid Korean summers. The gentle sponging continued downward from his face, to his jaw and then his neck. Sighing, the feeling decidedly sensual, he enjoyed the stroking motion.

"Chase? Are you awake?"

The angel's voice. His mind was functioning more quickly now, and his lids didn't feel like lead weights. Lifting them, Chase stared upward.

"You..." he croaked. How did she get prettier? Her cheeks were flushed, the color high, as if she had been running. And her golden skin had a sheen to it, emphasizing the beauty of her forest-green eyes. Chase lost himself in the warmth of them, noting the flecks of emerald in the darker green—and the look of care laced with amusement.

"Did you expect someone different?" Rachel asked with a low laugh. She sat back on her heels. Chase was alert this time, and it sent a prickle of delicious awareness through her. She felt his penetrating gaze, as if he were indeed an eagle sizing up his next quarry. Those blue eyes were so very readable, and she responded unconsciously to the invitation within them. Were all women as affected by his gaze as she was? Rachel managed a nervous smile.

"Can you speak?"

Slowly Chase brought up his hand, finding his brow bandaged. "Yeah...I think I can. What the hell happened? I remember taking small-arms fire and then bailing out."

Rachel poured a little more water over the parachute silk in her hands, swabbing down his neck and getting rid of the dried blood. "I saw you eject. The plane rolled on its side just after you leaped out, and your head hit the tail."

Scowling, Chase gingerly felt his bandaged wound, wincing. The area was tender and he had a horrendous headache. "I hit the tail?"

"Yes. It knocked you out." Rachel lifted aside the collar of his tan flight suit. Dark hair covered the area just below his collarbone. She swallowed hard, ensnared by his blatant masculinity. Quickly finishing her ministrations, Rachel retreated a few feet from the pilot. She felt heat crawl into her cheeks.

Her touch had been incredibly delicate. Chase had the urge to bring Rachel to his side and explore the softness he was sure she possessed. It was a stupid thought at a time like this, and Chase reprimanded himself. There was something about her slenderness, her unconscious grace, that struck him in the heart. How could a woman be so ethereal and yet possess such strength? And there was strength in her, Chase admitted sourly. It was obvious in her small but defiant chin and the way she squared her shoulders.

"You're Rachel McKenzie. The nurse."

"Yes."

Chase added, "They told us at Taegu, my air base, that four Americans were captured. My CO mentioned you by name." The scowl deepened on Chase's brow. "The others? Did they get away, too?"

She saw disapproval in his face and heard it in his voice, because she'd been captured. Internally Rachel went on guard. There were a lot of men who thought a woman's place was at home, stateside, and not mixed up in a war. "I hope so. We went in different directions when you started strafing the truck column." Rachel's voice shook. "We owe you and the other pilots our lives."

Chase slowly eased up on his elbows. The pain increased abominably in his head. "Nobody wants to see our people fall into enemy hands." He studied the terrain. "Where are we? How far are we from that column?"

"I'd estimate we're four miles from where the convoy is stalled." She pointed to the hill behind them. "I came over that ridge. The convoy is on the other side." Rachel felt another increment of safety since her escape. There was an alertness to his eyes that hadn't been apparent before. Still, Chase was pale and appeared hyperalert, a symptom of concussion.

"Then we've got to move. We can't stay here. If those North Koreans send out a patrol in this direction, they'll find us." He turned slowly, the pain increasing across his brow, making his eyes water. "We need to go that way. South."

Rachel stared at where he was pointing. "That's east, not south."

His mouth tightening, Chase could no longer fight the pain in his head. "You're a nurse, not a soldier," he snapped irritably. "South is that way." He jabbed his finger in that direction again.

Holding on to her anger, Rachel met and held his gaze. Beads of perspiration were dotting his furrowed brow. Chase was wrong about the directions and she knew it. But the concussion had sullied his senses. In a day or two, he might be reasonable and realize she was correct. Her own emotions were shredded, but Rachel hung on to her deteriorating patience. "I may only be a nurse, Captain, but I'm fully capable of knowing my directions. The convoy was heading due north. I went east, over the hills to escape." She pointed behind them, toward the entrance to the valley. "That's south. We need to go in that direction."

The set of her jaw reminded him of a bulldog. Chase glared at her. "You're wrong. South is where I said it was in the first place."

Her nostrils flaring, Rachel gritted out, "Captain, I'm not going to sit here arguing with you. Whether you realize it or not, that concussion has scrambled your senses but good. We're heading out of this valley, to the south."

Disbelief jagged through Chase. What a little hellion she was. He almost said it. How could someone with such an angelic-looking face be such a stubborn little shrew? "You may be going that way, but I'm not," he ground out.

"Yeah?" Even though there was a strident tone to her husky voice, a challenge in it, Rachel's heart sank. She knew better than to go on the offensive. A belligerent look came to the captain's face now, thanks to her loss of patience. Well, did it really matter? "Listen, our lives are at stake. There's no way you're going in one direction and I'm going the other. You can't even walk by yourself, so you're coming with me whether you like it or not."

Anger sizzled through Chase. "Lieutenant, you're way out of line. I damn well know which way is south. I fly this countryside every day. I know which direction our lines are located, you don't." He shouldn't have cussed in front of her. Women were to be protected; there was no excuse for cursing. Chase wanted to apologize but didn't get a chance.

Getting to her feet, Rachel wrapped the can in the silk and then attached it to a rear loop on her fatigues. Holding out her hand to him she said, "Get up, Captain. We've got to move or they'll find us. And then we'll both be heading *north*, together."

Such a small, delicate hand. Chase stared at her long, thin fingers and blunt-cut nails. Healing hands, he realized, attached to one of the most stubborn women he'd ever encountered. Rachel's insult about both of them heading north stung him. "I'm giving you an order, Lieutenant. I want to go that way."

Grabbing his extended hand as he jabbed a final time to the east, Rachel hauled Chase to his feet. "Write me up on court martial charges for disobeying a direct order from a senior officer when we make it back safely to our lines, Captain. I'm not going east. And neither are you." She pulled his arm around her shoulders, feeling him sag weakly against her. Groaning, she muttered, "We're both going south. Now, come on!"

Chapter Three

Chase ground his teeth, fighting back pain incurred by standing. He sagged heavily against Rachel, thinking that she would buckle beneath his weight. But she didn't. Again her strength impressed some small corner of his barely functioning mind. They tottered forward, weaving like a pair of drunks through the wooded area.

Sunlight lanced the branches, blindingly bright to Chase's ultrasensitive eyes. It must be because of the head injury, he thought. He didn't like his state of weakness or the fact that he was having to lean on a woman for support. To top it off, they were heading in the wrong direction!

"You're going the wrong way," Chase forced out, each step jarring waves of pain through him.

Her lips compressed, Rachel staggered beneath his weight, keeping them upright. "I don't have energy to waste on arguing with you right now, Captain! Try to stand up more! You're killing me!"

"I can't, dammit! My legs are weak," Chase muttered defensively, struggling to right himself more. Normally he was strong as a bull with a constitution to match. Dizziness assailed him and he fought it, trying to lessen Rachel's load. "You make me cuss," he growled. "Normally, women don't bring that trait out in me."

"I don't care if you cuss or not!" Rachel glared up at his sweat-bathed face. "You think my ears haven't heard a few curses? I treat wounded or dying men every day. Believe me, Captain, I've heard it all."

Each step was agony. "That's what I mean," Chase gasped raggedly. "Women don't belong in a theater of war. It's stupid."

"This conversation is stupid. Use that anger and focus it on moving each foot forward!"

What a pain in the neck she was. Chase glanced down at Rachel. Her mouth was set, her eyes narrowed and nostrils flared. Sweat was running down her temple, and it niggled his conscience. Rachel couldn't weigh much more than a hundred pounds soaking wet, and here she was helping him and his two-hundred-pound bulk.

Ahead, Chase could make out walls of rock with a narrow opening between them. They kept inside the tree line. Once they left the last grove, Rachel guided them among the sentrylike rocks that stood in clumps at the exit point out of the valley. Everything kept blurring and then coming back into focus. Nothing made sense to Chase. Deep down, he wondered if Rachel realized the magnitude of her mistake about their direction. No woman he'd ever met had a good sense of direction. Many were unable to read a map or even find the right street in a city. She could be leading them directly into an enemy trap.

Suppressing a groan, Rachel doggedly pulled Chase along. His flight suit was stained with sweat, and she was concerned with his possible dehydration. At the pool, she halted, sitting him down between two huge rocks to keep him out of view.

"Stay here, I'm going to get you some water."

Chase looked up, holding his head between both his hands. "Where?"

"It doesn't matter where!" Rachel put her hands on her hips, tired of him questioning her every decision. "Just sit there, will you?"

Chastened, he felt like a two-year-old being scolded by his mother. Rachel looked endearing in the bulky fatigues she wore. It hurt to nod his head, and he was unwilling to fight verbally with her any longer. If they survived the patrols for the next day or two, he'd assume command and get them back on track.

Checking the hills for patrols, Rachel found none and made a dash out to the pool, dipping the can into the water. Her conscience needled her as she hurried back to Chase. She shouldn't be snarling and snapping at him. He was even paler, and as he lifted his head at her approach, she saw the pain in his eyes.

Kneeling next to him, Rachel placed one hand on his back in a conciliatory gesture. She could feel the strength of his taut muscles beneath the khaki flight suit, and a wild urge to skim her hand along the breadth of his shoulders struck her. Stifling the desire, Rachel offered him a slight smile and pressed the lip of the can to his mouth. "Drink," she coaxed in a whisper, her head inches from his.

The water was warm but delicious. Chase hadn't been aware of how thirsty he was until now. His attention alternated between drinking the water and Rachel's closeness. Forcing himself to pay attention to the water, Chase still couldn't ignore her musky scent or the beauty of her attentive features. Rachel had to make four trips back to the pool before he was sated. There was an economy to her graceful movements, Chase decided grumpily. He enjoyed the opportunity to watch her walk toward him as she tied the can to the parachute silk cloth attached to a loop on the waistband of her fatigues.

Her baggy clothes couldn't hide the rounded curve of her hips or her long legs. There was a nice athletic balance to Rachel, yet Chase wouldn't say that she was a tomboy. No, her hair, fine strands of ebony brushing her shoulders, gave her a decidedly feminine cast. And those thick black lashes framing her glorious and defiant eyes made him aware of the scalding heat that simmered impatiently in his lower body. He longed to drown in the rich green of her eyes and explore her on a heated, intimate level.

Rachel crouched down, her back against the other rock, a mere foot separating them. She allowed her arms to rest on her thighs and closed her eyes, catching her breath. Although her legs had recovered from the initial escape attempt, she felt them protesting again. A careless smile pulled at her mouth.

"And I thought I was in such great shape." She laughed with derision. "My legs feel like rubber bands."

"Mine aren't much better." Chase followed the curve of her thighs, thinking that he'd like to run his hand down their length, sure of their firmness. The unexpected thought sent a jagged bolt of longing through him, sharpening his hunger for her as a woman.

Barely opening her eyes, Rachel studied him. "You have an excuse. You're injured."

"Women aren't supposed to be athletically fit."

One eyebrow raised at an imperious angle. "Oh?"

Chase gave her a flat look. "You aren't a man."

"What's that supposed to mean, Captain?"

He saw the set of her jaw and realized she was getting her back up again. "Women are soft. They aren't expected to be physically fit."

He was like a little boy in Rachel's eyes, sitting there spouting something that someone had taught him. "Oh, yeah? Who do you think tamed the Wild West? It was the women who really settled the West, making homes and raising families."

His jaw dropped. And then his eyes narrowed. "Who are you?"

A grin leaked out and Rachel laughed. "A woman, Captain Trayhern. Where I come from, women are admired for being strong, competent, intelligent and just as capable as a man. It's obvious to me you grew up with the attitude that a woman's entire life ought to be spent pregnant and hovering over a hot stove."

Her laughter was pleasant, and her lively eyes made Chase's heart pound hard in his chest. There was a winsomeness to Rachel, a quality he'd never seen in another woman. She was part child, part woman and some other part that was far too independent for his tastes.

"Well, my mother would disagree with you," he flung back sourly. "She raised three sons and is proud of it."

"I think a woman should be proud of herself whether she's a mother or not," Rachel said lightly, enjoying his discomfort at being on the defensive. Chase looked as if he could take a few blows and survive nicely.

"And that's why you're over here?"

Wiping the sweat off her face with the back of her sleeve, Rachel nodded. "My parents taught me to be self-sufficient and believe in myself and my dreams, Captain. I'm here in Korea because I know men are dying. I'm very good at what I do as a surgical nurse." She spread her hands out in front of her, studying them for a long moment. "Sometimes, speed is the determination of whether a man will live or die on that table. A good surgery nurse doesn't fumble the instruments the doctor needs. She's fast, cool and calm even if the world's folding in around her." Lifting her eyes, she held Chase's gaze. "I belong here in Korea helping those men because I'm good at what I do, Captain."

Disgruntled, Chase averted his gaze, the pain rolling through his head. He closed his eyes, grateful to be sitting quietly. "I don't care how good you are, war is no place for a woman."

Rachel snorted. "Captain, war is no place for a man, either. The boys who come through our MASH unit are just as injured psychologically by what they've seen and done as any woman would be if she was caught in the same circumstance."

She was too damn smart for her own good. Chase muttered, "I wish I had an aspirin."

"I wish I had one to give you. Your head has to be hurting a lot."

"Sledgehammers."

"I know." Rachel reached over, settling her hand sympathetically on his slumped shoulder. "We have to keep going. Maybe, if we're lucky, we'll find our lines soon."

Chase raised his eyes, nailing her with a disgusted look. "We're a good fifty miles inside enemy lines, Miss McKenzie. And the shape I'm in, we aren't going to be getting back fast. It will take us three or four days, providing a North Korean patrol doesn't find us first."

"Oh, dear..." She removed her hand from Chase's shoulder.

Chase heard anxiety in Rachel's voice. It surprised him, because she appeared completely self-sufficient and in command, even if she was headed in the wrong direction. "You got any Irish blood in you?"

She managed a grimace. "Yes. Does it show?"

He melted beneath her softening features. Maybe Rachel McKenzie wasn't a cold, efficient machine after all. Chase rallied, trying to smile for her benefit, but it turned into a line of pain. "You don't have red hair, but you've sure got spirit."

His attempt at a smile buoyed her gloomy mood. Suddenly Rachel felt shaky inside. The feeling was new to her, and it left her confused. "Come on, we've got to get going," she whispered in a strained tone.

The feeling in the pit of her stomach worsened by the minute as she thought about how far away Chase said their lines were. Rachel kept swallowing, feeling a lump form in her throat as she pulled, tugged and supported Chase Trayhern up and over the last hill leading out of the valley. Half an hour later Rachel stared at the country before them.

The wind was whipping through the restricted pass, and she looked into it, blinking, to see what lay ahead. The land was even more rocky and steep than what they'd come through. Scrawny trees dotted the harsh, dehydrated landscape. Rachel tried to ignore the continued unsettled feeling within her and study the region. As far as she could see, hundreds of caves appeared as dark holes carved into the hills. The sun was dipping into the west, and she squinted against it.

"Caves," she told Chase, keeping her grip firm around his large waist.

"Good. We should find one large enough to hide in for the night," he muttered. Every step increased his pain. Chase wanted nothing more than to stop and sleep.

Licking her dry lips, Rachel took a firmer grip on his arm around her shoulder. "Come on, Captain, I see a possible candidate for us. We have to get down off this hill. We're sitting ducks."

"Suits me," he growled, forcing himself to pick up each booted foot and place it squarely in front of him.

"How's your head?"

"Worse than any curse words you've ever heard."

"And probably worse than any cuss word you could concoct, Captain." She swallowed hard, the nausea stalking her in earnest. What was wrong with her?

Chase hurt too much to speak, each sound magnifying a hundredfold inside his head. He gritted his teeth, leaning heavily on Rachel.

The first cave at the bottom of the hill fit the bill in Rachel's estimation. It was barely five feet high but was almost ten feet in length, able to accommodate and hide two people. After throwing a few rocks into it to check for animals, Rachel helped Chase get in-

side. The floor consisted of smooth stone and pow-
dery dust. She made sure he was well hidden, by the
shadows, from possible patrols that might investigate
the surrounding hills. The roof of the cave allowed her
to crawl around on her hands and knees, but not to
stand.

To Rachel's utter delight, there was a pool of water
in the rear and a small stream that disappeared into the
rock wall. Chase lay down, using his arm as a pillow
for his head.

Her nausea was becoming nearly unbearable.
Rachel felt as if she had stomach flu and hurried out
of the cave without explanation.

Chase scowled, watching her brush by him. What
was wrong with Rachel? He propped himself up, following her progress out of the mouth of the cave. She
was pale, her eyes dark. Before Chase could speak, to
tell her to be careful and watchful of possible enemy
patrols, she crawled the last few feet to the dry grass
in front of the cave. The sounds of retching followed.
If he hadn't felt so damned faint, Chase would have
gotten up and gone to help her. Feeling helpless, he
had no choice but to lie back down.

He waited, keying his hearing to her return. It was
a long time, and Chase fretted inwardly. Patrols would
be out looking for them. The longer she stayed outside, the greater the chance of being spotted. Finally
he heard Rachel enter the cave. He opened his eyes,
pushing himself up on one elbow.

"You all right?" he asked, his voice gravelly.

Rachel held his narrowed, demanding look. "I—
yes." There was a tremble in her voice. And her hands
were shaking. She had gathered an armful of dried
grass to make a pallet for Chase. Actually Rachel had

spent the time alone trying to control all her escaping emotions. Pulling the huge swatches of grass had helped calm her nerves. "I threw up," she admitted, embarrassed. "I don't know why."

"Welcome to combat," Chase muttered. Her face was drawn, her eyes bleak. She winced at his blunt statement. "Throwing up is one of many reactions," he explained, trying to soften his tone.

Relief jagged through Rachel and she held the grass a little tighter, needing something that symbolized stability. "It is?"

"Yeah."

"I didn't know...." Her voice trailed off, absorbed by the wall of rock.

"How could you? It isn't every day your unit gets overrun by North Koreans and you get captured." Chase held her tenuous gaze, finding her features utterly vulnerable now. All the bravado Rachel had displayed earlier dissolved under the realization of what had happened to her over the past twelve hours. Delayed reaction to the mortar shelling, capture and escape had caught up with her, Chase realized. He patted the floor beside him.

"Listen, come and lie down for a while. You need to rest. This has been one hell of a day for you."

The invitation sounded wonderful. "I—I am tired." Exhausted would be a more appropriate word. Rachel saw Chase give her a tender smile, and it sent a sheet of warmth through her cold, trembling body.

"Come on," he urged. "I may be a miserable bastard with a blinding headache, but I won't bite you. Lie close, it's cold in this place."

Nodding, Rachel crawled forward. "I can give you the grass—"

"You use it. Come on, think of yourself for once."
He noted that her long, expressive fingers were white.
The amount of fear she must be feeling was overwhelming her. Chase took some of the proffered grass,
spreading it out thinly across the surface.

Rachel gave him a grateful look and lay down, her
back toward him. She used her arm as a pillow as he
had. "Thank you," she whispered. Even now, tremors
ran through her, and she drew her knees upward,
wanting to retreat into a fetal position.

Lying there in the silence, Chase listened to her
choppy, uneven breathing. He wanted to reach over
and pull her close to him, but he didn't dare. They
were strangers. He was a man and she was a woman.
If he tried it, she'd probably be shocked and properly
outraged. Fighting the desire to drag her against him,
to share body heat and help her up and over the combat reaction, Chase glared out into the gray dusk.

"When I shot down my first MiG, I landed and
promptly threw up in the cockpit of my plane," he
began in a roughened tone. "My mechanic, Sergeant
Owens, came over and shoved the canopy back and
looked at me. He's an older fella, and must have at
least fifteen years in the service."

Chase's voice washed across her like a warming
blanket, soothing the ragged edges of her composure.
"W-what did he say?" she asked in a strained voice.

"Slapped me on the back and congratulated me."
Chase closed his eyes. "He said, 'Welcome to combat, Lieutenant. Some men heave their guts out.
Others have bad dreams. Some cry. That's the way it
is, sir.' A real short, succinct lesson about war, isn't
it?"

A whisper of torn breath escaped from Rachel. "Yes. My stomach was upset for a long time. I thought I was getting the flu."

The ebony tresses lay sleekly against her shoulders and neck. Chase had a wild desire to reach out, thread his fingers through that beautiful, tangled mass and comfort her. Tearing his thoughts and desires from Rachel, he muttered, "No one said combat was fun. It's hell. A very personal hell."

Sliding her arm against her grumbling stomach, Rachel asked, "Does this feeling ever go away?"

"Yeah, if you go to sleep, you'll feel partly human when you wake up." His brows drew downward. "But I can't vouch for the memories or the fear. They hang around a lot longer."

Closing her eyes tightly, Rachel admitted, "I'm scared to death, Captain. I didn't realize it until I threw up. I was so busy making sure we weren't seen and taking care of you, all those emotions just got shoved down inside me for a while."

"Call me Chase. And I'm scared, too. Fear's a healthy thing. It'll keep us alive and get us out of this mess."

The desire to turn over and crawl into his arms was overwhelming. Rachel's eyes widened at the yearning deep within her. Chase had a rough timbre to his voice, and this time it was filled with incredible tenderness. Realizing he wasn't an ogre all the time took another layer of weight off Rachel's shoulders.

Sighing, she closed her eyes. "I'm so tired, Chase. I've got to sleep...."

"Then do it. We shouldn't both sleep. One of us needs to stand guard. I'll wake you up in four hours and then you can take the watch."

He was right, Rachel realized with a jolt. They were in enemy territory with no promise of getting back to their lines or getting out of this alive. She wrestled with the fear again, everything foreign to her. "Four hours," she repeated tiredly. And within moments, she spiraled into a dreamless sleep.

Rachel awoke with a jerk. Sunlight was streaming across the valley outside the cave, striking the withered ocher landscape. Heart pounding, she sat up, looking to her right. Chase was snoring softly, asleep. Fear stabbed through her. He hadn't awakened her in four hours. When had he fallen asleep? The possibility of the enemy finding them while they both slept was great.

Crawling to the mouth of the cave, Rachel flattened out on her stomach, perusing the windswept terrain. A few birds were singing, but she saw no other sign of life. Relief rolled through her and she got up, moving back to where Chase lay.

Without thinking, Rachel smoothed several limp strands of his hair away from his bandaged forehead. In those velvet moments, her heart blossomed with an incredible array of feelings as she gazed down at his face. Even in sleep, Chase's brow was slightly furrowed with pain. His mouth sent unbidden desire through Rachel and she stared at it, wondering what it would be like to kiss him, to feel his masculine strength.

Right now, Chase looked almost boyish. The rumpled strands of his hair, although short, added to his look of vulnerability. His antagonism stemmed, Rachel was sure, from being wounded and in pain. The shape of his mouth told her he wasn't always a grouch. No, his mouth promised strength coupled with great tenderness. Her hand came to rest on his shoulder as she drank Chase into her mind and heart.

The night before, Rachel had been on the receiving end of his tenderness and care. Chase hadn't had to share the story of his first combat experience with her or admit he'd been sick afterward. Despite his masculine stance toward women in general, he had been sensitive enough, concerned enough, to overcome his considerable male pride and share something of value between them.

"You're something else, mister," Rachel whispered. "Something else..." She couldn't compare Chase to any man in her experience. Of course, over the years, men had made passes at her, even stolen kisses. Rachel had been taught that the gift of herself was to be saved for marriage and her husband. Therefore, the groping hands of a number of boyfriends had been turned aside with studied insistence.

Looking at Chase, Rachel wondered if her resolve was strong enough. There was an intense sensuality to his mouth, to his whole body! She ached to spread her hand across his massive chest and explore it, not as a nurse, but as a woman. Sure, she knew the names of the bones and muscles. But Chase beckoned and stirred fires that lay beneath medical expertise.

Stymied by the new, unexpected feelings, Rachel closed her eyes. She had to think. She had to separate her emotions toward Chase and be clear about their escape effort. Because of the severity of his head wound, he wasn't capable of staying awake at night. She would have to be their eyes and ears, catching quick naps during the day in order to stay awake at night to protect them.

Her stomach growled loudly, and Rachel pressed her hand against the region. She was starved. The stream in the rear gave her an idea, and she moved quietly out of the cave and into the sunlight. Chase was sleeping soundly. Let him. At least one of them would wake up in a good humor.

Chase blinked, the light hurting his eyes. It took several minutes to realize where he was. His mind wasn't functioning very well at all, the pain a constant sledgehammer within his head. Grunting, he rolled over onto his side. Where was Rachel?

His mouth was thick and gummy, a croak coming out instead of her name. Dizziness assailed him briefly as he sat up. Rubbing his hand across his jaw, he realized belatedly that he needed to shave, the bristles sharp against his palm. His eyes adjusting to the sunlight, he looked around the silent maw.

Where the hell was Rachel! Dammit, didn't she realize the enemy was close? Where was she? Out powdering her nose? His anger rose with the incessant pain in his skull. Thirsty, he slowly got to his hands and knees, working his way back to the stream, drinking his fill.

Chase realized with renewed grimness that he was in no state to travel by himself. Just that small amount of crawling to and from his grass pallet had proven that. That would mean another day of leaning on Rachel, depending on a woman. He frowned, drawing up his legs and resting his brow against his knees. Good thing she couldn't read minds; she'd surely get her back up over that last thought.

Why did her independence and lack of need to lean on a man bother him so much? He barely knew her.

They weren't engaged. Matter of fact, there was nothing between them. In his mind's eye, Chase pictured her natural grace, the way her hips swung freely from side to side and the defiant way she held her chin, just daring someone to challenge her.

A grin leaked through his tightly set lips. What a beautiful hellion she was. He'd like to tame her, watch her defiance melt into cries of pleasure. Would her eyes deepen in color, a velvety green to match the richness of fulfillment he would give to her? Or would they lighten in color, like sunlight splashed across the surface of a lake?

Where was Rachel? Chase lifted his head, becoming more concerned. A good ten minutes had passed, according to his watch. Had a patrol discovered her? Was she captured, refusing to tell them where he was hidden? Ugly and unwanted pictures flashed through Chase's mind.

His anger was turning into genuine worry. Chase rarely worried about anything. But his Irish lightweight was out there somewhere, causing him a hell of a lot of unnecessary consternation. Suddenly, with a muffled curse, Chase rolled onto his hands and knees and started to crawl toward the glare of sunlight. He wasn't used to the avalanche of unbridled emotions that came with his decision to try to locate Rachel. The pain in the region of his heart was as real as the pain in his head. He knew why his head hurt, but he was stymied by the ache that was widening every moment in his chest. Whether he liked it or not, Rachel meant something to him. Not knowing whether to be happy or sad about that discovery, Chase forced himself forward.

Chapter Four

"Where the hell have you been?" Chase exploded.

Rachel froze at the lip of the cave, her hands filled with food for them. Her mouth dropped open and then she snapped it shut, her green eyes blazing as she held the pilot's furious gaze.

"Where have I been?" She glared at Chase. Her voice grew strident in uncharacteristic fashion. "Who do you think you are, bellowing at me like I'm some child to be punished?" Thrusting her hands forward, she shoved the food under his nose. "These are mussels. I found them in the stream in back of the cave. I don't know about you, but I'm starved and I intend to eat these slimy things!"

Chase watched her move by him and sit down on the grass pallet. His anger cooled by degrees as he made his way back to join her.

"It's almost eleven hundred," he grouched, sitting cross-legged, opposite her. "When I woke up, you were gone. How the hell did I know you were out foraging for food? For all I knew, the enemy had captured you."

"You're the one who overslept. What did you want me to do? Wake you up and tell you where I was going?" Rachel tried to stop the hurt and accusation from leaking through her voice, but she couldn't help it. Like a child finding treasure, she had happened upon the mussels in the stream. Finding enough food for both of them had made her confidence soar. When Chase bellowed like a wounded bull, demanding to know where she had been, it had spoiled her joy. Did it ever occur to the thick-headed pilot that she didn't have pencil and paper to leave him a note?

Chase stared down at the black and gray mussels, digesting her righteous anger. "Look, I'm a bear today. My head hurts and I'm hungry." That was as close to an apology as she was going to get from him.

Rachel flicked a glance up at him. "People aren't usually at their best when they're injured, Captain."

"Call me Chase," he ordered tightly, trying to defuse the anger that hung between them.

Rachel shoved six mussels toward him. "I don't feel very friendly toward someone who can only yell at me. You're not my father. We're both adults in a bad situation, so let's start acting like it."

He glared at her. "I was worried, okay?"

"Worried?" Rachel grabbed the first mussel, using a thin stick to try to force open the shells. "You have a funny way of showing it."

"I like you and I was concerned."

Startled, Rachel jerked a look up at Chase. It was true. She could see the concern, not anger, in his blue eyes. Heat rushed into her cheeks, and she quickly dipped her head, pretending to work at opening the mussel. "Oh..."

He wanted to throttle her. "You're touchier than that plane I fly."

"Flew," she corrected, trying to pry the shells open.

"All right, flew." Chase sat back, shaking his head slightly. "Has anyone ever told you you're stubborn, bullheaded, and a know-it-all?"

Rachel eyed him. "Many times. Usually, men who are defensive about my ability to think and speak for myself, *Captain*."

Irritation rippled through Chase. Still, he admired Rachel's skill at being able to find them food. How many people would have overlooked the stream, not thinking of edible creatures other than fish? He picked up a mussel and, using a penknife he always carried in his pocket, opened it.

"Where'd you learn to hunt for mussels?" he demanded sourly, revealing the mussel's fleshy interior. Chase handed the opened shell to Rachel, taking the one she was having no success with.

Rachel stared. He had a knife! Reluctantly she took the proffered mussel. "My dad taught me how to survive in the woods if I ever got lost." She eyed the meat, thinking how slimy it looked. Her stomach growled. Could she eat it?

"Where?"

"Maine."

"No wonder you're so bullheaded and independent."

Rachel grinned, noting that the surliness in Chase's voice had disappeared. She watched as he expertly opened the rest of the shells in quick succession. "Back where I come from, I'm seen as self-sufficient, not any of the unflattering adjectives you've labeled me with."

"Are you always this feisty?" Chase looked up, snared by the amusement in her eyes. There was a crooked smile on her full, firm lips . . . lips he wanted to taste, subdue and pleasure.

"Are you always down on women?"

"Touché." Chase folded the penknife and slid it back into his pocket. "I happen to like women very much." And then he smiled boyishly for the first time. "After all, I'm single, relatively good-looking and they seem to like me, too."

Rachel gave him a flat look. "Typical arrogant fly-boy. Your ego's as big as that inflated head of yours."

Chase popped the first of the mussels into his mouth, relishing the meat. "Lady, you have to have a healthy ego to fly a prop plane up against a jet-powered North Korean MiG."

He had a point, Rachel realized, still eyeing the mussels unenthusiastically. She really did have to eat them if she was going to have any energy to walk and help Chase.

"Go on, eat," Chase encouraged, popping a second and then a third one into his mouth. "They're good."

Wrinkling her nose, Rachel muttered, "I hate clams and such." She shivered. "They're so slimy!"

Grinning, Chase said, "I don't believe it. Lieutenant Rachel McKenzie has a weak spot in her armor after all. I'll be damned."

"You," Rachel retaliated heatedly, "don't know the first thing about me. Just because I don't like to eat slimy creatures doesn't make me weak!" Gingerly she picked up the flesh between her fingertips, holding it before her.

Chase took pity on her. He saw the agony in Rachel's eyes. "I know enough to see you're going to have a tough time swallowing them."

With a little sound of defeat, Rachel put the flesh back into the shell. "I can't eat it. I'm afraid I'll throw it up."

"No, you won't. I thought that at first, too, when I learned to eat them a long time ago. I lived in a lot of places, growing up, because my father was in the military for thirty years. Once, we lived near the ocean. Mom is a Massachusetts native, and she taught us how to hunt for clams on the beach and eat them."

Grimacing, Rachel muttered, "I'm glad for you."

"Maine has lots of beachfront property, too."

"I lived inland."

There was something vulnerable about Rachel at that moment. Chase reached out, placing his hand on her slumped shoulder. "When was the last time you ate?"

She shrugged, stabilizing beneath his firm touch. "I don't know. The ROKs and Aussies retreated around dawn yesterday. We'd been up through the night ferrying our patients to the helicopters, getting them out of there before the enemy overran our unit."

Chase saw her tuck her lower lip between her teeth. "It's a wonder you're still able to walk," he said quietly. "You've been without food for over twenty-four hours, then."

"I guess," Rachel admitted wearily. "To tell you the truth, our concern was getting the patients to safety. None of us wanted them to fall into enemy hands."

There was a quiet kind of courage about her, Chase realized, seeing Rachel in a new and interesting light. "And I'll bet you worked harder than anyone." His fingers tightened perceptibly on her shoulder. So much bravery in such a small powder keg of a woman.

Lifting her head, Rachel stared over at Chase. "I was the head surgery nurse. It was my responsibility to make sure everything was taken care of."

"And you never stopped to eat."

"No . . . stupid, huh?"

He managed a thin smile, trying to cover his pain. "Commendable in my eyes." Squeezing her shoulder, he reluctantly pulled his hand away. If he kept it there any longer, Chase knew he'd be unable to resist stroking the clean line of her jaw, trailing his fingers down the length of her lovely neck in an exploratory gesture.

Rallying beneath his sudden, unexpected tenderness, Rachel tried to smile. "Commendable or not, I've got to eat these things."

"Put them in that stream back there for about ten minutes. The water's cold. It will firm them up."

Taking the mussels to the stream, Rachel found a spot to place them in the water, then sat waiting. In the shadows, Chase's face was strong and hard looking. Meeting his gaze, however, Rachel felt the warmth reach out from him and gently hold her captive. She wrapped her arms around her drawn-up legs.

"I haven't even asked how you feel," Rachel offered softly.

"Better and worse," Chase admitted, pointing to his head. "I don't feel as dizzy, but I feel grouchier." He gave her an apologetic look. "You already know that, though."

Rachel smiled acceptance of the unspoken apology. "It's understandable. You've got a four-inch gash that needs to be sewn shut. Your skull isn't broken, but you really scrambled your brain when you hit the tail of your plane."

"I've got good news and bad news for you, then," Chase answered with a careless grin. He dug into another pocket of his flight suit. "The good news is, I've got a needle and thread." He produced a small first aid kit. "There's a pair of scissors in there, too. The bad news is, I know what you're going to do with them."

Delighted with the discovery of the medical items, Rachel crawled back to where he sat, opening the case. "I didn't know you guys carried things like this." Indeed, the kit contained antiseptic, bandages and various other first aid articles.

"Don't sound so happy. I don't really want anyone to touch my head."

Rachel smiled, holding his unhappy gaze. "Your head will hurt less when I get done patching you up, Capt—Chase."

Rallying beneath her attempt to be friendly, he shrugged his broad shoulders. "While your mussels are chilling to the perfect eating temperature, why don't you sew up my thick skull, doc?"

Rachel didn't need another invitation. Chase sat stoically, lips compressed, eyes narrowed, not uttering a word of protest as she cleaned the wound and sewed it shut. She had lost count of how many times she had sewn up the minor wounds of men. To ease their discomfort, Rachel always chatted with them in soothing tones. It was no different with Chase.

"You said your father was in the service?"

Chase closed his eyes. Although Rachel was delicate, it was still painful. "Yeah. I come from a hundred-and-eighty-year family tradition of military service. He was a general in the Army when he retired. My two brothers and I went into various branches of the service. Boyd's in the Marine Corps, Steve's in the navy and I'm in the air force."

Laughing huskily, Rachel said, "Are you the oldest?"

"How'd you guess?"

"Because you're bossy and a know-it-all."

Chase grinned sardonically. He was delighted with her lightning-quick retorts. "Then you must be first-born, too."

"I was an only child."

"That explains it."

"What?"

"Taking over," he explained. If the sewing hadn't been so damned uncomfortable, Chase would have enjoyed Rachel's closeness. Her body was fractions of an inch from his shoulder and arm. The musky scent of her made him dizzy in a new and enjoyable way. It would be so easy to curve his arm around her, drawing her against him.

"Taking over is fully acceptable if a man does it— he's called a leader. But if a woman tries to lead, she's called bossy and told she doesn't know her place." Rachel leaned over, catching the agony in his stormy eyes. So far, Chase hadn't uttered a groan. "Or, am I putting words in your mouth?"

He grimaced, holding her smiling gaze. *Saucy wench. You've got the upper hand right now, but that will change. And when it does, I'll be the one who's smiling.* "I guess it's all right if a woman leads. Once in a while."

Chuckling, Rachel completed the job, dressing the wound and wrapping a clean bandage around his head. "If I hadn't led us, we'd be captured right now. Don't you think you ought to reevaluate women and their abilities?"

"Maybe," Chase grumped. He shot her a dark look. "You're still going the wrong direction, you know."

"My father taught me directions when I was seven years old. You're still disoriented and in shock from your wound, Chase. In another day or two, you'll see that we are going the right direction—south." Rachel delighted in their parrying with each other. She couldn't even be defensive about his last comment. Somehow Chase made her feel giddy and happy as no other man had. Gently knotting the bandage, Rachel dropped her hands to her thighs, sitting next to Chase.

Carefully touching his newly bandaged head, he muttered, "I feel better. In fact, almost normal."

"You aren't, not yet." Rachel gave him a pleading look. "Just trust me, Chase, will you? I know which way is south." She opened her hands to him. "Am I not worth trusting? Who got you out of that parachute and to safety? Who found us food?"

Grudgingly Chase realized Rachel was right, but he couldn't admit it. "Speaking of food, why don't you eat those critters. We need to get going. We're still not very far from where that convoy was strafed."

Curling her lip, Rachel nodded. She made her way back to the icy stream. With great reluctance, she picked the first mussel out of the water. To her delight, the flesh was much firmer and far less slimy.

"They taste a little like chicken," Chase encouraged. "Just close your eyes, pop it in your mouth and chew it. Think of a big fat roasting hen while you eat. Maybe that will help."

Rachel followed his direction. The first one was the toughest, but it went down easily to her surprise. She kept her eyes tightly shut, visualizing that chicken. Soon, all six were gone. Letting out a long breath of air, she glanced sheepishly over at Chase.

"Okay?" he asked, watching her come back to where he sat.

"I think so." Running her fingers through her hair, Rachel realized it needed a combing. "How's your head?"

"Better. It's not aching so much."

"Good." She crawled to the opening and looked out of the cave. "When I was out scouting around, I noticed there aren't many groves of trees. We're going to have to stick to the edge of this valley and use the huge rock formations for cover."

He nodded. Rachel was practical—another commendable trait. "You're right. Did you see any patrols?"

"No." She chewed on her lips. "I get this awful feeling they're close, though."

He snorted. "Women's intuition?"

"What's wrong with that?"

"It's unreliable."

Rachel glared at him. "You're so pigheaded!"

"Keep your voice down, sound carries."

That did it! Rachel scrambled to her feet, crouched over in the cave. She glanced around, making sure they were leaving nothing behind. "Come on, it's time to go. I don't happen to agree at all with your assessment of my intuition."

Without a word, Chase followed her out of the cave. He told himself that Rachel was upset over nothing. Intuition was women's emotionality at best. He wasn't about to trust his skin to her feelings, but he said nothing.

Rachel bristled as Chase placed his arm around her shoulders, leaning on her for support. "One of these days," she muttered fiercely under her breath, "you're going to eat your words, Captain. Just because I sense things differently doesn't mean I'm wrong! Come on, we've got some miles to make up for."

Chase didn't have the heart to argue. Let her anger give her the stamina for both of them. The sunlight was bright, peeking between building thunderheads. He winced, squinting. The concussion made his eyes extraordinarily sensitive to light, and he was unable to look around for signs of patrols as Rachel guided them between rock formations.

The ground was uneven. Around them, Chase saw turrets of rocks, reminding him of castles thrusting upward hundreds of feet tall. They were traversing a narrow valley with sparse vegetation and trees. Everything was yellowed and shriveled from lack of rain. Numerous caves dotted the hillsides, the brush clinging to them indicating water nearby.

Thirty minutes later, Rachel spotted an enemy patrol. Her breath caught in the back of her throat, and she jerked Chase to the right, pushing him behind one of the turretlike rock formations.

"Enemy!" she breathed sharply, shoving him between two large rocks until he disappeared into the shadows.

"Where?" Chase whispered, unable to look over the rocks. He saw Rachel's face go pale. She was hurriedly gathering brush.

"About half a mile south of us. They're coming our way."

He gripped her hand as she threw a large branch above his head. "Hold it. What are you doing?"

Fear was making her shaky. "Hiding you."

His grip tightened on her slender wrist. Chase saw the fear in her eyes. "What about *you*?"

"I'm going to be a decoy and lead them away from here."

His lips drew back from his teeth. "Like hell you are!" Chase exploded softly. "Get in here! There's enough room. We'll hide together."

Shaking her head, Rachel jerked out of his viselike grip. "No! Now shut up and lie on the ground. Hurry!"

Real anger wove through Chase. He rolled over onto his belly, hugging the ground. The North Koreans wouldn't find them. Why was Rachel willing to become a target? Clenching his fists, he closed his eyes as she hurled thickets of brush on top of him. Chase wanted to throttle her. This wasn't a game. Is that how she saw this exercise? A child's game of hide-and-seek?

As he lay there, his breathing harsh, Chase felt the layers of reason rip away to the real truth of his concern. Dammit, he liked Rachel. More than a little bit.

She was the most courageous, foolhardy woman he'd ever met. Chase wasn't sure how he felt about that. Within moments, he could barely see her legs outside the brush enclosure that surrounded him.

Rachel got down on her knees. "Chase?" she hissed.

"Yeah?"

His voice vibrated with anger. Right now, it didn't matter to Rachel. Her voice came out off-pitch. "Look, I'm going to try and lead them away. It's our only chance—"

"Then be *careful*!" He saw the terror etched on her face, her beautiful lips compressed. Disagreeing with Rachel was fruitless. Time was precious and Chase didn't want her wasting it arguing. "Stay low, and don't compromise yourself for me. Understand?"

"I'll be careful," Rachel promised raggedly, jerking a look over her shoulder. "They're coming, Chase. I've got to go. I'll be back...."

Chase wanted to hold her and tell her to take it easy, that everything would be all right. But none of that was true. Helplessness overwhelmed him. It was one thing for a man to be lost behind lines. To have a vulnerable, beautiful woman like Rachel putting her life in jeopardy was more than he could handle. He glared up through the branches.

"Dammit, you'd better come back in one piece! This is crazy. You could be hiding in here with me."

A tight smile edged Rachel's mouth as she rose unsteadily to her feet. "I'll be back, Captain. I'm not done haunting you yet."

She was gone. Chase watched Rachel spin around, leaping like a graceful gazelle between the rock formations, moving to higher ground until she disappeared from his view. The emergency ripped away Chase's defenses. A powerful emotion shattered through him, one that focused on Rachel and what she meant to him. He barely knew her, and yet he was reacting like a protective husband. Glowering down at the gray and brown earth, Chase laid his head on his hands, hearing the voices of the enemy patrol coming closer. Shutting his eyes, he prayed, something he did only in dire emergencies. But he didn't pray for himself; he prayed for Rachel's flight to safety.

Her breath coming in heaving gulps, Rachel leaped from one small boulder to another, scaling the hill. At the crest, hidden behind a turret, she crouched. Below, Rachel could see the twelve-man patrol, their dark brown uniforms blending with the grays and yellows of the valley.

To Rachel's despair, they were headed directly toward Chase. Without thinking, she picked up a rock, hurling it behind the patrol. The rock sailed down the hill, landing about three hundred feet behind them. The patrol was jumpy, whirling around. The rock struck a turret, exploding into hundreds of smaller fragments.

Standing up, Rachel deliberately exposed herself to the patrol. She heard them shout, gesturing excitedly in her direction. Good! Whirling around, she headed down the reverse side of the hill, running with cadence, watching where she put her feet. One slip and she could hurtle down the rock-strewn slope, spraining an ankle or worse, breaking a leg. Either way, Rachel could be captured—or killed.

She heard more shouts and knew they were climbing the hill in pursuit of her. So much of her father's training came back to her. Rachel listened to her instincts, weaving them with the common sense her parents had taught her. The hill was steep, flowing immediately into another rocky slope.

The sun was high overhead, telling Rachel it was noon. If she could outwit the patrol, find a place to hide and remember where Chase was hidden, she could wait until dusk to find her way back to him. Taking huge breaths through her mouth, Rachel pushed her body to its physical limits. All the time she was intent on evading the enemy, her heart was centered on Chase. The possibility of losing him kept Rachel honest with herself. She liked the guy. A lot. *Just let me get back to him. Let me find him safe tonight....*

Chase lay unmoving, cramped and stiff. Dusk was upon him; the patrol had left hours ago. But they could call in trucks loaded with more squads to search the area carefully. He remained where he was. Frustration and fear gnawed at him. Where the hell was Rachel? Was she safe? Had they found her? Two hours earlier, he'd heard rifle shots ripping through the silence of the valley. Sweat dripped from his furrowed brow. Dammit, she *had* to be safe! Her angel features hovered hotly before his mind's eye. The contralto warmth of her voice haunted him.

"Chase!"

His eyes flew open. Was it the wind picking up or did he hear Rachel's voice?

"Chase!"

"Here," he said, his voice cracking. It was Rachel! He pushed upward, getting to his hands and knees, moving the entire group of thickets that had hidden him.

"Thank God," Rachel whispered, running to the spot. Quickly she tore away the brush, uncovering Chase. In the dusky light, she could see the shadowed harshness of his face as he staggered to his feet. Never had he looked so good. With a little cry, Rachel threw her arms around him, hugging him, holding him.

"You're safe," he growled, his arms closing around Rachel, holding her tightly against him. Chase felt a little cry come from her. He pressed one hand against her hair, the other against her long, curved back. "God, I was worried sick," he admitted thickly, lost in the musky scent of her hair, the sweetness that was only Rachel.

"I'm okay...okay..." she quavered. Her cheek pressed against the dampness of his flight suit, Rachel felt and heard the powerful beat of Chase's heart. She tightened her arms around him, wildly aware of his strength and the protection that emanated from him like an intense beacon of light. He'd been just as frightened as she had. When his hand slid down her spine to capture her hips against his, a gasp of shock escaped her.

"No..." Rachel protested, placing her hands flat against his chest, pushing away. Heat stung her cheeks, and she was unable to look at him for several moments afterward, trying to grapple with her unraveling emotions.

"Sorry," Chase muttered, opening his hands toward her. "I—well, I was worried. I thought they might have got you and..." His voice failed him. Rachel had felt incredibly alive and warm in his arms. Hunger for her thundered through him. Savagely he reminded himself that they were nearly strangers to each other. Rachel didn't feel like a stranger, though. She had fitted perfectly against his frame, each of her delicious curves molding to his harder planes.

Watching her from beneath his lashes, Chase added, "I got carried away. I was just glad to see you. Are you all right?" He saw several small scratches on her left cheek, the blood having dried a long time ago.

Rachel stepped away from Chase's overwhelming male presence, rattled by the powerful feelings the contact had created. "I know...I got carried away, too. I'm glad you're safe." Everything about him sang through her like a sweet song that her body knew intimately. "And I'm fine," she added as an afterthought, completely disoriented by what she had done in throwing her arms around Chase.

Chase appraised her more critically. "What happened? I heard rifle fire about two hours ago." He kept his voice low, constantly perusing the darkening hills for patrols.

Rachel sat on a flat rock, needing to rest. Chase looked remarkably well—a hundred percent better than when she'd left him hours earlier. "I threw a rock to distract them," she told him, watching him crouch nearby. "I played the wounded-mother-bird trick on them and they fell for it."

"And the gunfire?"

Rachel shrugged. "I don't know. I was on the other side of the valley when it happened. Maybe they were killing some poor animal for food."

Nodding, Chase knew that was possible. "That was a crazy, stupid stunt you pulled. You could have hidden with me."

The anger wasn't in his voice, and Rachel saw the torment in his dark blue eyes. "Our boot prints are all over this place, Chase." She pointed to the tread marks imprinted in the dirt around his hiding place. "If the patrol had made it to this point, they'd have known we were there. I had to distract them before they saw these prints. If we'd had more time, I could have used a piece of brush to hide our tracks, but we didn't." Rachel shoved several strands of hair out of her eyes. "I didn't have a choice."

Chase considered her argument. Damned if she wasn't right—again. And her woman's instincts had forewarned her of the enemy's nearness. He held her gaze, noting the exhaustion in her eyes. "Maybe we ought to have you teach our guys survival tactics."

She smiled, hearing the admiration in his tone, allowing his deep voice to wash across her like a healing blanket. "Thank my dad. He was the one who showed me a mother kildeer flapping her wing on the ground as if it were broken, to draw us away from her babies."

"One of these days, I'd like to shake your dad's hand and tell him he helped save my neck," Chase admitted ruefully, meeting and matching her smile. The ache to reach out and fold Rachel into his arms was excruciating. Chase reluctantly tabled the desire, realizing it was wrong under the circumstances. Hell, their embrace had been wrong, too, but he hadn't cared. They had come together like spontaneous combustion. It wasn't safe to hold her, Chase realized, because he had little control over his emotions toward Rachel. And she deserved his respect, not his groping.

"I found some water at the end of this valley," Rachel said, pointing in the direction. "On the other side is a village, a small one."

Chase studied her in silence. He saw the longing in her eyes; she couldn't hide how she felt about him, either. Their relationship was mutual and hope sprang strongly in his chest.

"Chase?"

"Huh? Oh, yeah. We should head toward the water and stay clear of the village."

Rachel saw the faraway look in his eyes and wondered what was going on inside that head of his. "You look better."

"I am." He touched the bandage. "And my headache is gradually going away."

"Good." Rachel stood up, stiff and sore. "Feel like taking a stroll with me to that water?"

He rose to his feet. "I never turn down an offer from a beautiful woman."

She colored fiercely as he slid his arm along her shoulder. "I'll bet you don't." Rachel gripped his wrist, prepared to take his weight.

"Now you're accusing me of being a lecher," Chase complained good-naturedly, meeting and holding her lovely eyes that sparkled with accusation.

Rachel propelled him forward, surprised that he wasn't leaning as heavily on her as before. Perhaps tomorrow Chase could walk on his own. "I haven't met a fly-boy yet that wasn't a groper, Captain," she returned evenly. "Even when they're wounded and just coming out of anesthesia, they're reaching for you."

A chuckle rumbled through his chest. They would have to stop talking soon, and Chase didn't want to.

"Can't blame the guys. You're a beautiful and desirable lady."

Ordinarily Rachel could handle such a compliment, but when it came from Chase, her womanly instincts responded differently, scaring and beckoning to her at the same time. "You're probably the biggest groper of them all," she muttered.

He smiled down at her but said nothing.

Heat spread through Rachel, and she drowned in his very male smile. Suddenly Chase seemed dangerous—almost more dangerous than the enemy they were trying to evade. Rachel dodged his conceited gaze, keeping her eyes on the rocky terrain ahead of them.

Chapter Five

"I've got to rest," Rachel groaned. She felt Chase halt immediately. His hand cupped her shoulder and he drew her against him, allowing her to relax. The gesture was simple and implicit: Rachel was to lean on him, if only for a moment. The darkness was serrated by thickening clouds, pregnant with rain, thin slices of a quarter moon shafting through the ragged ceiling here and there.

Unresisting, Rachel buried her face in the folds of Chase's flight suit, allowing him to take her weight. They had traveled through the valley, drunk their fill of water and moved on down into the next valley. Progress was good because the moonlight had allowed just enough light to see their way, without exposing them to the eyes of possible enemy patrols.

Chase pressed his bearded cheek against Rachel's head, inhaling the scent of her, branding on his senses the memory of how the sleekness of her hair felt. "Come on, let's call it a night." He looked at his watch: it was midnight. Throughout the evening, his eyesight had improved. His headache no longer blinded him with pain, and most of the dizziness had disappeared.

Rachel knew she should push away from Chase. It wasn't proper. But every muscle in her body was protesting fatigue, and right now Chase felt far more powerful and capable than she did. Finally Rachel forced herself to move away from him. To have Chase hold her while she fell asleep would be a dream come true. Ashamed of her torrid thoughts, Rachel chastised herself.

Her stomach grumbling loudly, she followed Chase to a small cave carved into the hillside. After throwing several stones into the maw with no response from within, he gestured for her to follow him.

The cave was smaller and narrower than the previous night's haven. Rachel eyed it apprehensively. There was barely enough room for two people—unless they huddled against each other. Rachel didn't want that. She didn't trust herself or Chase.

"Isn't this too small?" Her voice seemed thin and scratchy even to her own ears.

"Beggars can't be choosers." Chase craned his neck, studying the dark terrain below them in the valley. "Any closer to that village and we risk being detected." He motioned to the hole. "I'm afraid this is it for the night."

Panic ate at her. "But—it's so small."

Chase heard her strident protest. "Rachel, I'll keep my hands to myself, I promise you." He held her uncertain gaze. Right now, she seemed more little girl than woman. Could he blame her? "Are you engaged?"

Her eyes widened. "No. Why?" And then she realized why he was asking the question, feeling stupid that she hadn't figured it out sooner.

"Women who are about to get married usually aren't so naive," he muttered.

Rachel stood openmouthed, stunned by the inference. "Captain, I may be green as grass, but I've been around men long enough to know a few things!"

He grinned lopsidedly at her heated response, watching a flush suffuse her cheeks. "Calm down, Rachel. I wasn't attacking your chastity. You're jumpy, that's all. I was just trying to figure out if you didn't trust me out of ignorance or out of knowledge."

Stung, she glared at him. "Just because guys mess around all the time before marriage doesn't mean we do. And just because I'm 'ignorant' doesn't mean I'm stupid about these matters. That cave is too small. The only way we could fit into it is if we scooted up against each other. And I'm not about to do that!"

Chase swallowed his grin, realizing she'd fly into more of a rage if she saw his response. She was frightened. Of him? Of herself, possibly? He wasn't sure. And it was obvious he couldn't ask her. Rachel resented the unvarnished truth when it came to sex, but that wasn't her fault. It was a man's duty to protect a woman from that side of life.

"Okay," he muttered, "I'll sleep out here and you sleep in the cave."

In a quandary, Rachel searched for a way out of the unexpected problem. "I'm starved. I can smell food coming from that village. I saw a few cooking pots outside some of the huts. Maybe I can steal down there and get us some food." The plan gave her time to figure out sleeping arrangements.

Chase's eyes rounded. "You aren't going down there." His order came out in a strangled sound, laced with fury.

Jamming her hands on her hips, Rachel gave Chase a black stare. "There's no water nearby. No mussels. We can't possibly continue tomorrow without finding something to eat tonight."

Chase rankled at her logic. He advanced upon her, gripping her proudly thrown-back shoulders. "Listen to me, you stuck your neck out once today and got lucky. You go down there—" he thrust a finger in the direction of the village "—and you could get caught. Use your head, Rachel."

With a little cry of frustration, Rachel pulled from his grasp, taking several steps backward. "Lucky? What I did today wasn't luck! It was a premeditated plan that I pulled off successfully." She shook her head, completely disgusted. "And I suppose *you're* going down there to get us food?"

"I wouldn't even consider it," Chase ground out. "It's too risky."

"I'm starved," Rachel flung back hotly. "Forget it, Chase, I'm going."

"You're such a hellion," he snarled. "You won't listen to anybody!"

She compressed her lips, wildly aware of his concern. Rachel knew the real reason she wanted to go—to avoid the cave and Chase's arms. But how could she admit that? Right now, he looked like an enraged bull ready to take a china shop apart. Memory of his strong fingers searching, gliding down her spine, eliciting shivers of need from her, frightened Rachel into action.

"I'm going. I'll be back as soon as I can."

Chase opened his mouth to protest, but Rachel turned and ran down the slope, disappearing among the huge boulders that stood sentry all around them. "Damn her," he muttered, walking slowly toward the cave.

Later, after he'd cooled down, Chase tried to see Rachel, but the shadows deepened as the clouds became opaque, blocking out the moon's gossamer light. Instead, Chase busied himself with grabbing large handfuls of dried grass to make a pallet in the cave. When he had enough, he stood listening. No sound came from the village, only the inconstant, humid breeze across the hills.

Rain would fall soon, he thought, gathering more dried grass for a second pallet outside the cave entrance. Did Rachel realize the Koreans had dogs in their villages? One bark would alert the people, and she would be discovered. Damn her! When she got back—if she got back—they were going to have a heart-to-heart talk about who was in charge and who wasn't! She was such an independent wench. He admired her gutsiness and courage, but not her inability to listen to reason.

Rachel hesitated beside the last boulder, studying the village thoroughly. The moonlight was gone, leaving only darkness with vague shapes here and there. The thirty thatched huts were quiet, the people in bed. Hopefully, asleep. She flared her nostrils, drinking in a spicy scent of nearby food. Where?

Easing from her crouched position, she positioned herself at one end of the village. Near the door of the closest hut, Rachel saw a brazier with a black kettle suspended above the dying coals of a fire. Next to it was a big black dog with one ear missing. She froze as the dog's one ear pricked up in interest, looking toward her.

Swallowing against a dry throat, Rachel tensed. She watched the dog, a mangy, thin mongrel the size of a German shepherd, get up and trot to where she was hiding. Groaning inwardly, she froze, waiting for the dog to howl out a warning.

To her surprise, the black dog didn't bark. Wagging his tail, he approached. Rachel held out her hand, making sure to keep her fingers closed against her palm. Her mother had taught her as a child never to extend fingers to an animal—it was a sure way to lose them. Besides, the animal was less likely to try to bite into a much larger fist.

Expecting the dog to growl or bite, Rachel held her breath, speaking softly to him. Relief fled through her when he relished her hand with his thick, warm tongue. Closing her eyes, Rachel felt her heart bang violently against her throat. The dog nudged closer, burying his head against her breast, his tail wagging furiously. In that instant, she was reminded of Chase, of his ability to show his feelings, something many men couldn't do. They shared something special, Rachel realized, patting the dog absently. And Chase seemed to know what it was, even if she didn't.

Rising slowly, Rachel focused on stealing the kettle that contained the food. The dog stayed at her thigh, happy to escort her down the slope toward the hut.

The area was quiet and deserted, wind whipping leaves and other debris across the center of the village.

What if someone woke? There had to be other dogs. What if they barked? Rachel planned alternate escape routes in case a villager appeared. Her mouth grew dry as she stepped onto the level, well-swept ground. The kettle was a large iron pot, the aroma coming from it mouth watering. The dog surged ahead of her as two of his friends appeared from around a hut near the center of the village.

Rachel froze. She saw the hackles rise on the backs of the other two dogs. If they barked... The black dog touched their noses, as if telling them she was a friend. All three of them came back, circling her, brushing against her legs, begging to be petted. Rachel patted them, her gaze nervously perusing the community. *What a situation*... Chase would probably shake his head if he saw that she'd made friends with the guardians of the village. He was probably waiting on the hillside, wondering when the barking would wake the occupants.

Chase sat at the lip of the cave, arms dangling between his legs. The moment he heard a sound, he was on his feet, hiding behind a large boulder.

"It's me...."

Recognizing Rachel's husky voice, he straightened.

"And my friends..."

Scowling, he stepped from behind the boulder. She was coming up the hill with three dogs at her heels. Maybe he should have laughed, but Chase didn't feel amused, only relieved. Rachel was grinning broadly, carrying the kettle in triumph.

"Chow's on," she huffed, coming up to him.

He took the handle of the kettle. "You didn't wake anyone?" he growled. Chase chastised himself for the anger in his tone. He saw the smile dissolve on her strained features.

"No, of course not." Rachel gestured around to the dogs. "They're from the village. I guess they think they're going to get the leftovers after we've eaten our fill."

Glowering at the animals, Chase saw the black dog's hackles rise. "Pet the bastard before he starts barking at me," he ordered tightly, grabbing the kettle and heading back to the cave entrance.

"It's okay," Rachel soothed the black dog, smoothing down his hackles. Holding on to her anger over Chase's sulky nature, she followed him to the grass pallet near the cave. The dogs hung back at a respectful distance, as if taught not to get too close to the dinner table. Rachel crouched down opposite Chase, motioning to the pot.

"I smell meat and rice. Look how much is in there."

The pride in her voice was unmistakable. Chase frowned and dipped his fingers into the unknown mixture. He drew out a glob, smelling it cautiously. "Smells okay," he grumbled.

Rachel used her fingers, taking out a small portion. "Smells wonderful!" And then she grinned. "Anything's better than slimy mussels."

Her spirit was irresistible, and Chase managed a sour smile, tasting the fare. "Good..."

Good? Rachel ate the first bite, savoring the spicy fare with hungry relish. It was a combination of cabbage, rice and meat—and it was delicious. They both ate in starved silence, dipping their fingers into the pot again and again. Her eyes watered from the spices in the mixture. Rachel was sure hot peppers figured in the recipe, but it didn't matter.

Stuffed like a Christmas goose, Rachel took the tin can from the back of her belt, filling it with food. She covered it with a piece of silk. Chase gave a nod, approving of her idea. He pulled the first aid kit from his pocket, emptying the contents into another pocket. He handed the box to her.

"Fill this, too. We don't know when we'll get another meal."

Rachel agreed, stuffing the plastic box full of the food. She got up afterward, gripping the kettle handle. "I'm taking this back down to the village where it belongs."

"Why?" Chase wondered if she had a death wish.

"Because," Rachel explained patiently, "tomorrow morning they'll think the dogs got into the food, not us. If they knew we were here, they might call the soldiers. It's a dead giveaway that we were in the area, Chase."

He rubbed his brow. What the hell was the matter with him? Of course Rachel was right. "I think this concussion is really fouling me up," he muttered in apology.

"I understand," Rachel responded softly. "I'll be back as soon as I can."

Chase snapped his head up. Silhouetted in the darkness, he could barely make out her features. "Take these mutts with you. We don't need them following us."

"Right."

"Rachel?"

She turned, looking across her shoulder. "Yes?"

"Be *very* careful."

Rachel saw the glimmer in his eyes, his concern burning straight through to her heart. "Of course."

Chase watched her disappear, the faithful dogs at her heels. If they weren't in such a dangerous situation, he'd have thought it an endearing picture. Rachel had a way of taming the most ferocious of beasts— even him. Sighing, he stood waiting tensely for her return.

The rain started minutes later. Chase cursed under his breath, moving to the dryness of the cave. The temperature was dropping, and his flight suit wasn't enough to stave off the chill brought by the rain. He sat cross-legged, anxiously awaiting Rachel. Time crawled by. Chase kept looking at his watch. Each minute felt like a miserable hour.

Rachel appeared out of the darkness, her once buoyant page boy hanging limply around her face. She was soaked, Chase discovered, as she crawled into the confines of the cave. Her fatigues were drenched, and she was shivering involuntarily.

"Come here," he ordered roughly, gathering her into his arms despite her protests.

Between the fear of being discovered and the cold rain, Rachel was chilled. As Chase reached out, dragging her against him and then settling onto his back, all her protests died away. He was warm, and Rachel closed her eyes, snuggling closer.

"We shouldn't be doing this," she chattered, burying her head beneath his chin, trying to control her shaking limbs.

"Be quiet," he breathed, running his fingers against her wet hair, squeezing the water out of it. "Etiquette only goes so far. This is one time we're going to ignore social conventions."

The caress of his hand against her hair and back soothed her fears. Her hand stole up his chest, her fingers coming to rest against his dry flesh just below his neck. His leg folded across hers, bringing her tightly against him. The gesture was wildly intimate, and she tensed, too tired to fight or pretend to be outraged.

"Relax," Chase growled, running his hand up and down her back, creating circulation in her chilled flesh. He felt her tightness dissolve, the curves and slopes of her body fitting beautifully against him.

The rain drummed at a hard, steady rate outside the cave. Rachel loved the sound, and she nuzzled upward, her lips resting against the bearded curve of Chase's cheek. He smelled of perspiration and of maleness. Inhaling deeply, Rachel succumbed to his ministrations to warm her.

"I'm so tired, Chase," she murmured against him.

"I know you are. Go to sleep."

His strong fingers found each source of tension in her back, and Rachel moaned as he began to gently massage those areas. How did Chase know where each sore muscle lay? Was he an expert on women's backs? Probably. Drowsiness pulled at Rachel and she allowed Chase to take her full weight. That last thought pulled at the corners of her mouth, and Rachel spiraled deeply into sleep.

Chase awoke with a jerk. He heard roosters crowing in the distance from the village below. Blinking, he raised his head, looking out of the cave. The rain had stopped, and a wall of thick fog lingered outside, muting the forthcoming dawn on the horizon. The air was chilly and damp, but he was warm.

All his attention focused on Rachel, who lay in his arms. A groan came from within him as he raised up on one arm, studying her in the dim light. Her lips were parted, making her seem excruciatingly vulnerable. Gently he smoothed away several strands of hair from her cheek. Her skin felt like velvet beneath his fingertips, and he stroked her cheek one more time.

A small sigh whispered from Rachel's lips as he caressed her flesh. A sharp heat centered in his lower body, and Chase felt himself growing with real need of Rachel. As he lay there, his hand resting on her shoulder, absorbing her into him, Chase tried to order himself not to feel, not to want.

You want her, Chase. In the worst way. Why? Rachel's not like the other women you've known. He tried to throw the reasons in front of himself as he gently brought her back against him, wildly aware of her pliancy in sleep. If she were awake, she'd fly like a wild bird out of his hands, accurately reading the intent in his face, in his hands. His fingers sliding up the dry sleeve of her fatigues, Chase continued to caress her.

Rachel awoke in a languorous heat, responding to Chase's quiet, evocative caress. She felt the stroking motion of his fingers gently kneading the flesh of her arm and shoulder. It was a dream . . . a torrid dream, she told herself. Chase would never do that in real life. A moan of pleasure sighed through her, and she enjoyed each firm touch that aroused her senses to sharpened life.

Rachel's moan struck Chase hard, his need turning into a fiery, demanding ache. He saw the slight smile hover around Rachel's lips although she was still asleep. He tried to tell himself that stroking her arm and shoulder was harmless enough. His gaze never left Rachel's face. She was an angel, her hair a black halo around her clean features and those thick black lashes lying against her flushed cheeks, enticing him.

His attention centered on her lips, and Chase tried to breathe, strangled by his own desires surging hotly upward through him. Just to feel her once, to taste her texture, was all he wanted. A hiss came from within Chase as he fought himself. He couldn't! Rachel's face lingered before him like a beckoning mirage. Just one kiss wouldn't hurt anything....

Rachel stirred, feeling the moistness of breath against her face. Her lashes barely lifted. Where did dream end and reality begin? She wasn't sure, drowning in the stormy blueness of Chase's eyes that held hers captive with sizzling need. He was so close, the beard making his face hollowed, darker, more harsh. His male scent entered her flaring nostrils as she saw him lower his head those last few heartbeats to meet her lips.

The heat of her dreams melded hotly with reality as she felt Chase's mouth brush her lips. A sigh rippled from Rachel as his butterfly touch grazed her. Instinctively she leaned upward, wanting more of him, wanting to revel in his maleness. She felt him run his tongue across her lower lip. A shiver of yearning fractured through her like sunlight on a chilled day. His mouth claimed hers a third time and she felt his strength molding and cajoling her to celebrate their mating. Heat radiated outward from his mouth as he cherished her, drank her into himself, and Rachel closed her eyes, a moan coming from the very depths of her awakened femininity.

His breath was hot and punctuated against her face, his mouth searching, exploring in urgent, hungry need of her. Rachel returned his kiss with equal fervor, just as starved as he. The experience was so new, so wonderfully pleasurable. She felt him smile against her. Fulfillment riffled through her as his mouth searched, inviting her to explore him in return.

The dream ended abruptly when Rachel realized what she was doing was wrong. Placing her hand against his chest, she pushed him away, her lips throbbing, on fire.

"No..." she whispered, staring up into his hard, intense features. She shivered, vividly aware that her breasts were aching with a strange sensation. Her breath was coming in ragged gulps, and she lay frozen, snared by his gaze. Confused by the heated signals of her body, Rachel could only look helplessly up at him.

Without thinking, Chase reached out, caressing her hair. "I'm sorry," he said thickly, "I got carried away...." *Dammit,* Chase chastised himself. He saw the bewilderment in Rachel's wide eyes. But he also saw the emerald fire within them, telling him that she had enjoyed the unexpected kiss as much as he had. Slowly Chase removed his arm so that she could scoot away from him.

With nettlelike heat, Rachel's blush emphasized the shame she felt over her wanton actions. Getting up, she left Chase's side and made her way out into the foggy dawn, disappearing into the wall of mist.

Congratulations, you stupid bastard. Chase shook his head in disgust. Rachel was flushed and shy, unable to face him. He watched her disappear from view. Anger drenched his throbbing flesh. Had this whole fiasco turned him into nothing more than a caveman lusting for a mate? Self-reproach effectively quenched his remaining desire as he crawled out of the cave.

The fog was thick. Chase could barely make out the rocks six feet away from him. That was the only good thing about today; no one would be able to spot them. Chase closed his eyes, dragging in a deep, unsteady breath. Lord, how sweet Rachel tasted. She hadn't been kissed too many times. The thought pleased Chase a great deal. Her lips had been soft and pliant, ready to be formed and sculpted by his. She had been swift to learn, returning his exploration with equal fervor. That realization sent another shaft of heat through him. Sweet and hot. Just as passionate inside as outside. The discoveries left Chase shaky.

Rachel collided unexpectedly with Chase on the way back to the cave. He reached out, grabbing her by the arm so that she wouldn't fall. His hand was like a burning brand to her sensitized flesh, and she jerked away, putting several feet between them. The fog swirled and eddied silently between them, symbolizing her inward chaos.

Chase stood, reading every feeling in her face. Her lips were still pouty and provocative from the kiss they'd shared. He saw the guilt and hurt in her eyes. "Look," he began awkwardly in a low voice, "I'm sorry, Rachel. It was my fault. I got carried away...."

Rachel chewed on her lower lip, the scent of Chase embracing her like a rare, exotic perfume. She rubbed her arm where he'd made contact with her. Her feelings were in disarray, roiling heat throbbing between her thighs. "I—"

"It was my fault. I'm the man. I know better." He was blithering, wanting to smooth over his error in judgment. The look on Rachel's face, the distrust, stabbed at him, a blade driven through his heart.

"And you did it anyway," Rachel flung back, her voice unsteady. "I was asleep...I thought it was a dream."

Chase managed a self-deprecating smile, unsure of what to do or say. "I think we were dreaming the same thing, then."

Setting her lips, Rachel forced herself to stare him in the eye. "Captain, you were awake, I was not."

Shrugging, Chase said defensively, "You enjoyed it as much as I did."

"That," Rachel whispered fiercely, "is beside the point!"

"Then, you don't deny it?"

"You're impossible!" Rachel exploded in a hiss. "It shouldn't have happened! A lot of the men here in Korea think that a nurse is fair game. Well, we aren't!" She clenched her fists. "You're just like those guys. You don't respect me, you think you own me and can get away with whatever you want."

"Rachel," he began lamely, holding up his hand, trying to stop her tirade, "keep your voice down."

She circled him warily. "Maybe I'd be safer if we were caught! I thought you and I were supposed to be on the same side in this lousy war!" Storming toward the cave, Rachel disappeared into the fog.

"Dammit," Chase growled, touching his head. The ache had returned with renewed intensity. He glared in the direction she'd gone, giving himself a chance to simmer down. The blame was on his shoulders not hers, he admitted sourly. After all, he had awakened her with the kiss. Abruptly Chase turned on his heel, stalking back to the cave.

Rachel frowned at him when he appeared out of the fog. "Just keep your distance, Chase. I'm picking up our stuff and then we're leaving." Rachel steeled herself against his sad-eyed look. She handed him the plastic food container and crawled out of the cave.

"Are you ready?"

He nodded, dropping the case into a large pocket of his flight suit. "Yeah, let's go."

Rachel turned to walk away, but Chase caught her by the arm. "Hold on," he ordered. "Today I'm taking the lead. You stick close behind me."

"Are you sure?" Rachel searched his face. There was high color in Chase's cheeks and his eyes looked clear. She had to tear her gaze from his, lowering her lashes.

"I can make it on my own today. Right now, with this fog, we have to take it easy, and rely on our hearing. Sounds will be muffled and if we run up on a patrol, we won't know it until the last minute. If you hear anything, grab my arm to get my attention, but don't speak out. Understand?"

Part of Rachel felt relief. Today Chase would help shoulder some of the load she had been carrying. "Fine," she mumbled, still angry and confused by his kiss. "South is that way," she said.

Taking the lead, Chase didn't argue with her. He kept a swift steady pace, circumventing the village below them. He could tell by the frayed light on the horizon which direction was east. Within moments, he realized that Rachel had been heading south all the time. It had been the concussion playing tricks on his senses. Today he felt much better. Wasn't their torrid kiss proof of his awakening desires? *What a mess.*

Despite his new duties as leader, Chase mulled over the mistake he'd made with Rachel. How could he get her to understand how desirable she was to him, that the kiss didn't mean he disrespected her? It was as hopeless as fighting city hall, Chase decided morosely. One look at the jut of Rachel's chin told him she thought he was one of those "gropers" she'd told him about yesterday.

As they climbed out of the valley and headed into the next one, the sun rose. Very slowly the fog began to dissipate, thinning here and there for hundreds of feet around them, creating worrying conditions. His senses becoming even more alert to their dangerous surroundings, Chase continued to run a number of conversations around in his head. He had to convince Rachel that he respected her virginity and her. More than anything, he wanted to figure out a way to make her come to him, not run in terror from his embrace.

Chapter Six

Rachel was blindly following Chase's footsteps when he suddenly turned, pulling her against him. Her mouth opened and he clamped his hand across it, shoving her down to her knees.

Crouched next to Rachel, Chase kept his hand in place as they huddled in the swirling fog. "Enemy," he whispered raggedly. He saw her eyes change from fury to fear, and he eased his hand away from her lips. Keeping his arm around her shoulders, Chase tensed, waiting.

Tasting the blood where her lips had been pressed hard against her teeth, Rachel nodded, her heart accelerating in beat. Voices! She strained, barely able to hear the North Koreans, marveling at Chase's ability to detect them. Before Rachel could do anything, Chase pinned her savagely to the ground. Rachel gasped, her face shoved into the weeds, the air knocked from her lungs as he threw himself across her.

The fog swirled thinly, moving as a slight breeze came off the hillside. Chase kept Rachel beneath him, watching the enemy patrol barely four hundred feet away. Only the fog hid them, and the sun's rays were rapidly dissipating the vapor. Chase clenched his teeth. His grip on Rachel tightened, signaling her to remain frozen.

Keeping his head pressed close to hers, Chase watched the patrol through narrowed eyes, barely breathing. In some distant corner of his mind, he was aware that their breathing had synchronized. The scout for the patrol halted, turning and looking directly at them. Chase went rigid, preparing himself to jerk Rachel up and run, if necessary. *Don't let them see us...don't...*

The scout frowned and rubbed his eyes. A hundred crowded thoughts poured through Chase's mind. He was aware of Rachel's groan, realizing he was too heavy for her. Simultaneously a pulverizing realization that she meant more to him than anyone he'd ever known skimmed across his heightened senses. The scout craned his neck, zeroing in on them.

Rachel's too young to die. So am I. God, don't let them see us. Don't... The rest of his prayer was cut short as the scout shrugged and turned away, leading the patrol up and over the crest of the rocky summit.

The instant the patrol disappeared, Chase rolled off Rachel. She struggled to her knees. Worriedly he assessed her, unconsciously reaching out, smoothing the hair away from her face.

"Are you okay?" he demanded huskily, gripping her shoulders.

Dazed by the suddenness of Chase's actions, Rachel nodded jerkily. Her fingers went to her cheek. She felt warm liquid smearing across her skin.

"Damn," Chase muttered, drawing her hand away from her cheek. When he had thrown Rachel to the ground, she'd struck a twig, opening a long scratch that was now bleeding heavily. "Hold on," he told her, digging into his back pocket, finding a cotton handkerchief.

Rachel found herself in Chase's embrace, being held as if she were a small but dearly loved child. The adrenaline that had shot through her earlier was making her shaky. Rachel tried to hold the handkerchief in place, but it fell from her grasp.

"It's all right," Chase crooned, "I'll take care of you."

For once, it was easy to trust someone other than herself to do exactly that. Rachel lowered her gaze, unable to meet Chase's burning blue eyes. He reminded her of a warrior, taut and prepared to do battle. This was another side to Chase Trayhern, the pilot who bravely challenged the enemy when necessary. His touch was exquisitely gentle as he wiped the blood from her face.

"Damn patrol almost got us," he muttered, his head bent fractions of an inch from hers. "I'm sorry I had to throw you down. There wasn't time to tell you...."

Rachel sighed, resting her head against his shoulder. "It's okay."

Rachel's gesture shattered Chase; he read it as a sign of renewed trust in him. Without thinking, he wrapped his arms around her, giving her a squeeze that communicated his care.

"This is getting worse," she admitted hollowly, allowing Chase to embrace her. Right now, Rachel needed his care, her limbs feeling shaky and weak. "I—I was scared to death."

Chuckling softly, Chase released her and studied the crest of the hill for a moment, making sure the patrol wasn't going to return. "Angel Eyes, I was scared too." Chase wanted to take back the words. He glanced down at her. Rachel's forest-green eyes were wide with wonder.

Nervously Chase folded the handkerchief, making a square out of it, pressing it to her cheek to stop the bleeding. He hadn't meant to let Rachel know his treasured name for her.

"Is that what you call all the women you date?" she joked lamely, warmed by the beautiful endearment.

Heat stole into Chase's cheeks and he avoided her searching look. "No. Usually women don't remind me of things like that," he murmured, concentrating on keeping an even pressure on the injury. Stealing a glance at her, Chase bashfully admitted, "But I've never seen a lady with such beautiful green eyes in my life. When I became conscious after bailing out, I thought I was dead and was seeing my one and only angel before they sent me to hell. In my mind, I kept calling you Angel Eyes because your eyes calmed my fears."

Touched beyond words, Rachel stared up at Chase. The tremble in his voice, the flush to his cheeks, told her everything. For once Chase Trayhern wasn't flaunting his superior male ego. No, in those seconds, he was excruciatingly human and she longed to reach out, frame his face and kiss him.

"I've never been called such a beautiful name before."

Chase's gaze softened and he stared down at her. "I've never met such a beautiful or courageous woman before," he rasped unsteadily. It would be so easy to press the advantage and kiss her. Chase remembered their last kiss, aching to do it again. He wanted to show Rachel the beauty of love between a man and a woman, to explore that passionate world together.

Rachel's womanly instincts told her to move, to ease out of Chase's seductive embrace that begged her to stay and kiss him again. His words fell like heated promises across her, as she reluctantly pulled away, sitting up opposite him.

Awkwardly Chase handed her the handkerchief. The moments strung gently together as he wrestled with proper words instead of the more natural ones that would convey his naked desire for Rachel. She was so pretty in those minutes. Her black hair framed her face in mild disarray, her cheeks were flushed and her eyes were a soft green. His gaze fell to her mouth, and Chase groaned inwardly; he felt the turgid flow of blood, making him want her all over again.

"Come on," he whispered gruffly, helping Rachel to her feet, "let's get out of here."

Nodding, Rachel fell into step behind Chase. The bleeding had halted, and she clenched the handkerchief in her hand. Chase increased the length of his stride until she was almost running across the rocky hillside in order to keep up with him. But her body was becoming accustomed to the hard physical demands, and she kept up the pace. Even as they crossed the treacherous, enemy-infested valley, Rachel couldn't erase the feeling of being in Chase's arms.

"Let's take a breather," Chase told her, finding a grove of trees and using the thick trunks as cover against possible enemy patrols. He sat down, his back against the rough bark. Rachel sat two trees away, keeping her distance. Looking at his watch, Chase realized it was nearly two o'clock.

"We've been moving fast," he commented.

With a grimace, Rachel gently rubbed her calves, working the knots out of them. "Don't I know it."

Managing a sour grin, Chase agreed. "We've probably made twelve miles already today. That's good."

"That's killing." Rachel managed a returning smile, thinking how handsome Chase looked. His face glistened with sweat, emphasizing the strong lines of his features, bringing out the intense blues of his narrowed, keenly intelligent eyes.

"We'll rest a good half hour." Chase wiped the sweat off his brow with the back of his sleeve. "I'd give anything for some water."

Rachel rolled her eyes. "Wouldn't that be heavenly?" She dug out the can of food wrapped in the silk. "I'm starved."

So was he, Chase discovered, pulling out the plastic box from his pocket. "Let's eat now and keep up our strength."

Hungrily Rachel agreed, using her fingers to scoop out the food. "We'll be lucky not to get food poisoning."

"Typical nurse, thinking of the medical ramifications," Chase teased, thrusting his fingers into the rice dish.

Smiling, Rachel focused on the food, more hungry than she could ever recall. After finishing, she confided, "When I was a kid, I used to think wiping my fingers on my trousers when we were out camping was great." She examined her fingers with distaste. "Now, I wish I had a stream to wash them in."

In that moment, through Chase's eyes, Rachel looked like a little girl. His smile deepened, and he straightened out one of his legs in her direction. "Wipe them on my flight suit, I don't care."

Laughter bubbled up within Rachel and she leaned forward, wiping her greasy fingers on his lower pant leg. "Don't ever let it be said that you aren't an officer and a gentleman under some *dire* circumstances, Captain. This calls for a medal of some sort."

Her touch was evocative, fleeting. Chase yearned to have Rachel skim his entire body with those slender hands. Hooding his eyes so she couldn't read his less than gentlemanly thoughts, he teased, "What? A greasy-fingers medal? Aren't many of those given out, you know."

Rachel had to put her hands over her lips to stifle a real laugh, her eyes dancing with merriment. The corners of Chase's mouth pulled into a heartbreaking smile, the heat lancing through her like sweet summer rain. Every nuance of her body responded to his smile, leaving her breathless.

"How did a nice girl like you end up in a place like this?" Chase prodded.

Tipping her head back against the tree, Rachel studied him through her lashes. "After I graduated from nursing school, I wanted to make a difference, Chase."

"You could have made the difference in a hospital stateside."

She shook her head. "You don't understand. I've always lived a life of extremes. I never did anything halfway. My parents will tell you that from an early age, I was always putting myself into exploratory situations. I wasn't content to play with my dolls in the living room. I had to have a tree house instead."

"Your father must have thought you were a tomboy."

"My parents never saw me that way. They accepted my curiosity as normal, and encouraged my exploration."

"Unusual."

"If it had been a boy doing the same thing, it wouldn't have been seen as unusual, Chase. Everyone would have expected it."

Nettled, Chase saw her point. "I guess..."

"It's a good thing my parents allowed me to be all those things, because they've played a major part in our escape so far."

Again he nodded. Still, her flagrant independence bothered him.

Rachel smiled to herself. She saw the bullish set of Chase's mouth, realizing that he was fighting the truth about her. "Well, what about you? Were you raised like a typical boy?"

Chase nodded. "With my father being in the military, we got a pretty broad and interesting education early on."

"You're proud of your father, aren't you?"

Chase smiled. "Yeah, I am. And I'm proud to be carrying on our family tradition."

"Every son went into the service. Any daughters?"

Chase nodded. "They stayed home and made good wives while their men went off to war."

Rachel winced and gave him a sour look.

Chase scowled. "Look, the military is no place for a woman."

"Why not?"

Jabbing his finger down at the soil, Chase said, "Because you can get killed, that's why. Besides, women can't take the blood and horror."

She sat up, her arms dangling over her knees. "Men can't either, Chase."

Frowning, he muttered, "I don't believe it."

"I see blood day in and day out."

"You're different."

"No, I'm a woman. We're far better equipped emotionally in my opinion, to handle the ups and downs of life."

"War is more than 'ups and downs,' Rachel."

"Is it? Your family has made a career of it."

Eyes narrowing, Chase stared at her. "My family has not made a career of war. We believe in freedom and see ourselves as patriots willing to go to war if necessary to defend our way of life."

Shaking her head, Rachel absently picked at a dry blade of grass between her legs. "Chase, every day I see young boys, eighteen and nineteen years old, come through our MASH unit shot up. I see the terror in their eyes. I wish I could take you on night rounds, listening to them screaming out in the middle of a nightmare." She held his gaze. "War is no place for anyone. And men don't handle it very well, either."

"Look, women don't understand these things."

"What, war? I understand it just fine, Chase. In fact, as a nurse, I understand it far better than most people."

"So, what's your point?" She was smart and quick-witted, traits Chase admired in a man.

"My point is, war is a crime against *all* human beings."

Rolling his eyes, he muttered, "Brother, are you in the wrong place, then."

Her nostrils flared. "Chase, you're acting like you have blinders on. Can't you see what I'm saying?"

"No. Look, the Commies are trying to take over South Korea. We've got to stop them."

"Do you realize we're the only species that fights its own kind? When I sit out in the forest, I watch the animals and birds for hours. They never attack one another."

"We're fighting for freedom," Chase said stubbornly. "Animals don't have that to worry about."

Rachel leaned back. "I guess I want peace over war," she uttered wearily.

The tremble in her voice unstrung Chase. He reached over, gripping her knee, giving it a small squeeze and then releasing it. "I think that's the difference between men and women. For myself, it's exciting as hell to be staring an enemy pilot in the face, getting ready to do battle."

A one-cornered smile tugged at Rachel's mouth. "Fighting through a machine can be highly impersonal. The men on the ground in the trenches don't have that protection. War becomes personal on the front. I honestly believe there are some men who are warriors by nature. But if you spent one day at my

MASH unit, you'd discover how many men aren't of that nature."

Rising, Chase said, "Well, when we get out of this mess, you'll be heading stateside, where you belong. Come on, let's go."

Rachel slowly stood, realizing the war hadn't really touched Chase—yet. She hoped it never would. But until it did, he wouldn't understand or see what she had experienced. Another even more insidious thought leaked through; something Rachel had been trying to ignore.

As she walked at Chase's side, Rachel broke out into a cold, unnerving sweat. It was a reaction to fear, something she'd experienced off and on since her capture. Would they get out of here alive? Rachel had tried so hard to maintain a positive view of their situation, but the days without proper food and rest were fraying her optimism.

Needing to talk, she blurted, "Chase, do you think we'll make it back?"

He glanced over at her. "I don't know."

Her stomach knotted hard. "Well...I mean, we've done well so far."

"We're in a wartime situation, Rachel. I wish I could promise you things are going to be fine, but I can't. We've just got to be on our toes and hope like hell we find our lines before the Commies find us."

Rubbing her stomach, Rachel frowned, a terrible, cold panic growing deep within her. "I see," she said faintly, bowing her head, keeping her attention on the countryside around them.

As much as Rachel tried to concentrate on remaining alert to possible enemy patrols, her anxieties multiplied until, by the end of the day, her emotions were frayed and she felt herself unraveling. Rachel had no experience to draw upon to know how to combat her spiraling fear.

The temperature dropped dramatically when the sun slid behind the horizon, and Rachel was shivering despite the fast pace of their walk southward. They had crossed another valley and had trekked close to thirty miles that day, in her estimation. Her breath came out of her mouth in ragged white wisps as they climbed a grassy hill. The moon had just risen, the sickle shape larger than before, casting a glow that reminded her of a molten river of silver across the landscape.

Glancing down at his watch, Chase slowed. It was midnight. He turned, looking down at Rachel. The scratch on her face was puffy, marring the beauty of her features. Looking into her eyes, he saw weariness and something else. There was a haunted quality to Rachel, something he'd not seen before. Recalling their earlier conversation, Chase knew that the reality of their dangerous situation was hitting Rachel in earnest. Yet, the stubborn set of her lips told him she would keep going without complaint if he asked it of her.

"Ready to call it a night?" His voice was low, barely audible. They hadn't run into any more patrols, although they had seen a convoy on a dirt road speeding north late in the day.

"Am I ever," Rachel whispered. Her legs felt rubbery, and she was shivering. Placing her arms around herself, she rubbed her arms vigorously, trying to create better circulation.

"It's freezing out here," Chase muttered. He looked around, spotting a ledge and a small crawl space beneath it. Capturing Rachel's hand, he turned, leading her toward it. Chase's hand was warm in comparison to hers. Rachel remained close, needing the heat of his body. She fought the other reasons; being near Chase aroused her in new and wonderful ways that she desperately wanted to explore with him. Rachel remembered her mother's words: A woman saved herself for the man who was going to be her husband. The silly thought invaded her spongy senses that Chase, despite his warlike beliefs, was really a decent man at heart. He didn't enjoy killing. To him, it was like a game of wits, nothing more or less. In her present state, she wanted to be in his arms, to huddle up next to him, feel his strength and hide from the tearing fear that lived within her.

As Chase released her hand, knelt and cleared the pebbles from beneath the overhang, Rachel allowed his presence to envelope her fatigued senses. When he turned, motioning for her to join him in the small space, she hesitated.

"Come on!" he whispered.

"Chase, there isn't room in there for both of us."

With a growl, Chase pulled Rachel into the niche. "It's too late and we're too tired to argue. I'm not going to take advantage of you." He folded her into his arms, her length against his. Seeing the disbelief in her large green eyes, Chase held on to his fraying temper. "Look, just because I stole a kiss once doesn't mean I'm going to do it again." *Liar.* Right now with her head resting against his arm, her body fitted comfortably against him, Chase entertained that very thought.

Rachel tried to protest, but it was impossible. Chase was warm, and his arm around her shoulders was taking away some of the chill. She was afraid that if she admitted how badly she needed to be held, Chase might take advantage of the situation. Burrowing her head beneath his chin, her cheek against his chest, she felt some of her fear melt away.

Grinning crookedly, Chase relaxed, contentment flowing through him. If he told Rachel how good she felt against him, she'd push away and spend the night outside the ledge. "Trust me," he soothed deeply. "Come on, let's sleep, Angel Eyes. We're too tired to do anything." Well, that wasn't quite true. As Chase ran his hand up and down her back to create warmth in her, he thought it was a good thing Rachel couldn't read his mind.

"This isn't right, Chase."

He heard the indignation in her protest. "I know it isn't, but it can't be helped. I'm not going to let you sit out there trembling. It would make me feel like a heel."

Rachel took a deep, ragged breath, pressing closer. "I—I'm cold, Chase..." *And scared.* The words never left her lips. She didn't want him to think her weak.

"Take it easy, Rachel. Use my body heat to warm yourself."

Though her conscience shouted that it wasn't right, fatigue won the argument. Rachel surrendered, sinking deeply into his embrace. As Rachel lay with his arm acting as a pillow, her face pressed into the folds of his flight suit, she laughed to herself. For being a nurse and knowing so much about anatomy and the male body, this was certainly a different sensation.

"Better?" Chase asked in a low voice, his mouth very near her ear.

"Yes..."

He smiled, hearing the pleasure in her husky voice as he continued to slowly rub her back. "Warmer?"

Rachel gave a slight nod, her hands nestled between her breasts. Her lids felt weighted, and she acquiesced, falling into a deep sleep, unaware of anything except Chase's arms holding her safe.

How long Chase lay with Rachel in his arms, wanting her, he didn't know. Every inhalation of her breath brought her soft breasts against his chest. Her scent moved maddeningly around him, enticing him, cajoling him to do something about it. *Why couldn't she be less beautiful? Married? Anything?* He glared into the darkness, telling himself all the reasons why he should leave her alone.

At the end of two hours, Chase was more awake than before. Though he was mentally tired, his body was begging him to love Rachel. The moonlight slanted beneath the overhang, illuminating Rachel's sleeping features. She looked angelic in sleep, he thought, staring down at her, absorbing her into his heated bloodstream.

Her full, beautifully formed lips were slightly parted in sleep, alluring and beckoning. Her softly winged brows were frames for her wonderful green eyes. He liked her chin and the strong line of her jaw. And Rachel's burning, unquenchable spirit drew him powerfully to her.

Reaching out, Chase gently drew several strands of ebony hair away from her injured cheek, tucking them behind her delicately shaped ear. He'd never met a woman like her, so full of life, possessing her own opinions and displaying an incredible confidence. She was no wilting lily, that was for sure.

Frowning, Chase allowed his hand to rest against the crown of her hair. Something special about Rachel had eaten at him hourly over the past few days. Chase had tried to define it. She was a rare butterfly and he was chasing her with his net, trying to capture her. His eyes darkened as he ruthlessly assessed his feelings.

There was no way to break the connective cord he felt strung between them. So much of what he felt defied definition. Chase knew only that when he talked with Rachel, he was eager to communicate and explore any topic with her. He might not agree with her on the war issue, but it excited him that she had an opinion on it in the first place.

A slight deprecating smile formed on his mouth as he gazed longingly down at her. Chase felt his heart expanding outward, exploding with a warm sensation unlike anything he'd ever experienced. Chase wanted to tell her he admired her, even if he didn't agree with her.

His smile deepened as he watched her breasts rise and fall slowly against the less than flattering fatigues she wore. There was no way to hide her femininity. Of their own accord, his fingers began threading through strands of her hair. Each strand was like silk: strong, resilient, yet smooth and sleek, like Rachel herself.

Rachel stirred in her sleep, trying to escape the terror that stalked her. She felt Chase's fingers sliding through her hair, combing it gently, releasing a deluge of stored longing from her heart. No one had ever touched her with such reverence, such overwhelming tenderness.

As she opened her sleep-filled eyes, Rachel stared up into the dark blueness of Chase's intense gaze. Her breath snagged in her throat and she was unsure whether it was a moan of pleasure or a cry to tell him to stop touching her. Drawn into the cobalt depths of his eyes, Rachel felt her terror dissolving, leaving her real feelings and needs exposed for the first time.

As if sensing Rachel's reaction, Chase laid his hand on her shoulder, offering her a helpless smile. "Lady, I can't sleep with you in my arms. I don't know where dreams and reality begin or end with you, Angel Eyes...."

The gritty words washed across her, permeating her skin, heating her blood and putting her in direct touch with an ache deep within her. *Angel Eyes.* The endearment moved through her like sunlight, and Rachel raised her hand, pressing it against Chase's chest. She felt the strong muscles beneath her hand tense, and she wanted more to explore than push him away.

"Chase..." For the first time, Rachel realized that she could die. Her optimism was gone. In its place was a terrible knowledge that she could die today—any day, before possible rescue. And so could Chase. Rachel stared up into his face—incredibly tender despite his harsh features. She would never know what it would be like to love him. The feeling struck her deeply, and she raised her hand, tentatively sliding her fingers along his beard-roughened cheek.

He frowned, watching Rachel's eyes. Chase saw very real fear in them, but he also saw desire—for him. Just the butterfly touch of her fingers against his flesh made him groan. Trying to separate desire from her actions, he gripped her hand.

"Rachel, what's wrong?"

She took a ragged half breath. "I—I just realized that we could die, Chase."

Nodding, he guided her hand to his lips, pressing a kiss into the small palm. "I know." He felt the rise and fall of her breasts against him, sensing her need of him. His own hunger sharpened as she reacted to his kiss. The wild urge to kiss her pleading lips drove him beyond his massive control. His hand tightened on her shoulder momentarily. Shadows highlighted Rachel's clean features, making her excruciatingly tempting.

Rachel released the breath, seeing the intent in Chase's narrowing eyes, wanting the promise she saw in them. Life over death. As she closed her eyes, feeling the tentative brush of his lips on hers, Rachel realized what life was all about. Chase's mouth plundered her, the terror dissolving beneath his quickening breathing and worship of her. A moan slid from her throat as she felt him begin to unbutton her shirt. His fingers were trembling... but so was she.

Burying herself in the primal needs of life, Rachel surrendered to the building fire that extended from her thighs up to her taut, aching breasts. Her lashes fluttered as Chase pulled back her shirt, exposing her bra. Somewhere in her dizzied senses, Rachel acknowledged her womanly instincts, promising her life above death.

The shirt came off, and so did her cotton bra. Rachel gasped as Chase's roughened fingers caressed her breast, but it was a sound of pleasure, not shock.

Leaning down, Chase trailed a series of kisses from Rachel's soft, pouty lips, down her slender neck to her finely sculpted collarbones, then her small, firm breasts. Stunned by her unexpected decision, he gloried in her, wanting her more than any woman in his life. His knowledge that their lives hung in a fragile balance consumed him. If he had to be captured or die, he didn't want it to happen before he could love Rachel. The words were almost torn from him, but as she pressed her breasts against him, all thought was erased.

"I need you," he rasped thickly, sliding his hand down her torso, his hand cradling her belly, asking entrance. Burying his face in her hair, he felt Rachel moan, her mouth moving insistently across his neck, jaw, and finally to his mouth. As he fumbled with the buttons on her fatigue trousers, Chase's senses spun. Rachel was just as fiery in loving as she was at living her life. The discovery only made him want her more.

Her trousers were next. Rachel had unzipped his flight suit, running her fingers through the mass of dark hair across his chest. Chase was beautifully and brazenly male to her excited senses. He slid out of his uniform, and the instant his warm, hard flesh met hers, Rachel sank into his arms. Chase gently maneuvered her onto her back. Lifting her lashes, Rachel stared up into his face in the shadowy light.

"Love me," she pleaded, her voice cracking. "Please..."

Urgency pounded through Chase. Time...they didn't have any left. Now was all that counted. He saw the desperation, the need coupled with desire in her eyes. As he covered her, a fleeting thought crossed his whirling mind. Rachel deserved to be courted, to have her first time be beautiful—to be introduced into the realm of lovemaking with delicious slowness and tenderness. Chase crushed the thoughts as they arose. They might never get back—never have that chance. As he felt Rachel open her firm, velvety thighs to him, he framed her face with his hands. He could only give her what they both needed now under terrible, uncertain circumstances.

Rachel felt Chase's large hands close around her face, and she opened her eyes, looking up into his, drowning in them. Trying to prepare herself was impossible. Her blood pounded demandingly through her, driving her to couple with him. Tenderness and concern burned in Chase's eyes as he held her gaze. She felt him press against her, felt the pressure as he sheathed deeply into her. Her lashes fluttered closed, her breathing suspended.

Chase felt her tense, and his hands grew tight against her, unmoving. But she was hot liquid silk around him, and he clenched his teeth, sweat running down his temples as he tried to stop long enough to give her time to accommodate him. Fighting to get beyond his own screaming needs, Chase leaned down, plundered her parted lips, drawing all her attention to his tongue lushly stroking her.

Heat drove through Rachel as Chase kissed her deeply, hungrily. Her hips moved provocatively beneath him, and a groan tore from deep within him. Each stroke moved him into her welcoming confines, and he felt Rachel begin to enjoy the rhythm. In the ensuing moments before their mutual release, he tried to make it good for her, a welcoming into the world of desire. As Rachel tensed, a soft cry echoing from her throat as she arched into his arms, Chase used his experience to prolong the sensation for her. She deserved that, and more. And, as she went limp in his arms, the last of his control dissolved into a steamy fire of need, and he buried himself deeply, forever, into Rachel's loving body.

Minutes later, Rachel slowly became aware of their breathing, of the fact she lay against Chase's damp, hard body. He had gathered her up in his arms, wanting to keep her warm against the coolness of the night. Slowly her senses were returning. The glow of the climax still throbbed between her legs, the sensations wonderful, slowly dissolving with each heartbeat.

"You're cold," he muttered, concerned, raising on one arm and locating her shirt. Drawing it across Rachel's back and shoulders, he looked down into her shadowed features. Her lips were full and well kissed, still beckoning him. With a gentle smile, Chase outlined them with his finger. "Lady, you're something else. I want you all over again." And then he laughed ruefully, shaking his head. "You're incredible. We're incredible together...."

Rachel blinked, hearing the gritty tone in his voice. Reality was quickly pushing back the beauty of what they had shared. My God, what had she done? Shakily Rachel pulled out of his arms, quickly slipping on the shirt.

"Rachel?" Chase saw the sudden uncertainty in her eyes. Her fingers trembled as she rebuttoned her shirt. "Hey? What's wrong? Talk to me." He reached over, gripping her hand as she reached for her trousers.

"Don't!" It was more a plea than an order.

Chase slowly sat up, scowling. "Rachel, don't do this to me...to us. We have to talk."

Her hands were shaking badly as she got the trousers on and buttoned them up. "There's nothing to talk about, Chase," Rachel whispered hoarsely. It hurt to look over at his stunned features. She saw the confusion and lingering tenderness still in his eyes. Biting down hard on her lower lip, she tried to gather her strewn emotions. "I—it was my fault," Rachel blurted. "I—I was scared, I needed to be held for just a little while."

Biting back a curse, Chase dressed, zipping up his flight suit, then sat watching Rachel intently for several seconds before speaking. "Look, it was good between us."

Running her fingers through her hair, lovingly mussed by Chase only minutes before, Rachel felt defensive. Why had she done it? Oh, God, why? Was it the war? The terror of getting caught?

"Dammit," Chase growled, capturing her wrist, "talk to me, Rachel!"

She jerked out of his grip, anger in her low voice. "I just did! What else do you want? You ought to be satisfied. You got what you wanted all along."

Shaken, Chase sat up. "What are you talking about?"

"You took advantage of our situation, Chase, and you know it!" She was trembling, her arms wrapped around her, but it wasn't from the freezing night air, it was her reaction to Chase as a man.

He glared at her. "We *both* did, Rachel. And I'm not sorry, but apparently, you are."

Her head hurt. Unable to hold his accusing look, she turned her head away, staring out into the darkness. "You shouldn't be sorry at all, Chase. I never expected you to be." Oh, why was she behaving like this? The urge to run out of the cave, and keep on running forever, struck Rachel. She was behaving like a teenager, not a mature woman. Why had she invited, even asked Chase to love her? Tears welled in her eyes, and Rachel forced them back.

"Look, it happened," she snapped at him. "Let's just let it go at that. That's the way you want it, anyway."

His nostrils flared with real anger. "How the hell do you know what I felt or want from you? In case you've got a short memory, you enjoyed it, too."

"You're just like the rest, Chase. You want to marry a nice girl, but you're willing to take any warm body that comes along in the meantime." Her emotions in utter chaos, Rachel added painfully, "And I just happen to be the warm body this time around. So, it's done." Unable to remain close to him for fear of falling back into his arms, Rachel scrambled out from under the overhang. "Let's just forget it!"

"You're being ridiculous, Rachel," Chase protested. He crawled out, straightened and gripped her by the arm. "I can't help it if I like you, can I? We aren't school kids, either, you know."

Stung, she pulled from his grip, getting to her feet. "I don't want to talk about it!"

Just as he opened his mouth to speak, artillery shells were fired south of their position. Chase snapped his mouth shut, his attention zeroing in on the artillery. He saw Rachel jump outwardly as the first shells landed less than half a mile from them.

"That's our guys!" he crowed triumphantly, grabbing her by the arm. "Come on!"

"Wait!" Rachel was jerked along, having no choice as Chase dragged her at a dead run along the grassy, wet slope of the hill. More shells landed, the explosions loud, puncturing the cold night air, like drums being beaten against them. She slipped in the dew-laden grass.

Chase felt Rachel fall and let go of her hand, chastising himself for running too fast. She couldn't possibly keep up. Leaning down, he kept low, hearing another barrage of fire.

"Stay down," he ordered, gasping. Gripping her shoulders, he added, "That's our guys. Our lines are closer than I thought. All we have to do is reach them, Rachel. They can't be more than five miles away." He buttonholed her with a dark look. Rachel was shaken and pale, wincing every time a shell landed and exploded. "Can you make it?"

"Y-yes. Chase, are you sure it's our guys?"

"Positive. If it was North Korean, they'd be firing toward the south, not from that direction."

Rachel glanced around, the night suddenly lighting up with spectacular yellow, orange and red tentacles of fire arcing outward, casting long shadows where they crouched in the grass. "Does this mean the enemy is nearby?"

He nodded, skimming the area, looking for patrols. "Yeah, it does or they wouldn't be peppering this place." Another shell screamed overhead. Chase threw Rachel down, covering her with his body. The shell landed frighteningly close. He cringed, feeling rocks and dirt pelting them, the debris raining over a large area.

As soon as the debris stopped, he rose. "Come on," he ordered, "we're getting the hell out of here. We're right in the middle of a push by our troops. Ready?"

Gripping his large, steadying hand, Rachel got to her feet. Nodding, her eyes large with fear, she followed him. Thankfully Chase shortened his stride so she wouldn't fall again. The shelling grew more intense, the explosions pulverizing the hill they had just left behind.

Rachel tried to steady the unraveling terror inside herself as the nearness of the shells screaming overhead and return fire by the enemy increased. Sudden light from the explosions shattered the darkness, lighting their way, exposing huge craters of freshly torn earth.

Rachel's lungs felt as if they were on fire, each gulp a huge, tearing effort from deep within her chest. Chase was tireless, seeming to gather strength from the run. Her legs were getting rubbery, and Rachel wondered how long it would be before she fell, unable to get back up again. How far had they come?

Just as she thought she'd collapse, Chase jerked her down into the grass. For a brief second, Rachel saw men with rifles advancing toward them, barely five hundred feet away. Her heart banged away in her throat. She huddled next to Chase, a scream begging to be released. The soldiers came closer. Chase's fingers dug deep into her arm, warning her to get ready to run.

I'm going to die. The thought struck Rachel hard. Her senses were screamingly heightened, the shadows dancing around them. The soldiers were advancing directly at them, rifles held ready. *Chase!* Rachel jerked her chin to the left, photographing him in her memory. His features were bathed in sweat, granite hard, and remorseless as he focused on the men approaching them. *I love you.*

Rachel didn't have time to consider where that irrational thought had come from. Suddenly Chase gave a yell, leaping to his feet, throwing one hand above his head. She froze, trying to prepare herself to die. Instead, he grabbed her by the arm, pulling her upward. Stumbling, Rachel grabbed at Chase's arm as he dragged her along.

"Hey! Americans! Americans!" Chase's voice thundered across the yards that separated them from the troops. Joy surged through him when he recognized the U.N. soldiers, the patches on their arms indicating they were from Australia.

As he closed the last few yards, grinning broadly, Chase saw the officer smile and raise his hand. They were saved! Saved! He grinned down at Rachel. Her face glowed with relief as she staggered to a halt against him. Sweeping his arm around Rachel's shoulders, Chase couldn't remember ever being this happy.

As he reached out, shaking the captain's hand, Chase wanted only one thing: safety for Rachel. Somehow, in the past couple of days, their bond had fused into something so powerful that Chase gladly would have given his life to make sure she got home safely.

Home. The word hung provocatively in front of Chase as he pumped the Aussie's hand. *Home and Rachel. God help me, but I love her. I love her....*

Chapter Seven

"Clean bill of health, Lieutenant McKenzie." Dr. Wells smiled, taking the blood pressure cuff off her left arm.

"Thanks, Doctor." Shakily Rachel tried to smile. She was sitting on a cot in a tent not far from the headquarters area for the Australian battalion. She was in shock and knew it. In the past half hour, her life had turned from certain death back into life again. Where was Chase? They had been separated earlier and sent to different tents. Perhaps they were interrogating him. He ought to have medical attention.

The lantern suspended above them threw weak light against the walls of dark green canvas. Rachel rolled down the sleeve of her fatigues, fastening the cuff with trembling fingers. "Doctor, where did they take Captain Trayhern? He has a concussion." She sat on the cot, not willing to test her legs yet. Her ears ached from the continual bombardment of artillery loosing their shells of destruction northward.

Wells tucked the cuff back into his leather case. "We've got two doctors with this battalion, Lieutenant. Bob Friese is checking Captain Trayhern over right now. He said he wanted to send the captain to a MASH unit by helicopter and get X rays of his head. I agree with you, he's suffered a nasty concussion."

Rachel sat still as the doctor applied antiseptic to the scratch on her cheek. "He received it bailing out of his fighter," she explained.

"Word has it, you saved his life." Wells, a man in his forties, smiled benignly. "And from the looks of things, you're in shock from this experience."

"I know I am. Doctor, may I see Chase? I mean, Captain Trayhern, before he leaves?"

"Of course." Wells turned, calling a young soldier into the confines, and gave orders to have Chase brought to the tent. Just as the messenger left, another soldier entered the area, coming to attention.

"Lieutenant McKenzie?" he asked.

Rachel looked up at the youth. "Yes?"

"A message for you, ma'am." He handed it to her, performed a snappy about-face and left.

Frowning, Rachel read the dispatch. It was orders directing her to report to another MASH unit, this time much farther away from the ever-changing front.

"Orders?" Wells guessed, finishing dressing her scratch.

"Yes." She grinned lopsidedly. "They don't waste time, do they?"

Wells shut the sturdy medical case and straightened. He was dressed like the other doctors and nurses, in the same drab olive-green fatigues as

Rachel. "Nurses are invaluable, and there's a short-age. I'm not surprised that they've given you orders. I'm sure the general has been keeping an eye on this situation. We need brave women such as yourself here with us."

Heat stole into Rachel's face. Wells was sincere. She gently folded the message. "Anyone who is in a war is brave."

"No argument from me on that point," he said. Then he gave her a wink, preparing to leave. "I've got to go, there's plenty for me to do with this push tak-ing place."

"Thank you." Rachel watched Wells disappear out the flaps, the constant boom of artillery shattering the stillness around her. It was nearly dawn. So much had happened so quickly. Where was Chase? Rachel was preparing to test her legs when he entered the tent.

"There you are." Chase gave her a tentative smile and ambled in. "How are you doing?" Chafing be-cause circumstances had intruded on their argument after making love, Chase wanted somehow to turn the clock back, to give them time to talk. Nervously he wiped his hands down the legs of his flight suit.

Rachel's heart picked up a painful beat, and she held his searching blue gaze. Memory of his lips on hers, his hands worshipping her breasts, making her body sing like a beautiful instrument, would not leave her. "I—fine. Post letdown, to tell you the truth."

Chase came over, sitting on the cot opposite Rachel. He touched his head, which sported a new white dressing. "The doc says you did a great job sewing this thick skull of mine back together."

Nervously Rachel ran her fingertips along the bor-der of the orders she held. "You deserve only the best,

WOW!

THE MOST GENEROUS
FREE OFFER EVER!

From the
Silhouette Reader Service™

GET 4 FREE BOOKS WORTH $11.80

Affix peel-off stickers to reply card

FOUR FREE BOOKS

4 4

4 4

FOUR FREE BOOKS

PLUS A FREE VICTORIAN PICTURE FRAME

AND A FREE MYSTERY GIFT!

NO COST! NO OBLIGATION TO BUY!
NO PURCHASE NECESSARY!

Because you're a reader of Silhouette romances, the publishers would like you to accept four brand-new Silhouette Special Edition® novels, with their compliments. Accepting this offer places you under no obligation to purchase any books, ever!

YOURS

We'd like to send you four free Silhouette novels, worth $11.80, to introduce you to the benefits of the Silhouette Reader Service™. We hope your free books will convince you to subscribe, but that's up to you. Accepting them places you under no obligation to buy anything, but we hope you'll want to continue your membership in the Reader Service.

So unless we hear from you, once a month we'll send you six additional Silhouette Special Edition® novels to read and enjoy. If you choose to keep them, you'll pay just $2.74* each—a saving of 21¢ off the cover price. And there is *no* charge for delivery. There are *no* hidden extras! You may cancel at any time, for any reason, just by sending us a note or a shipping statement marked "cancel" or by returning any shipment of books to us at our cost. Either way the free books and gifts are yours to keep!

ALSO FREE!
VICTORIAN PICTURE FRAME

This lovely Victorian pewter-finish miniature is perfect for displaying a treasured photograph—and it's yours *absolutely free*—when you accept our no-risk offer.

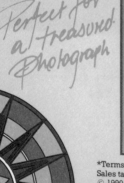

Perfect for a treasured Photograph

Plus a Free mystery Gift! follow instructions at right.

*Terms and prices subject to change without notice.
Sales taxes applicable in New York
© 1990 HARLEQUIN ENTERPRISES LIMITED

WE EVEN PROVIDE FREE POSTAGE!

It costs you *nothing* to send for your free books — we've paid the postage on the attached reply card. And we'll pick up the postage on your shipment of free books and gifts, and also on any subsequent shipments of books, should you choose to become a subscriber. Unlike many book clubs, we charge *nothing* for postage and handling!

Chase." So much needed to be said, but Rachel felt time slipping away. "Dr. Wells said they were going to send you by helicopter to a rear MASH unit for X rays."

"Yeah. I told them I was okay, but they didn't believe me." He gave her a longing glance. "You look kinda pale. Are you sure you're okay?" Chase had to force himself not to get up and go over to hold her. He saw how washed-out Rachel's flesh appeared beneath the lantern light. And she was tense, moving a piece of paper constantly between her fingers.

"Really, I am. I know I'm in shock, but I was more worried about you."

"Typical nurse," he joked huskily. "What about you, Rachel?"

Tilting her head, she gave him a puzzled look, trying to steel her emotions. "Me?"

"Yeah. I'd think you'd be going home now."

"Home?"

Chase scowled. "Yeah, stateside. I mean, this has been one hell of a hardship on you. No woman should have to go through what you did."

With a little laugh of frustration, Rachel held up the paper toward him. "Stateside, huh? These are my orders, Chase. I'm to report in to a MASH unit south of here tomorrow morning."

His eyes widened and he sat up. "What?" It was crazy! His hands knotted into fists on his thighs. "You're not serious?"

"Of course I am," she said quietly.

"But—Rachel, you damn near lost your life!" The words came out in an explosion of disbelief.

"Stop shouting at me, Chase!" Damn him! Why couldn't he understand this was where she wanted to be, helping the men who were wounded? She saw the anger and question in his eyes. "You can be so bullheaded sometimes." Her voice quavered. "Whatever gave you the idea I'd tuck my tail between my legs and run for home?"

Sputtering, Chase got to his feet. "Rachel, use your head! This is *not* a place for a woman. And you, more than anyone, should know that!" He threw his hands upward. "You ought to be going home."

"I'm a nurse," Rachel began tightly, glaring at him. "A damned good one, if I don't say so myself. I'm needed here." She wanted to choke Chase. He was stuck on the idea that a woman's place was at home, in a kitchen or raising children.

"Then do your nursing stateside." Helplessness washed over him. She was incredibly beautiful when she was furious, the set of her lips pouring fire through his body.

"You don't understand a thing, do you, Chase? You've just spent the last couple of days with me behind enemy lines. You've seen that I can hold my own just like any man."

"What's that got to do with anything?" Chase shouted. He loved her. He wanted her safe, and she was sitting there like a pouty three-year-old, stubbornly refusing to cooperate!

Lurching to her feet, Rachel crossed the tent, sinking her finger deep into his chest. "Wake up, Chase! This isn't the Middle Ages. This is 1951! I have *every* right to be here in Korea, just as you do. You're here to kill. I'm here to save lives." Her nostrils flared, her words coming out in punctuated snatches. "I was hoping you'd understand. I was hoping for so much. All you see in me is what you consider weakness and inability." She backed away, the defiance in her tone dissolving. "Look at *me*, Chase. Not that image in your head about women in general. I'm an individual. Weigh me on my own merits, not what someone has pounded into your head."

Smarting beneath her attack, Chase threw his hands on his hips. "Damn you," he whispered harshly, "you won't listen to anyone, will you?" This wasn't how Chase wanted their meeting to end. He wanted more than anything to embrace her, hold her and yes, maybe steal a small kiss from her. The hurt in Rachel's face and the huge tears in her eyes tore at him.

"I won't listen to anyone who thinks they know what's best for me, Chase Trayhern! Why don't you just leave? All we do is argue anyway."

He hesitated, trying to think of words to heal the widening rift between them. As he stood, hearing their ragged breathing in the momentary stillness, Chase realized there was no bandage to treat their situation. Rachel wasn't going to back down and leave Korea. The set of her jaw guaranteed that.

"Captain Trayhern!" An orderly slipped into the tent, coming to attention. "Sir, a helicopter is waiting to take you to the rear."

"Fine. I'll be there in a moment, Private."

"Yes, sir."

Rachel watched the soldier leave, positioning himself outside the flaps. She saw the agony in Chase's set features. "This isn't good for you," she muttered. "Losing your temper increases blood pressure. Your head's probably pounding."

Anger and frustration ballooned within Chase. "My head hurts like hell." His heart ached even more. "If you'd listen to reason—"

"Leave, Chase," Rachel whispered wearily, sitting back down, collapsing on the cot. She could feel her heart breaking with such incredible pain that it felt like genuine cardiac arrest. She avoided his pleading gaze.

"But—"

Lifting her head, she shook it. "No."

Chase opened his mouth to launch into further argument, but he saw the defiance glittering in her narrowed green eyes. "It's just that—"

"I'm not a child, Chase. I'm not the little girl you see me as. Until you can get rid of that image, there's nothing to share between us."

The words hit him hard. He snapped his mouth shut, turned and jerked open the flaps of the tent. Damn her! Damn her to hell! Every step across the harrowed earth multiplied the pain in his heart. The orderly led the way to the helicopter. Chase rubbed his chest, trying to will away the agony ripping him apart. Rachel's tear-filled eyes haunted him. *Little girl.* He hadn't treated her like that! She was just upset by the trauma and unexpectedly making love with him, that was all.

Chase strode the last few feet and boarded the helicopter. Strapping in, he sat fuming. An icy sensation tore through him. He didn't even know where Rachel was being stationed! The helicopter lifted off into the dawn sky, the unit below them growing smaller and smaller. Anxiety coursed through Chase. How in hell was he going to find out where Rachel would be? Somehow, he'd locate her unit. This wasn't the end. He glared toward the red and pink ribbons of color along the horizon. Time, they needed time, and they had none. Absolutely none...

* * *

"Ready, Lieutenant?"

Rachel sniffed, fighting back the tears. The private smiled uncertainly, holding the flap of the tent open for her. She got up, looking around. Half an hour ago, the tent had rung with heated and angry words. Following the private, she walked carefully over the rutted earth. A jeep had been rerouted for her use, and the private would drive her south toward her new MASH unit. Her new home. Not the home Chase had in mind.

As Rachel climbed into the passenger side of the jeep and settled into the seat, she released a long, painful sigh. The sky was a deepening crimson color, highlighting the few clouds with pink edges. Her heart felt as if it had been ground up and destroyed.

The jeep lurched forward, gears grinding, tackling the tank tracks and bumping along the poor excuse for a dirt road. Rachel held on for her life as she was tossed around, bruising her hips and rear. This was one ride she wasn't going to enjoy. Columns of Australian troops, their young faces darkened and blank, carrying their rifles on their shoulders, marched slowly toward the front. War surrounded her. Yet Chase's argument and anger kept pounding through her head like an artillery barrage.

Gradually the reminders of war were left behind, and the jeep was able to speed up as the road improved. Rachel relaxed, trying to focus on the bare-limbed trees preparing for the forthcoming winter. That was how she felt, as stripped and vulnerable as those trees. She loved Chase. The word warmed Rachel, but the reality of his stance shattered her hope. Why couldn't Chase see her as an individual instead of lumping her in under the title *woman*? She was many things. Why couldn't he see that?

The memory of Chase's kiss, the strength and tenderness of his mouth teasing hers, compounded Rachel's pain. She closed her eyes, a tiredness thousands of years old settling around her shoulders. How could she have fallen in love so quickly? Was it possible? Didn't love take at least a year to blossom? Searching her experience and her mother's advice, Rachel came up with few answers. Her father had courted her mother two years before he had asked for her hand in marriage. Most of the women her age insisted upon a one-year engagement after discovering they loved a man.

Rubbing her aching temples, Rachel wondered if the trauma of the capture and escape had influenced her emotions to that degree. How could it? With another sigh, she opened her eyes. Perhaps time would give her the answers. Her mother always said time would tell everything. She didn't even know where Chase was stationed or have an address where she could reach him. Her misery multiplied. It was really the end. He'd made no attempt to get her new address or even mention the fact that he'd like to get to know her better.

Where was her mind? Her reason? Rachel realized then how much she'd fallen in love with Chase. It had been a one-sided affair. Of course, he wanted her physically, but that wasn't real love. At least she knew the difference. A coldness invaded Rachel, and she felt the pain jag through her. There was no way to fight her grief, her loss of the only man who had ever stolen her heart. Rachel laughed sadly to herself. She was right back where she'd been: a nurse in a MASH unit. It was as if this had been an incredible dream and nightmare combined, which hadn't really existed at all.

Time, she told herself. *I need time to grieve for what I've lost in Chase. I need time to forget him....*

Buddy Dawson couldn't die! Chase awkwardly unstrapped from the Mustang he'd just landed at Taegu. His wingman had gotten hit over a target, and Buddy was down. Chase climbed out of the cockpit, walked down the wing and leaped to the muddy ground. Rain slashed at his face as he ran toward the ambulance parked next to Buddy's fighter.

Ever since he'd left Rachel, nothing had gone right. Now his best friend was wounded. Clenching his fists, Chase climbed into the ambulance. There was a MASH unit five miles away. After looking at his unconscious friend, Chase closed his eyes, a terrible feeling moving through him. Buddy was incredibly pale, his red hair stark against his pasty flesh. All Chase could think about was Buddy's three-month-old baby—a daughter he'd never seen. Reaching over, he unbuttoned the pocket on Buddy's leather jacket, pulling the photo out to protect it. Chase's fingers closed around the photo, his eyes never leaving his friend's face.

The rain was coming down harder, the muddy road a thickening mire rutted with deep trenches, slowing the ambulance considerably. By the time they arrived at the MASH unit, Chase was beside himself. The doors flew open and he leaped out, stepping aside to allow the orderlies to take Buddy inside a huge dark green tent. Cold water stung Chase's frozen features as he watched them throw a protective blanket over Buddy.

"Hurry up!" he roared. "Dammit, hurry up!"

The corpsman grabbed Chase, dragging him away from the ambulance. "Take it easy, sir," he gasped, watching the wounded man being taken inside.

Jerking off the corpsman's hold, Chase shouldered past him. "Get out of my way," he snarled. The photo of Cindy Ann Dawson remained in his pocket, safe from the rain's damaging drops as Chase entered the Surgery tent.

The bright lights hurt his eyes, and he halted at the entrance in confusion. The place was a beehive of activity, with several nurses in dark green surgery gowns moving around Buddy. Two doctors were prepping him for immediate surgery. Chase felt a hand on his shoulder.

"Captain, you can't be of any use here," the corpsman said gently. "If you want, you can wait in the admissions tent. It's across the way. There's hot coffee over there and a place to sit down."

Torn, Chase watched the nurses, masks in place on their faces. Shouts filled the tent, escalating Chase's tension. The five people around Buddy's cot looked like a nest of green-clothed hornets stirred up and flying around in frantic urgency, shoving tubes into his friend, poking him with needles and clapping an oxygen mask over his mouth and nose.

"Sir?"

Chase resisted, his gaze clinging to Buddy's slack face. His fingers wrapped protectively around the photo in his pocket. He saw one nurse suddenly jerk her attention in his direction, but he paid no heed, all his focus centered on Buddy.

Rachel's eyes widened. She snapped her gaze from Chase back to the man on the cot. Giving orders quietly to her team of nurses, Rachel shut out the shock she felt at seeing Chase again. Her heart took a ragged plunge at realizing he was standing no more than ten feet away. In those agonizing seconds, Rachel saw a man who was pale and drawn, not the cocky pilot she'd known before. The look in his eyes shredded her composure. She glanced down at the pilot they were working feverishly to stabilize. She guessed he must be a good friend of Chase's. The war had finally become personal to him.

Within the next two minutes, they had the pilot transferred to the operation theater, the doors swinging shut. Rachel was the head surgery nurse, quickly getting her instruments ready for the two doctors who were going to try to save this man's life.

"Shrapnel," Dr. Todd growled to his partner, Dr. Davis.

"Busting tanks when it happened, according to the corpsman," Davis added. He shot a glance over at Rachel. "Ready?"

"Let's go," she whispered, hands hovering over the myriad of items that could possibly save the man's life. The minutes congealed into a tense ballet between Rachel and the doctors. She kept taking blood pressure readings, watching it drop repeatedly. The pilot had lost too much blood. Although they were pumping as much whole blood as possible back into his body, they were losing the battle for his life. The main artery in Dawson's leg had been severed. Rachel wondered how he had been able to fly back and land the plane before fainting from loss of blood. Chase slammed back into her mind. The look of agony in his eyes haunted her as she handed clamps to Dr. Davis. *Chase.*

* * *

Chase prowled the admissions tent like a caged animal. The place was deserted, the rain pelting down on the canvas, creating a dull background sound. He kept looking at the photo of Buddy's daughter and praying. Buddy had to live! He had a home and a family waiting for him. His wife was only twenty, and they'd been married less than two years. He kept looking toward the wooden door. The urge to find out how Buddy was doing was killing Chase.

Glancing at the watch on his wrist, he realized it had only been forty minutes since they'd arrived at the MASH unit. Chase paced restlessly, rubbing his brow where an ache was centering. Just as he was about to head back over to the surgery tent, the door quietly opened and closed. He jerked to a halt in the center of the tent, his gaze swinging to the figure standing inside the door. It was a nurse, her surgery gown darkened with rain and splattered with blood. Chase's eyes widened as she took off her mask and pulled the sweat-stained green cap from her head. Black hair, shining beneath the lantern light, tumbled around her shoulders.

"Rachel!" Her name came out explosively, raw and primal.

She stood uncertainly, the mask and cap dangling in her left hand. "Chase?"

He blinked once, as if not believing his eyes. "What—I mean, I didn't know you were here." His voice was terribly off-key.

Walking over to him, Rachel managed a strained smile laced with sadness. "I've been here a month." She frowned, gripping his arm, her voice lowering. "I asked the doctors to let me talk to you about Lieutenant Dawson."

Chase tensed, his eyes darkening. "Buddy?"

"Yes." Rachel swallowed hard, forcing herself to hold his anguished gaze. Chase knew what she was going to tell him—she could see him trying to prepare himself for the tragic news. She gripped his arm more firmly. "He was your friend?"

Chase couldn't speak. His throat closed up. Instead, he nodded, holding on to the photo in his right hand.

"I'm sorry, Chase. Buddy didn't make it. He'd lost too much blood. He went into cardiac failure." Her fingers tightened as she felt him stiffen, denial coupled with disbelief in his features.

"No!" His cry caterwauled off the tent walls. Chase spun from her grasp and walked to the other end of the tent.

Rachel watched Chase halt, his back to her. The shadows accentuated his hunched and shaking shoulders. He was crying. Without thinking, she walked over to him and placed her hand on his shoulder.

"Chase," she murmured in a strangled tone, "I'm sorry. So sorry..."

Just the firm touch of Rachel's hand on his shoulder made Chase turn blindly in her direction. His eyes were filled with tears, blurring her softened features and sad green eyes. "It can't be...it can't be." He held up the photo for her to look at, his hand trembling. "Buddy's got a new daughter, three months old. He's never seen her...he's got a wife. They've been married just a short time—" His voice cracked, the wall of pain welling up through him.

"Come here," Rachel pleaded, throwing her arms around him, pulling Chase against her.

The first sob ripped through Chase, shattering the rest of his composure. Rachel's arms were strong, holding him, her voice trembling next to his ear as he swept her into his grip. He held her hard, afraid that if he let go, the rest of his world would shatter, too.

The strangled, animallike sounds that jerked out of Chase tore through Rachel. She whispered singsong words as she repeatedly caressed his hair in a gesture meant to heal. Chase held her like a hurt child hiding in his mother's arms. His tears wet her cheek and neck, mingling with Rachel's own tears dribbling down her cheeks.

How long she stood holding him in her aching arms, Rachel didn't know. Finally Chase's sobs lessened, his breathing becoming steady against her neck as he held her. The fact that Chase would cry at all tore away Rachel's defenses. She blindly kissed his rough cheek, wanting to tell him in her own way that she applauded his courage to cry, to share this terrible tragedy with her.

"Come on," she whispered against his ear, loosening her arms from around his shoulders, "Come over here." Rachel guided them to a wooden bench near the coffeepot.

Chase wiped the tears from his eyes, following her. He gripped her hand, refusing to release it even after they sat down. Rachel remained close, putting her other arm around his waist. The lump in his throat was still there, and he helplessly studied the photo.

"This is Buddy's daughter," he choked out. "They call her Cindy."

Rachel cupped the photo, her hand beneath his. "She's a beautiful baby with a beautiful name," she whispered unsteadily.

Chase shut his eyes tightly, more tears beading and dropping from his lashes. "She'll never know Buddy...."

Resting her head against his shoulder, Rachel tried to comfort him. Words were useless. His fingers squeezed her hand until she felt pain, but she said nothing, understanding the depth of Chase's agony and loss. The rain continued in a deep, drumming pattern, as if the sky, too, were crying for the loss of Buddy. Gradually Chase retreated into silence, the grip of his fingers easing from her hand.

"Cindy will know her father through her mother," Rachel began haltingly. "I know it doesn't bring Buddy back, but she'll have letters and photos of him to share with her daughter."

Staring at the opposite wall of the tent, Chase allowed Rachel's husky voice to fall over him like a balm, easing some of his pain. "I—I just shot some film of Buddy a week ago." He closed his eyes. "I'll get it developed right away and send it to Susan, his wife."

Squeezing his hand, Rachel said, "I know she'll treasure those photos."

"I can write a letter," Chase went on, talking more to himself than to her. "I can write a special letter to Cindy. Even though she's too young to read or understand it, someday she will. I want to tell her about her daddy—how brave he was, how he fought to stay alive when most men would have died at the stick with that kind of wound." A shudder worked its way through Chase. He twisted his head, studying Rachel in the subdued light. How beautiful she was. And she was alive and here, with him. "Buddy was one in a million."

Rachel managed a wobbly smile. "Like you, Chase."

Some of the grief was sloughing off his shoulders. Being able to cry had helped. Chase gave her a bashful look. "I've never cried in a woman's arms before."

"For a man to be able to cry at all is something, Chase. I wish more of them could." Rachel lowered her lashes, unable to stand the burning blue of his eyes as they looked into her heart and soul. "I'm glad you did, and I'm glad it was with me."

Rousing himself from his crouched position, Chase straightened up, feeling gutted and numb inside. He noticed how tightly he'd been holding Rachel's hand and released it, examining her slender fingers. They were work worn and red, the skin chafed and in need of some care. He was struck by how hard Rachel worked.

"I didn't mean to bruise the hell out of your hand." Rachel's ability to handle emotional issues stunned him. She was being strong for him, and it brought to the surface just how much he loved her.

"Don't worry about it," she murmured. Rachel could see hope in his bleak eyes. Chase was over the worst of his shock. Buddy's death would haunt him for a long time, though. Right now, he was cycling up and out of the grief, and she wanted to make him feel better. "How about some coffee with a stiff belt of medicinal whiskey?"

Chase nodded.

Rachel got up, moving to the coffeepot. She opened the cabinet beneath the burner, removing a bottle of whiskey. "We use this for medicinal purposes after a particularly bad day or night." She took two tin mugs, filling them with hot coffee and adding a splash of liquor. "Some days are worse than others."

Gratefully Chase took the mug, the metal warming his cold hands and fingers. He sipped the steaming liquid, the whiskey burning away the lump in his throat, making him gasp.

"I forgot to tell you, that's two hundred proof moonshine," Rachel said. "Davis comes from Kentucky hill people, and he makes his special brew just for such occasions."

With a startled sound, Chase wiped his mouth, eyeing the coffee with respect. "It's got a kick to it."

She sipped the liquid cautiously. "How do you feel now?"

"Better," he rasped. Chase knew the moonshine had little to do with his improvement. Hungrily he sponged Rachel's face into his memory. Even draped in a large, tentlike surgery gown too big for her thin frame, Rachel glowed with inner strength and spirit.

Reaching out, he captured her hand. "We have to talk," he told her huskily. "Now."

Chapter Eight

"Miss McKenzie!" An orderly poked his head around the door, gulping for breath.

Rachel released Chase's hand, her heart sinking. "Yes, Al?"

"We need you back in surgery. We're getting three loads of wounded by helo in ten minutes."

Chase frowned, hearing the urgency in the soldier's voice. He looked up. Rachel looked serene and composed under the circumstances. Chase felt none of those things, the shock of Buddy's death hanging over him.

"I'll be there in just a few minutes, Al."

"Yes ma'am." The orderly disappeared out the door, leaving them alone once again.

Glumly Chase muttered, "Looks like duty calls." His voice was rough with emotion.

Setting the cup of barely touched coffee and whiskey on the counter, Rachel grimaced. "I'm sorry, Chase."

"Is it always like this?"

She nodded. "If we didn't have to sleep sometime during a twenty-four-hour period, we'd be in the surgery theater or over in recovery nonstop." Sighing, Rachel added, "We're shorthanded, Chase."

"And you're tired." Chase finally had surfaced from his grief enough to take in Rachel's condition. Faint shadows showed beneath her glorious green eyes. He felt a sad smile pull at the corners of his mouth. "Look, I know this is bad timing, Rachel, but I need to talk to you."

Rachel's heart picked up in an erratic beat. She didn't dare believe that Chase wanted to see her—not after their fight a month ago. But how many nights had she tossed and turned in torrid dream states, remembering it? Remembering him?

The sound of approaching helicopters drowned out the drumming rain. Chase saw Rachel tense, and it reminded him of a boxer preparing to do battle, only she was going in to fight to save lives. Getting slowly to her feet, he recaptured her hand.

"I looked all over Korea for you after we got split up. I never realized how many MASH units are over here. I thought it would be easy to locate you, but I was wrong."

Rachel stared up into Chase's craggy, worn features. "I thought you never wanted to see me again." His eyes were red rimmed and filled with pain. The last thing she wanted to do was leave his side. Right now he needed someone to help him work through his grief.

"I never said that, Rachel." He struggled with his grief and his need of her, trying to right the wrongs between them. "You may feel that way, but I don't," Chase whispered huskily, studying her chafed hand. "I know you have to go, Rachel, but tell me when I can see you. When can we have a few hours together to talk?" He heard the pleading tone in his voice and didn't care. What he felt for Rachel wasn't a game. Since their escape, he'd had a long time to look at how he'd behaved with her. She'd been right: He'd acted like a groper intent on only one thing. And he'd loved her, fulfilling that promise that she'd accused him of all along. Now, it was a Sword of Damocles between them.

Rachel hesitated, unable to get beyond the shock of seeing Chase or the feelings that still burned brightly in her heart for him. Incredible tenderness in his blue eyes reminded her of what they'd shared. It was all he wanted, she decided sadly. And it wasn't what she wanted at all. "I don't think we have anything to talk about, Chase."

"I do."

Rachel wavered, exhausted and emotionally drained. Rubbing her brow, she muttered, "A week from now. I get next Friday off."

"I'll be here. That's a promise, Rachel." Chase saw her eyes become dull with some undefined emotion. Wasn't she happy to see him? Would she allow him back into her life? She hadn't tried to contact him after he'd left in a huff, he acknowledged.

Reluctantly Rachel pulled her hand from Chase's grasp. "I've got to go, Chase." She opened the door, started to leave then turned back toward him. Her face was drawn with real worry. "Be careful flying next week. You're suffering badly for Buddy. Please..."

A sliver of his normal cocky grin surfaced. "I'll be real careful, Angel Eyes. I've got something to live for...." Chase saw her eyes go sad, and then she turned, disappearing into the rain. He stood, savoring the wave of happiness flooding through his chest, dissolving a portion of his grief. Glancing around, Chase glumly realized it was time to get back to the air base. He hadn't gotten permission from Hob to come here, and his commanding officer was probably wondering where the hell he was.

Pulling the collar of his flight suit up to protect the back of his neck, Chase ducked out into the miserable weather. His heart hurt, but a new sense of life pulsed strongly through him. He'd found Rachel! As he slogged between the dark green tents and inch-deep mud, he wanted to shout for joy. Water ran down his face in rivulets, outlining his features, dripping down the back of his neck, but Chase barely noticed the physical discomfort. His heart centered on the loss of his best friend, and hope for a future with Rachel. The weight in his chest told him which was affecting him the most, and he allowed himself to dwell on Buddy and the letters he would write to his friend's family.

"Rachel, you look great!" Annie Johnson, a twenty-three-year-old lieutenant in the nursing corps said, sauntering into the tent. She sat down on her cot, running a hand through her short blond curls.

"Thanks, Annie." Nervously Rachel applied lipstick to her mouth. She used the tube sparingly, applying it only when she had duty in recovery. The boys over there appreciated her feminine appearance. All the nurses did their best to give them hope by looking feminine, and it made the men rally.

"Who's this guy coming to see you?" Annie teased, stretching out for a few minutes of rest, her hands behind her head.

"You know—I told you about him. Captain Chase Trayhern." Rachel picked up the brush, running it through her recently washed hair. Sunlight pierced through the window of the door, making the inside of the tent brighter, emphasizing the shine to her hair.

"Oh, the groper."

Rachel groaned. "Annie, don't you dare call him that." She turned to her friend. Annie was smiling broadly.

"You called him that yourself."

"That was over a month ago."

"Think he's changed?"

"No," Rachel muttered. She stepped back from the mirror. Cosmetics were rare, and each nurse hoarded what she'd brought with her from the States. She asked herself why she cared what she looked like for Chase. She shouldn't.

"This is one of those times you wish you had a dress," Annie drawled.

Muttering under her breath, Rachel took another look in the mirror. "Chase doesn't care what a woman wears."

"Oh, one of those. The day's gorgeous. What have you got planned with the captain?"

Nothing fit right. Rachel flattened the collar on her fatigues. It remained wrinkled. "We're just going to talk. There are no plans. I'm sure he has some, but I don't intend to fit into them, whatever they are."

"Talk?" Annie tittered. "Come on, Rachel!"

"Annie!" she said in an exasperated tone, looking at her watch. It was ten in the morning, the time Chase had said he'd arrive. Looking out the dirty window of the door, she didn't see any unfamiliar jeeps winding their way toward the MASH unit.

"Well," Annie added dramatically, "I'll be gone from the tent for the rest of the day, should you want to 'talk' in here."

Heat stung Rachel's cheeks as she turned and studied her friend and roommate. "It's not like that between us," she protested.

"Sure..."

With a groan, Rachel opened the door, stepping out into the brilliant sunlight. "I can't stand this waiting around, Annie. I'm going for a walk in the field behind our tent." The field, filled with autumn flowers and multicolored leaves, reminded Rachel of her home in Maine.

"Okay, I'll tell the captain where you are, in case he comes here first."

Rachel waved her thanks, heading toward the field. The nurses' tents were located at the southern end of the compound. Beyond that was a friendly village, not far away. On her rare days off, Rachel walked to the village and set up a first aid station in one of the huts, giving inoculations or taking care of simple medical problems of the children or their parents.

The day was utterly beautiful. Rachel lifted her face to the sun, feeling its warmth steal through her. After five days of continuous rain, the sun was a welcomed respite. Stepping into the ten-acre field, she saw it was alive with the color of a myriad of fall flowers. Delighted, Rachel walked through the field, occasionally stooping to cup a flower in her hands and smell its fragrance. The bees were busy getting the last of the pollen to make honey for their hives before the icy winter fell upon them.

Ten o'clock became ten-thirty and then eleven. From the field, Rachel could see any traffic entering and leaving the unit. None of the vehicles contained Chase. Worry gnawed at her. Had he crashed his plane? Been shot down? If he had, she would be the last to know. Chewing on her lip, Rachel sat on a group of rocks, facing the road in the distance.

Taking a strand of withered grass, she shredded it absently between her fingertips. Why was she putting so much into seeing Chase again? *Because,* her heart whispered, *you love him.* Rachel shook her head, staring down at the stalk of grass now in shreds at her booted feet. Chase could have changed his mind about coming. After all, he'd been in shock over Buddy Dawson's death. Upon returning to the air base, he may have decided against seeing her again. One small part of Rachel hoped that was the case. She didn't want to see Chase if he was going to continue his past campaign to bed her. There were more important things in life than a toss in the hay.

Groaning, Rachel slid off the rock, grabbing another strand of grass and turning her back to the road, heading deeper into the oasis of beauty. Chase made her feel like melting honey in his hands, Rachel admitted. He made her feel like a woman, something no other man had ever evoked. But that was all he really wanted from her. Marriage wasn't in his future. And she had no plan to try to force him into a marriage just for some sex.

"Angel Eyes!"

Gasping, Rachel whirled around. There, at the edge of the field, stood Chase in his tan flight uniform and brown leather jacket. He had just climbed out of a jeep, a huge bouquet of flowers in his hand. Rachel's heart snagged and she watched his progress toward her. If her eyes didn't deceive her, his uniform looked *pressed*! Chase wore the garrison cap at a cocky angle on his head. Trying not to smile at the pains he'd taken with his appearance, she waited with trepidation, her hands suddenly damp and cool. How handsome he looked!

More than anything, Rachel saw life again in his blue eyes. The bashful, uncertain expression on Chase's face as he approached her, holding out the field flowers, unstrung Rachel.

"They're beautiful," she murmured, taking them. "Thank you." Their hands met, touched.

"You're beautiful," Chase returned huskily. He released the bouquet, watching as Rachel held the flowers at her breast, inhaling their scent. Indeed, she was ten times more lovely than he could ever recall. Was it the spare use of makeup? The dancing warmth in her lovely green eyes or that shy smile on her full lips? He wasn't sure and didn't really care. What mattered was that they were here—together.

"I never expected flowers," Rachel whispered, caressing the bouquet.

Chase glanced around, throwing his hands on his hips. "My mother taught me to give a lady flowers." He smiled, enjoying her response to them. "I can't believe it. I discovered a field about two miles from the air base and decided to pick you some." Chase made a gesture around the area, grinning. "But you've got the same flowers in this one."

Rachel walked toward the group of rocks and took a seat on a flat one. "Still, it's the thought that counts, Chase." He chose a rock right next to her. What did she expect? He was going to launch a campaign to get her into his arms and his bed once again.

Chase squinted against the sun, absorbing Rachel's face into his heart. "Hell, I could have had an extra twenty minutes with you by coming straight here. We could have picked the flowers together."

Rachel placed the bouquet in her lap, nervously touching the flowers. "You're incorrigible, Chase."

"Maybe." He studied her for a moment, his smile slipping. "How have you been?"

"Working hard as usual. You?"

"More missions than I'd like. Hob wants the squadrons flying twenty-four hours a day, softening up the enemy while the weather holds. I understand winters are hell over here."

"We're already preparing for frostbite cases when it decides to turn ugly around here," Rachel agreed quietly. The war was never far from them. Ever. Rachel gently cupped some of the flowers, inhaling the scent. "These remind me of life, not death."

"That's why I picked them. You remind me of the good things life holds. When I think of you, I can put the not-so-good things into perspective." Chase ached to reach out and slide his fingers through Rachel's loose, silky black hair when she leaned over to smell the flowers. His throat constricted as he mentally rehearsed what he was going to say to her.

"Uh...listen, I need to talk with you, Rachel." Chase dove on when she lifted her head, her eyes filled with incredible warmth. "We got off on the wrong foot with each other when we met. I mean, I wasn't

behaving properly, like a gentleman would to a lady."
He swallowed hard. "And you are a lady, believe me,"
he added huskily.

Rachel sat very still.

"I was out of my head," Chase continued, hoping
she would pin his actions on his concussion. But the
truth was, he'd wanted her. All of her. He still did.
Just being this close to Rachel, smelling the special
fragrance that was only her, was driving him crazy. He
clasped his hands, staring down at them, trying to
rearrange his scattered thoughts. "I don't know what
happened between us after we made love. Looking
back, I guess we can chalk it up to the stress we were
under."

Rachel glanced at him sharply. "Stress or not,
Chase, you were continually trying to get me in your
arms."

He shrugged. "Guilty as charged. But, dammit,
that doesn't mean I didn't enjoy making love to you.
I did."

Flushing, Rachel was unable to hold his pleading
stare. "That's not the issue, Chase, and you know it."

Mouth tightening, he muttered, "Then I wish you'd
tell me what is. I've been going crazy for the past
month. I've tried to look at what happened to us from
all angles. I don't see how you can be sorry it happened. It was good for both of us."

"That's just it, Chase. For you men, it's a one-shot
deal. Stalk the woman, capture her, then let her go
after you've bedded her down. Nothing asked, nothing received. No responsibility or emotional ties exchanged. Men have the privilege of loving and leaving.
We're under a double standard, Chase." Rachel held
his gaze, now marred with confusion. "I was sup-

posed to save myself for marriage, for the man I was going to spend the rest of my life with—'' She turned away, her voice choked. "And I threw it away because I was scared and wanting to be held for just a little while."

Clasping his hands between his legs, Chase released a long sigh, hearing the pain in her voice. "I did take something that didn't belong to me," he whispered. "For that, I'm sorry. You're right, Rachel, men get away with murder, and women are held accountable. But I'm trying to make myself responsible for what we shared. I'm here, with you. I want—"

"A man can divorce a woman, but a woman risks a lot more if she dares to divorce her husband."

Chase nodded, feeling the terrible reality of what he'd done in stalking and taking Rachel. "Isn't there something I can do or say to make it right between us?" He twisted a look up at her. Rachel's features expressed the same sadness he felt.

She shook her head. "I don't think so, Chase."

"Well, if I could?" God, how he wanted another chance with her. "Listen, when I loved you, it was you, not another woman in my head or heart. Having you in my arms was heaven, and that's not a line." And then Chase added grimly, "Or a lie."

A terrible ache wrenched her. The conversation was so painful to both of them. "Chase, I never said it was."

He heartened. "If I had it to do all over again, it would be different—better, for you, Rachel."

"No," she whispered, getting up, moving away from him. "It won't happen again."

Frustration thrummed through Chase. He scrambled to try to save the deteriorating situation. "We got in a terrible argument with each other at the Aussie camp. I—that was my fault." His brows dipped and he tried to remember the next memorized line that he'd written four days ago. "You were right. I was treating you like a girl, not a woman. And—I had no business telling you to go home to the states."

"What about the rest of the conversation, Chase?" she asked gently, suffering along with him, because she knew he was a proud man and it was tough for him to admit he was wrong.

"What other stuff?" Chase lifted his head, cradled by her soft green gaze.

"About putting me under a general category where women do this, but don't do that."

"Oh..." He cleared his throat a couple of times, nodding his head vigorously. "I've given that a lot of thought, too."

"It appears you have."

"Yes...I decided you're different from most women, and I shouldn't try to corral you into what most other women do or want out of life."

Rachel wanted to reach over and caress his sweaty cheek. Chase was struggling beneath all these weighty admissions. Were they lies to convince her back into his arms? She didn't know, feeling serrated. "Chase, more than anything, I want to be married someday and have two or three children. I love the idea of sharing my life with someone, of carrying his child and feeling that life within me. That's part of being a woman, not just what society expects of me. There is a difference. I've always rebelled against being looked at as nothing more than a brood mare. Life consists of so much more than that. I decided at a very early age that I deserved to live the way I wanted to and be my-self."

He gulped once, holding her gaze. "I understand that—I think," he said. "You do want to get married and have kids, then?"

Her smile was tentative. "As a woman, I want the right to do what I feel is best for me, not what some man decides I should do. But that doesn't mean I don't want a husband and family someday."

She was right, Chase realized humbly. He read so much in her eyes, fighting every desire to drag her into his arms and kiss her until she melted with passion. His thoughts were completely scattered, his memo-rized script erased under her quietly spoken admis-sion. He had visions of her decidedly pregnant, carrying *his* child. The thought was galvanizing.

Dipping his head, Chase had to break eye contact with Rachel or do something they'd both regret—again. Did she know the beauty of making slow, pas-sionate love in a field like this, getting back in touch with the earth and with all that was alive and beauti-ful? Damn, thinking was tough around her! All he wanted to do was feel the wealth of emotions Rachel aroused within him. "Look," he began, his voice low, "I want the right to know you better, Rachel. I know I acted like a cad before, but I want to make up for it, to prove to you that I'm not a groper. There's some-thing we share. I can't put it into words, I can only feel it." Chase closed his eyes, waiting for her to say no.

"When you left, I thought you never wanted to see me again."

Jerking his chin to the left, Chase said, "That isn't true, Rachel. On board the chopper, I realized I didn't know what unit you'd been assigned to." He shoved his fingers through his hair in aggravation. "You don't know how many times I was in the radio shack bugging the operators to make just one more call to one of the many MASH units in Korea." His eyes narrowed. "Every spare minute between missions, I was over there ordering those guys to put in calls, trying to locate you. I wanted to apologize, to start over, if you'd give me the chance."

"Oh, Chase..."

He managed a grimace. "I never stopped looking for you, Rachel. After cooling down, I realized I was wrong—about everything. You're your own woman. I didn't want to deal with that aspect of you. All the women I've known have been passive in comparison to you."

"I think if you'd stop lumping women under one label, you might find out there are quite a few like me."

Bashfully he smiled. "Yeah, you're probably right. You were right about which direction was south, too."

Rachel managed a thin smile. "You're too much, Chase. All these admissions in one day must be killing that proud fly-boy ego of yours."

"They are," he groused good-naturedly, grinning. She was so incredibly beautiful when she smiled. It was the first time he'd seen Rachel's lips move upward since seeing him again. His gloom dissolved. Chase wanted her more than ever—to see her laugh in his arms, to see her smile after making love.

Reaching down, he picked a blue flower from the field. "You're like this wildflower," he told her, "tough and resilient in ways a hothouse variety isn't. You're one of a kind, woman."

Sobering, Rachel stared at the flower he held. Chase possessed a large hand with long, strong fingers. A shiver of need wove through her at the memory of those fingers igniting fire within her, giving her unbelievable pleasure. The wind caressed the flower, bending it under the breeze's gentle bidding.

"We're all unique, Chase. Even though you're a man, I try not to make general assumptions about you," Rachel said, holding his gaze.

"I proved the groper stereotype."

Her eyes crinkled. "Yes."

"I couldn't help it, Rachel. I was out of my head."

"Chase."

"Well, maybe not completely out of my head. But Rachel, you're a beautiful lady. I like everything about you."

"Everything?"

He smiled, noting the seriousness in her voice. He handed her the blue flower to add to the bouquet in her lap. "Everything," he growled.

"Rachel?" Dr. Davis cocked his head, holding out his hand expectantly for the next instrument.

"Oh!" She handed him the needle and thread, embarrassed. Her thoughts weren't on the injured soldier who had come in earlier. No, they were on Chase. Where had the days gone? It had been nearly two weeks since she'd last seen him in that field of flowers.

Davis grinned, completing the job. "He's all yours, Miss McKenzie."

Trying to make up for her lapse in attentiveness, Rachel nodded. She quickly dressed the soldier's wound, a small cut on the arm, and released him back to his unit. Davis remained in the background, washing his hands in a basin.

"This is unusual behavior for you," he told her when she came over to wash her hands.

"I'm sorry, Brad, I should have been concentrating more."

A smile pulled at the corners of his mouth. "I understand from Annie you're sweet on some fly-boy captain over at Taegu. Trayhern his name? Annie said he called over here half an hour ago and is coming to visit."

Heat prickled her cheeks. Rachel was going to strangle Annie. Scrubbing her fingers, she muttered, "It's not what you think, Doctor. Captain Trayhern called and said he needed some medical help. Now, I don't call that a hot date, do you?"

Chuckling, Davis picked up a towel, drying his hands and then passing it over to Rachel. "Not exactly. Still, you're sweet on him, aren't you?"

Rachel tossed the towel into a nearby receptacle. "No..." she answered softly.

Davis studied her critically. "I think Annie's right: You like him, but won't admit it. I've got to give this captain credit, he's creative about finding ways to come calling."

Rolling her eyes, Rachel groaned. "I'm leaving! I've got half an hour before making rounds in recovery, Doctor." Crossing between tents, the mid-October wind tugged at her fatigues. The wind was sharper than usual today, promising a bitter winter ahead. Her mind and heart lingered on Chase. What was wrong? Did he really need medical help? Or was it a ruse? Worriedly she walked the well-trodden dirt path toward recovery.

A jeep pulled into view, and she saw Chase in the passenger seat. The driver was a young man with dark, curly hair. Her pulse leaped erratically as the vehicle ground to a stop in front of her, a cloud of dust following in its wake.

Chase smiled, thinking how pretty Rachel looked in her wrinkled fatigues. Nothing could hide her slender body from him. "Hey, I've got a patient for you." He climbed out, holding his leather jacket closed with his large hand.

Rachel smiled up at him, despite the nervousness she felt. She pointed toward admissions. The leather jacket was bulging with something inside it. Rachel gave him a curious look, but didn't ask what he was hiding inside its folds. "Sure. Come this way."

Chase fell into step beside Rachel, unable to tear his gaze from her. The wind played with her hair, and he longed to tunnel his fingers through those tresses himself. "How have you been? I haven't been able to get the time off I expected. Hob's turning up the heat on bombing missions to the north."

When Chase had left two weeks ago, Rachel had told him not to come back—that there was nothing left to explore between them. Now, inexplicably, Rachel was happy he was here. "I've been kept busy," Rachel admitted. She halted, opening the door into the large, roomy tent. "Come in."

Chase walked over to a wooden table and opened up his jacket. "This little guy came around my tent this morning."

Rachel stood on the opposite side, her eyes large with surprise. "It's a puppy!" Automatically she reached for the small animal. To her dismay, the dog was starved, his ribs sticking out pitifully from beneath his matted brown fur.

"I call him Fred," Chase offered, watching how carefully and lovingly Rachel held the puppy. Fred promptly whined and started licking her hand with an eagerness that made Chase wish it was him instead in her hands. "I heard whining outside my tent. He was sitting there looking like hell. I gave him some of my C rations, but he threw them up."

"Poor baby," she whispered, gently stroking Fred. Examining his floppy ears, she saw that mites infested them. "He's starved, Chase. Look at his eyes, they're almost matted shut because of malnutrition." She ran her hands down his accordianlike rib cage, her heart breaking. "And he's got mange." Fred's skin was ulcerated and flaking beneath her fingers.

"Will he make it?" Chase asked. The tenderness in Rachel's voice unstrung Chase. Would she ever respond to him like that? *Time,* he cautioned himself, *and patience.* Since their day in the meadow, he thought he saw a slight change in her. Nothing dramatic, but hopeful. Chase hadn't tried to kiss Rachel. It was as if she'd been waiting for him to start groping again, and he hadn't. This time, he saw trust in her eyes instead of wariness.

She placed Fred back in Chase's hands. "Hold on to him. I'm going to give him a B-12 shot and treat him just as I'd treat a malnourished villager." She went to the cabinet, pulled out a hypodermic needle and a vial containing the vitamin essence. Rachel stole a look at Chase's serious features. He looked tired and that worried her. Moving back to the table, she prepared the shot.

"How are you doing?"

Shrugging, Chase muttered, "The usual. Hob's short on aircraft, so we're flying double missions."

Rachel met and held his gaze. "You've got dark circles under your eyes. Maybe you need a B-12 shot, too."

He gave an adamant shake of his head. "Lady, those shots sting like hell! I'm fine, just a little short on sleep is all." Placing Fred on the table, he held the puppy still for Rachel.

As carefully as possible, she administered the shot to Fred's hindquarters. The puppy whined once, his brown eyes huge. Rachel patted him, murmuring affectionate praise. The puppy eagerly licked her hand.

"He's going to get a bath. Do you have time to hang around and help, or do you have to get back right away?" Rachel would need help. Chase looked vulnerable as he picked up the puppy and pressed it against his chest.

"I can stay for a little while. Hob knows I'm on a mission of the utmost mercy."

Smiling, Rachel led him behind another set of doors and into an area that contained two sinks and bathing facilities. She filled one sink with soap and water, the other with rinse water. She took Fred and carefully introduced him to the soapy water. The puppy happily stood in the basin, continuing to wag his long, thin tail. Chase came over, leaning against the sink, inches from Rachel. Hungrily he drank in her intent features. "You're a sight for sore eyes," he murmured, meaning it. When she raised an eyebrow, he added, "Now, that's not being a groper, is it? Can't I admit I like seeing you, talking with you?"

Heat rushed to her cheeks, and Rachel smiled, gently washing Fred with a soft brush. "It's nice to get a compliment," she admitted.

"Whew!"

She laughed.

"What do you consider groping, then?" Chase pressed.

Rachel slanted an amused look in his direction. She laid down the brush and took a comb, beginning to unknot huge hunks of hair hanging on Fred's dull coat. "What you did when we were behind enemy lines."

He sighed dramatically, noticing that they were alone. Crossing his arms, Chase watched her work for several minutes before speaking again. No wonder the men loved having Rachel for a nurse. Her touch was exquisitely gentle. He'd never forgotten the feel of her lovely hands running across his body. Fred was sitting in the hock-deep water, obviously enjoying her attention and ministrations. Suddenly Chase felt jealous of the dog. "Do you consider a kiss groping?"

"Well..." Rachel stammered. She looked up, drowning in the brilliant blue of his eyes. His mouth was incredibly strong and beautifully molded. Remembering the persuasive power of his mouth against her lips, she sighed, her feelings in turmoil.

"Great!"

Rachel gave him a warning look that spoke volumes. She lifted Fred out of the sink and transferred him to the rinse basin.

Chase followed her. "Look, what's a little kiss? If it's mutual, there's nothing wrong with it," he argued quickly.

Using a cup, Rachel rinsed Fred off. "Your kisses always go a lot further, Chase. That's what I have a problem with." Her heart was pounding unevenly, and she had the distinct impression that Chase was preparing to kiss her. Rattled, Rachel looked around. No one else was in the area. She didn't know whether to be glad or scared. His mouth was curved in a devil-may-care grin, melting her resolve, making her yearn to feel the strength of it against her lips once again.

Chase uncrossed his arms, holding them up in a gesture of conciliation. "What if I restrain myself, Rachel?"

She eyed him, placing Fred on a towel, beginning to pat the dog dry. Almost blurting out that she was more afraid that she couldn't restrain herself, Rachel dodged the question, refusing to answer Chase.

"Look," he urged, "we like each other. A lot. You know how hard I tried to locate you after we got to safety. Doesn't that prove something?"

"I guess..."

Chase sensed Rachel's sudden shyness. Checking to make sure no one was around, he gently took her by the shoulders, forcing her to turn and face him. Fred was wrapped in a white towel against her breast, looking up at him expectantly.

"Listen," Chase said huskily, drawing her as close as the puppy would allow, "I like you, Rachel." He caressed her tense shoulders. "I go to sleep thinking about you. I dream about you. Sometimes," he grimaced, "I find myself thinking about you instead of concentrating on flying."

Her eyes grew troubled. "No, Chase, don't do that. I'd never forgive myself if something happened to you on a flight—"

"Sh, Angel Eyes." He smiled tenderly, his hands drifting upward, framing her flushed face. "Show me how much you like me with a kiss. Just a kiss..."

Fred whined and lunged upward, his long pink tongue relishing Chase's jaw. Chase stepped back, surprised. Rachel burst out laughing. He grinned belatedly and joined her.

Sheepishly he wiped his jaw dry with the back of his hand. "I guess I had that coming."

The fear left Rachel and she relaxed as Chase placed his hands on her shoulders again. Laughter still danced in her eyes.

"Does that make Fred a groper?" Chase teased mercilessly, drowning in her lovely green gaze.

"I—" Rachel giggled, placing the towel over Fred's head to keep him warm—and contained. "I guess not."

Chase lost some of his merriment, his fingers firm against her shoulders. "I don't want you worrying about my flying. Okay?"

Hesitantly Rachel nodded, the air turning serious. "I'll try not to." She couldn't tear her gaze from his mobile mouth.

"May I kiss you?"

Chase's low voice tremored through her. "Don't," she pleaded softly, "do this to us." Rachel tried to move from his grip, but he kept his hands firmly on her arms. Weakness moved through her. She recalled Chase's skilled loving, and an ache began deep within her. Shaking her head, Rachel whispered, "This is all wrong, Chase. You want the kiss, that's all, nothing more."

He drew closer. "That's not true, Rachel. I'm treating you as an equal from here on out. I'm being a gentleman about this. What do you want?'' he murmured. "Tell me...."

His hot, gritty voice plunged through her, making her shaky. Chase was so close, so pulverizingly male. Her lashes fluttered shut as she leaned forward, answering his question. The first brush of his mouth was ethereal, almost reverent. Parting her lips, Rachel leaned upward, wanting more, urgency pounding through her. The second time, his mouth molded hotly against her own, erasing all thought, creating a lava-like world of heat that exploded through her lower body. His mouth was firm, seeking and searching hers. As his tongue traced her lower lip, a little cry vibrated in her throat. The effect was melting, her breathing becoming fast and erratic.

"Sweet,'' Chase whispered hoarsely, trying to control himself. "You're so sweet and clean, Rachel...." And he tasted each corner of her mouth, feeling her lower lip tremble in reaction. She was soft, womanly, and the pain in his loins grew unbearable. Chase tried to remain aware of Rachel's needs instead of his own. As he reluctantly drew away, he saw how red her cheeks had become. As her lashes lifted to reveal lustrous eyes dazed with pleasure, a shaft of longing nearly shattered his resolve. His hands tightening momentarily on her face, he smiled sheepishly, releasing her. "I've gone far enough,'' Chase said thickly.

Reeling from his sweet assault on her senses, Rachel could only stare up into Chase's craggy features. The burning fire in his eyes made her boil with want of him in ways she wasn't familiar with but longed to explore. "I—'' She was breathless.

Smiling, Chase took the puppy from her. "Come on, I think you'd better sit down before you fall down, Angel Eyes." He led her over to a chair.

Rachel tried to take a deep breath and found it impossible. Her thoughts were scattered, and all she could do was feel. When Chase crouched down in front of her, gently drying the puppy with the towel, her heart squeezed with renewed love for him. For all his swaggering male ego, he was a kind man underneath.

"I was wondering if you might take care of Fred for a couple of weeks. I can't keep him at my tent because I'm not there most of the time."

Rachel nodded. "Of course..." Her voice came out as wispy as she felt.

Chase looked up, realizing Rachel was twice as shaken as he was by their kiss. It served to warn him that it was definitely his responsibility to control his own needs for her benefit. He offered her an understanding smile. "See what I mean?" he posed softly.

Dazed, caught in the web of unfamiliar sensations racing through her, Rachel looked blankly at Chase. "About what?" she whispered unsteadily, touching her lips, still tingling with the memory of his evocative kiss.

"About us," he whispered. "We're good for each other, Angel Eyes. We're good together. All I have to do is convince you."

Sadness clawed at her momentary happiness. "Chase, you can't do this anymore. Please. It isn't going to work!"

He gloated, completing the drying procedure on Fred. "This is just the beginning," he promised her huskily. "Just wait and see."

Taking a breath, Rachel picked up Fred, letting the dog sit in her lap. "You aren't even listening to me!"

Trying to look contrite, Chase rose to his full height, barely suppressing the glowing smile of triumph he felt over finally getting Rachel to admit that she liked being kissed by him. "You're right."

Placing Fred on the chair with the towel draped around him, Rachel stood, her eyes blazing. "*We* aren't going to work, Chase. Look at you. You're like a little boy standing there after stealing that kiss from me."

"Well, you enjoyed it, didn't you?"

Angry at her own weakness where Chase was concerned, Rachel muttered, "Yes."

"What else is there, then?"

She paced the length of the room. "Commitment, Chase. Proving you're responsible, that's what!"

He opened his hands. "I thought I was. I'm here, aren't I?"

Rolling her eyes, Rachel stopped in front of him. "You're here to steal a kiss . . . anything you can get, that's all."

Wanting to throttle her, Chase stared down at her. "You're wrong."

"I wish I was, but I'm not. Just because I don't have much experience in the realm of lovemaking doesn't mean I don't see through men and their lines, Chase, so don't try and snow me."

Raking his fingers through his hair, he began to pace, mulling over her statements. "This isn't simple," he growled. He halted, giving her a significant glance. "You're not simple."

"Just another reason why we shouldn't see each other anymore, Chase."

"No way," he ground out. "Dammit, we've got monumental communication problems, but I'm not giving up on us, what we share, Rachel."

"All we share is sex, Chase. That's a lousy start to any relationship!"

Shaken by her cry, Chase watched sudden tears form in her eyes but not fall. Shoving his hands into his pockets, he stood there a long time. "What do you want from me?"

"How about a decent conversation without stalking me and trying to touch or kiss me?"

"God, Rachel, it's tough to keep my hands off you."

She glared at him. "Precisely my point. Please, why don't you go? I'm sure Hob will be needing you or something."

Angry with himself and her, he looked at the watch on his wrist. "You're right, I've got to go. Hob isn't exactly the good fairy granting wishes. He told me if I wasn't back in an hour, he'd skin me alive." Chase forced himself to walk to the door, though he burned to do anything but that. His hand on the knob, he turned, looking across the tent at Rachel. She appeared positively bereft and so did Fred. "One thing," he said. "What's your favorite color?"

"Color?" Rachel blinked, still fighting her own need for him and their impossible situation. "I— blue."

"Blue." He nodded. "That suits you," he murmured.

"Why?"

"Oh," he murmured, "I've got my reasons." He threw her a mock salute. "I'll be back, Rachel.

Somehow, we're going to talk our way through this mess I've created.''

Rachel felt hope burn strongly alongside the defeat she'd been feeling. Chase would never change. ''Please . . . be careful flying, Chase.''

''Let my best girl down by getting shot out of the sky? No way.'' He grinned. ''See you later, angel. Take good care of our puppy, huh?''

He was gone. Rachel stood in the silence, petting Fred's damp fur, acutely feeling the loss of Chase's presence. He was incredibly cavalier about the fact that he faced death every time he flew. Rachel picked Fred up and held him against her, burying her face in his fur.

Emotions, like a multicolored rainbow after a rain, skimmed through her opened heart. Rachel saw Chase trying to control himself and be a gentleman. But it was impossible. His respect for women was in the bedroom, that was all. And then there was the irrepressible little-boy spirit that she dearly loved. Lastly, there was the man who drew out her femininity like a spring blossom, and that frightened her. Rachel didn't know what to expect. Where did a kiss end and going too far before marriage begin? Chase had not mentioned marriage, nor would he ever.

Opening her eyes, Rachel smiled sadly down at the puppy who was enjoying her absent but loving caresses. Each time Chase left, the parting was more painful, less easy to overcome. Rising to her feet, Rachel took Fred over to the towel cabinet. Wrapping the damp puppy in a dry one, she left admissions, heading for her tent.

Chapter Nine

Chase could hardly control his eagerness to see Rachel. He stood in the admissions tent, a brown paper parcel beneath his left arm. Although she'd asked him not to come back, he wasn't going to give up. Instead, he'd radioed over and found out when her next day off was going to be. Rachel had been supposed to have the day off, but when wounded were unexpectedly routed by helicopter to this MASH unit, she'd been called back into the surgery until the crisis was past.

Glumly Chase stared out the door, weeks of fatigue stalking him in earnest. He blinked his burning eyes. Sleep had been at a premium since he'd last seen Rachel. In the distance now he could see their flower field. But most of the flowers had been frost-bitten, the color bleached from their petals. That was how he felt about Rachel. When he'd left two weeks ago, all the joy had disappeared from his life. And that kiss! Chase closed his eyes, his arm tightening around the package slightly. Rachel was innocent and sweet. Despite her spirit and independence, she had placed herself in his arms for that one devastating night that had rocked his world.

Chase grumbled to himself. All he thought about day or night, in or out of sleep, was Rachel. What little sleep he'd gotten was in snatches of two or three hours at a time. Still, Rachel was with him in those dreams. He twisted a look over his shoulder. He'd arrived two hours ago, and now he waited with thinning patience. Their day together was being eaten away by this latest emergency. At 1700 he had to be back at Taegu for a night mission. He ached to see Rachel again. He was starved for the sound of her voice, the warmth dancing in her green eyes and that playful smile on her sensuous lips. But he'd seen precious little of that side he knew existed within her. What would she think of him showing up here unannounced?

Two hours turned into three. It was noon, and Chase reluctantly headed into the officer's chow tent within the MASH complex after leaving a message at the desk with a corpsman about where he could be located in case Rachel came out of surgery. Exhaustion dragged at his every step. He longed to lie down somewhere and simply go to sleep.

At the chow tent, despair settled around Chase. He sat at a wooden table, his tray piled high with hot food, not really hungry. Normally he'd be delighted to have some "real" food instead of canned C rations.

The lowered voices of a few nurses and doctors lingered in the tent. The pleasant clank of utensils against the aluminum tray reminded him sharply of home. It was almost Thanksgiving, and he could remember the happy times when his family prepared to eat a huge midday meal of turkey. This year, he wouldn't be celebrating any holidays with them.

"Chase?"

Startled out of his reverie, Chase rose to his feet at the sound of Rachel's astonished voice. The table tilted and his tray started to slide. Rachel reached out and caught it. Chase promptly sat down, his face a dull red. He pulled the tray back to where it belonged.

"What are you doing here?"

He managed an embarrassed smile. "I came to see you."

She stood uncertainly, a tray balanced in her hands. Noting that several people were watching her, Rachel sat down opposite Chase.

Chase saw the purse to her lips. "Are you mad?"

"No."

"You look exhausted."

She glanced up at him. "So do you."

"Things are tough all over," he muttered, smiling.

Chase's smile went straight through her like sunlight on a dark, cloudy day. Unable to maintain her sour look, Rachel relaxed. "I'm sorry, I didn't mean to scare you out of your wits earlier. You were the last person I expected to see in the chow tent."

"That's okay...." Chase gazed happily at Rachel. In that moment, with her black hair shining and curved into a well-behaved page boy, she looked girlish. His heart exploded with such joy that it caught Chase off guard. "I managed to grab a couple hours and wanted to come over and talk."

The fork stopped midway to Rachel's mouth. "Talk?"

Chase felt heat crawling up his cheeks. "Yeah, *talk*. Not grope, stalk or kiss. Okay?"

She eyed him for a long time, trying to decide whether he was being honest. "Chase, a leopard doesn't change his spots."

"But those spots can be lightened?"

"Maybe..."

"Willing to give me a chance at just talking, then?"

Rachel smiled and shook her head. "You're tenacious, I'll give you that."

"Part of my family's genes. Do you have a couple of minutes to spare? You look pretty busy around here."

"We had four helicopters of wounded arrive unexpectedly." She ate lightly, noticing that Chase was sitting, simply staring at her. Rachel fought a similar urge. She had missed Chase acutely. There was a soul-shattering intensity in the look he gave her.

His throat constricted, Chase whispered, "You look more beautiful than I could ever imagine." All he wanted to do was lean across the table, frame her face and capture those soft lips, making Rachel his once again.

Chase would never change, but did she want him to? Rachel couldn't tell his line from his sincerity. She laid her fork on her tray. "You look tired, Chase. Have you been flying too many missions?" Indeed, the dark shadows beneath his eyes were more pronounced than two weeks ago. And Chase looked as if he'd lost some weight. Still, he was heart-stoppingly handsome in his tan flight suit, his garrison cap captured beneath one epaulet of the leather jacket.

What was left of Chase's appetite fled. "There have been a lot," he hedged, not wanting her to worry. Chase shoved the tray aside, folding his hands on the table, all his concentration on Rachel. He grinned bashfully. "It's probably a good thing you can't read my mind, Angel Eyes." The color rose in her cheeks, making her excruciatingly beautiful.

"You're right." Rachel touched her warm cheek.

"Did you miss me?"

She raised an eyebrow at him. "If I admit it, will I ever hear the end of it, Captain?"

Grinning, Chase shrugged. "Probably not. I've been charged before with having a swelled ego. How's our dog, Fred?"

"Becoming a fat little sausage. He's the mascot for the MASH unit now. He's figured out that if he goes from tent to tent, scratching on the door, he can get multiple meals."

Chuckling, Chase nodded. "The little beggar."

Her smile slipped. "You really do look exhausted."

"Things are heating up. The U.N. forces are actively pushing out of the Pusan area and expanding their perimeter before the snow falls. All the pilots are flying two missions a day. Sometimes three."

Rachel gasped. "Three? Chase, that's too many! Look at you. You've lost weight, and you've got dark circles under your eyes."

He nodded patiently, hope springing to life in him. If Rachel didn't care, she wouldn't be concerned about his condition. "It can't be helped, Rachel. It's just the way things are right now."

"Doesn't it affect your flying?"

"Sure." When he saw the anxiety in her eyes, Chase hastily amended the statement. "Well, sometimes. Remember, all we gotta do is fly. We have a crew chief who services the plane. Between missions, I go to the tent and sleep."

Distressed, Rachel took a few more bites then pushed the tray aside. Suddenly the possibility of losing him was too much to bear, despite their obtuse relationship. Rachel didn't know what to do with the unexpected feelings slamming through her. "Come on, let's go to my tent. It's too cold and windy to go for a walk in the field today." She waited to see him gloat or get that stalking look in his eye, but to her surprise, he didn't.

Chase extricated himself from the table he'd nearly tipped over earlier. "Sounds good," he rasped. He tucked the package beneath his arm, following Rachel out of the tent.

She glanced at the package. "What's that?"

Chase grinned. "This? Oh, a little gift for you."

Rachel's heart sank. Men always brought gifts to buy favors from a woman. Was this Chase's new tactic? Try to get a kiss by giving her a gift? "Really? What is it?" she asked suspiciously.

Gloating at the show of interest, Chase said, "You'll have to wait until we get to your tent to find out."

"You didn't have to get me anything."

I want to give you the world. Chase swallowed the words. Instead, he whispered, "I wanted to see your smile again. I thought maybe a gift would do it."

She heard the ring of truth in his words, and her heart expanded with renewed feelings for Chase. *Go slowly,* she warned herself. In a little while, she would know whether the gift was intended as barter.

The cold air snapped Chase awake, and he monitored his stride, walking at Rachel's shoulder. They wove through the large city of tents, working their way toward the southern end of the compound.

"Here we are," Rachel announced, opening the door to a small tent. Chase had to stoop in order to enter. She smiled. He was a giant of a man, there was no doubt.

Chase looked around, impressed. "This is almost like home." Two cots and two makeshift lockers for clothes joined a table. The plywood floor had rice matting on it, giving it a warmer feel than typically sterile barracks. He spotted some photos on Rachel's locker and went over to look at them.

"My mom and dad," she explained. "They live in Bangor, Maine."

Chase studied them for a long time. Then he turned and smiled gently over at her. "Looks like you're a pretty happy family."

"We are."

They were alone, and Rachel wasn't behaving as if he were going to attack her. Yes, trust was building between them, and for that, Chase was eternally grateful. He looked for the puppy. "Is Fred on his rounds?"

She nodded. "Usually, at this time of day he's over at the enlisted chow hall. Fred has made friends with the chief cook, Jerry Lister."

"The dog's no fool, is he?" Chase chuckled.

"No, but at night Fred comes back to our tent and sleeps between our cots."

"Lucky mutt," Chase said, noting color rising in Rachel's cheeks. He'd give his arm and leg to share a cot with her. Judging from her reaction, she read those very thoughts in his eyes. Wrestling to keep his promise, he placed the parcel in Rachel's hands. "Here, go ahead and open it."

"Thank you, Chase," she whispered, carefully feeling the package.

"Mind if I sit down while you open it?" he asked, heading for the cot. The air was chilly, although a wood-burning stove sat in the center of the tent.

"Go ahead. I'd offer you a chair, but we don't have any. That's Annie's bed. She's my roommate." Rachel barely contained her curiosity about the package. She sat on her cot, eagerly working out the first of many knots on the heavily wrapped package.

"Is she on duty now?" Chase asked, sitting down. The cot was large and even had a mattress beneath the green army wool blankets. He groaned with pleasure at the unexpected luxury.

"Yes, she won't be getting off until 1700." Rachel noted the weariness in Chase's features. Her fingers shook as she freed one knot after another. Why was it wrapped so well?

"That's good timing. I have to be back at the base by 1700 to fly a night mission." Chase patted the cot. "You gals have it made. What I'd give to have a cot like this in my tent."

"Become a nurse," Rachel teased. What was in the parcel? It felt like clothing. The urge to rip the brown paper was paramount, but Rachel didn't want Chase to think she was more kid than lady, so she diligently unknotted each string.

Satisfaction thrummed through Chase. "You're sure taking your own sweet time opening that. Mind if I stretch out on Annie's cot while you're working at it?"

Tugging at the stubborn array of strings, Rachel murmured. "Go right ahead. Annie won't mind."

Chase lay down, his hands behind his head. "This is wonderful," he muttered, closing his eyes.

"I've never seen a package so well wrapped," Rachel muttered. Glancing up, she saw a rugged smile on Chase's mouth. She resumed her efforts to open the package.

"I hope you like the present," he said, his voice slurring. "It's wrapped like that because it came all the way from Japan...."

Rachel stopped her unwrapping activities, glancing up again. Her features softened as she watched Chase fall asleep. Within seconds, he was snoring fitfully. Putting the unopened parcel aside, Rachel quietly got up and took some blankets from the end of her cot, placing them over Chase. She pushed several strands of hair off his furrowed brow. His flesh was tense, and she gently massaged his forehead until the lines eased and disappeared.

Fear trickled into Rachel's heart as she stood by the cot, watching Chase sleep. No wonder the pilots were getting shot out of the sky, flying so many missions without proper rest. It would be humanly impossible to remain alert under those circumstances. The urge to lean down and kiss him was almost too much for Rachel to ignore. Fighting her feelings, she turned and went back to her cot. As much as she wanted to open the package, she decided to wait. She wanted to share the experience with Chase. Walking over to her locker, she quietly opened it. There were a number of letters she'd been remiss about writing, and this would be a good time to catch up. An incredible sense of contentment washed over her. Rachel savored the new feeling, hesitantly admitting that just being with Chase was enough.

Sitting cross-legged on her cot after taking off her heavy combat boots, Rachel began to write. Occasionally she would look up, absorbing Chase's sleeping form into her heart. His snore was erratic, and she smiled, wondering if he snored all the time or if it was combat fatigue causing it. A warm memory of her mother chiding her father because he snored like a runaway freight train from time to time, entered Rachel's thoughts.

Home. The word struck her hard. Rachel missed her home and family. Thanksgiving was coming soon. This year, she would miss the pungent autumn in Maine and the early first snows. More than anything, Rachel realized, she would love Chase to share her world of beauty in those timeless woods where color and scent were a heady experience. What were his parents like? His brothers? He was so proud of the family military history and the fact that all the men had served with such great honors. She wanted to know much more about him.

If Rachel was honest with herself as she sat there with pen and paper in her lap, she longed to be in Chase's arms more than anything else. Torrid memories of his lovemaking were indelibly branded into her heart. Her hand trembled slightly as she started another letter, remembering his strength, his maleness. Rachel looked at her watch. She would wake him an hour before he had to return to Taegu. At least she was sharing this time with him, the experience oddly satisfying to her.

"Chase?" Rachel squeezed his shoulder again. "Chase? It's time to get up." She was careful not to shake him, having discovered long ago that men who had been in combat would often jerk awake, hands flailing, fists doubled—coming out of sleep fighting. More than once, Rachel had dodged a patient's fist by simply squeezing his arm.

Groaning, Chase felt Rachel's hand on his shoulder. His spiky lashes moved and he forced his eyes open to bare slits, studying her through them.

"Uh, what time is it?" He saw the concern in her features.

Straightening up, Rachel said in a quiet voice, "Four. That gives you an hour to get back to Taegu." Chase looked like a lost little boy, blinking his bloodshot eyes, disoriented. She held out her hand.

"Grab my hand, I'll help you sit up. I made some fresh coffee and I'll get you a cup."

Her hand was slender and small. Chase gripped it, feeling her chapped flesh as he sat upright. Releasing her, he rubbed his face wearily.

"Damn, I didn't mean to conk out," he muttered. "So much for my attempt to talk with you."

Rachel poured the coffee and set the percolator back down on the heating element. "You needed sleep more than anything else, Chase." She brought the aluminum cup over to him.

"Thanks," he whispered, taking the mug. It was hard to think, so he concentrated on sipping the scaldingly hot coffee. Chase heard Rachel sit down on the other cot. He noticed a number of letters, paper and pen strewn around her.

"Letters," Rachel explained in a gesture with her hand. "I'm behind on sending them."

With a grimace, Chase held the warm cup between his hands, looking haggard. "My mom and dad are probably having fits. I haven't written in a month."

"If your dad is in the military, I'm sure he realizes why you aren't writing."

Giving Rachel a long look, Chase felt warmth moving through his chest. "Dad retired at the end of the last war with thirty years of service. You've got a lot of insight about people."

"Second nature for a nurse."

Chase studied her. Rachel was relaxed, legs crossed, her black hair framing her flushed cheeks. The exhaustion he felt was torn away by a pulsing need to take her into his arms and kiss her. Chase lowered his lashes, paying attention to the mug of coffee, instead. More than anything, he didn't want Rachel to see what he was thinking.

"Look," Rachel said, patting the package at the end of her cot, "I didn't open it. It killed me to wait, but I wanted you to be awake."

Chase lifted his chin and managed a grin. "What do you know, a woman who can wait to open a gift."

Laughing softly, Rachel settled the package in her lap, carefully easing open the taped wrapping. "I suppose *all* women rip into a gift as soon as they get it, completely out of control. Caught again, wasn't I?"

Chase laughed with her. "I expected you to tear it open," he agreed.

Rachel held his smiling eyes, remembering how they changed and became intent when he kissed her. "Believe me, I wanted to," she admitted fervently.

Chase watched her pull back the crisp, crinkly paper. Her expression changed, her lips parted and a gasp escaped. He sat up, watching as she pulled the blue silk robe from the paper, holding it up.

"Oh…Chase…this is beautiful! Beautiful!" Rachel got off the bed, holding the turquoise-blue silk up to herself. The robe was exquisitely embroidered with colorful flowers. She held it against her. "It feels so sleek…."

Swallowing hard, watching Rachel move her hand in a graceful motion across the robe, he said in a strained tone, "Chuck Dancey, one of the pilots in my squadron, flew over to Japan for a week. I asked him to pick you up something sexy…er…in blue."

Rachel blushed, running her hand in a caressing motion across the silky material, marveling at its beauty and workmanship. "Chase, this is too expensive—" Was there another, even heavier price tag attached to it? More than anything in the world, Rachel prayed that Chase had given her the gift for the right reasons.

"You're worth it, Angel Eyes." His voice vibrated with feeling, and he saw her look up, her eyes a soft green that made him go hard with longing.

Helplessly Rachel sat down, unwilling to refold the robe. "It looks like it will fit," she whispered.

"Try it on," Chase encouraged. "Go on."

The buttons were silk knots, and she carefully eased each one free from its loop. "This is real silk," she whispered, looking at the label. "Chase, really this is too expensive to give as a gift—"

"No strings attached, Rachel, if that's got you worried."

Realizing she'd hurt Chase's feelings, she said, "I didn't mean it that way. It's just that—well, I've never been given such a lovely gift in all my life." Rachel inwardly breathed a sigh of relief.

"Oh." Satisfaction wreathed Chase's smile. Rachel slipped the robe across her shoulders, and in his mind, he was taking it off her, making slow, delicious love with her in the process.

Pirouetting around, Rachel laughed. "Well, I don't have a mirror. You'll have to tell me if I look all right. Does it fit?"

Heat pounded through his bloodstream as she made a graceful turn, her arms extended like a ballerina. "The robe," Chase choked out, "fits perfectly...."

Anticipation sang through Chase as she clasped her hands in delight. Then, unexpectedly, he got up and walked over, framed her face between his hands and placed his mouth against her lips. Her warmth and sweetness unknotted the terrible cold that always inhabited him since coming to Korea. The kiss was deep, quick and hot. He felt Rachel's hands push against his chest, and her muffled response.

"No!" Rachel jerked out of his embrace, her fingers against her wet, throbbing lips. "Damn you, Chase Trayhern! You *did* expect payment for this gift! Damn you!" she sobbed.

Stunned, Chase stood there. His hands dropped to his sides and he looked at her morosely. "What? I—can't help myself when it comes to you, Rachel. And I didn't bring you a gift to steal a kiss." How could he explain to her what had made him suddenly get to his feet and kiss her? "It was your smile, the happiness in your eyes that made me do it," he whispered. "God, can't you understand any of this, Rachel?" Was love so hard to understand? If he told her he loved her, she would throw it back in his face as a line he was using on her. Damn, it was so frustrating. He saw her eyes fill with anguish.

Fighting back real tears, Rachel pulled off the silk robe. "Here, take it. Give it to the next woman you want, Chase."

"Rachel!"

"Don't say a word, Chase! I've had it! You talk a good line, but when it comes right down to it, you don't respect me or my wishes."

Groaning, he bowed his head. "That's not true, Rachel."

Her heart was breaking, and the tears were going to fall any second. Rachel didn't want him to see her cry. "Please, just leave. You've got to get back to your unit." A lump formed in her throat, and the rest of the words were torn from her. "Don't come back anymore."

The effect of her words was shattering. Chase looked up into her flushed features, her eyes still velvet with what he was sure was love for him. It occurred to him that maybe Rachel didn't know she loved him. Or did she? He wasn't sure of anything anymore, except that he'd hurt and disappointed her—again.

Reluctantly he looked at his watch. With a sigh, he walked over to the cot, set the robe on it then shrugged into his heavy winter coat. The terrible feeling that he'd severed all his hopes crushed him. Unable to look at Rachel, he shuffled to the door. His hand on the knob, he barely turned his head.

"The robe's for you, Rachel. I want you to keep it. And don't worry, I won't be back." His voice became strangulated. "I'm sorry I blew it. We had a lot going for us...I just kept getting sidetracked by your beauty, your heart...."

Tears squeezed from beneath Rachel's lashes as she heard the door shut quietly, leaving her standing in the silence. The first sob racked her, and she pressed her hand against her mouth. Moving to her cot where the robe lay, she picked it up, moving it out of the way and lying down.

Why was she crying so hard? Why was it making her heart ache like this? Rachel wanted Chase in so many different ways but couldn't get it through to him. And she cried even more, realizing that whatever might have been, would never be. She had stood firm, not buckling to Chase's provocative touch and kisses. There was hurt even in victory, Rachel thought. They had both lost. And she would never see him again. How could she stand living every day, knowing that?

Chapter Ten

"Merry Christmas," Annie sang out to Rachel as she entered the surgery theater. She headed to an operating table where the latest casualty had been placed, prepping him for the doctors' arrival.

Rachel nodded, concentrating on organizing the instruments the doctors would need. It was Christmas, and snow was falling outside the surgery tent. She raised her arm, blotting her forehead where sweat ran into her eyes. Twelve hours had blurred her concentration. Dr. Doug Thornton looked up at her worriedly, his gloved hand open, waiting for the needle and thread.

Apologizing, Rachel handed him the items. She shut her eyes. In the past three days, there had been no rest for anyone. The North Koreans were making a major push toward Taegu, trying to capture the main U.N. air base. *Chase.* Rachel's heart plummeted again.

Every time she replayed their last conversation, fear vomited through her. How long since they had last seen each other? Six weeks. Six of the longest, worst weeks of Rachel's life. The pain in her heart wouldn't heal, wouldn't stop aching.

"Take a breather, Rachel," Dr. Thornton ordered. "I'll finish up. Go on now."

"Thanks," she whispered, moving toward the scrubbing area just outside the theater. Pushing through the swinging doors, Rachel pulled the mask down off her nose and mouth. Every table was filled, teams of doctors and nurses working frantically over patients. Rachel heard more helicopters arriving in the snowstorm. She knew it was nearly impossible for the aircraft to fly in such weather, and the pilots were taking great personal risk in order to bring the wounded back from the front so the men wouldn't freeze to death out on the icy reaches of the battle-field.

Rachel stripped off her gloves and washed her hands. Annie came in a minute later, looking just as tired as Rachel felt.

"Whew!" Annie muttered, "This is getting to be serious business. Glad that last case was nothing more than a patch job. I get ten minutes to rest." She pulled off her gloves, tossing them into a wastebasket.

"This is bad," Rachel agreed, and she dropped into a chair, tipping her head back against the wall. "I'm dead on my feet."

Annie scrubbed her hands vigorously. "I don't have any feet." She grinned.

"I heard more choppers flying in."

Groaning, Annie dried her hands and sat down next to Rachel. "Oh, no. More wounded, then."

Looking at her watch, Rachel saw it was two in the morning. She dropped her arm back into her lap, closing her eyes. "I'm afraid so. This is a terrible Christmas."

"The worst," Annie agreed glumly. "Too bad you and Chase broke up. It would be nice to spend a holiday with a loved one."

"We didn't have much to build on," Rachel said quietly.

"Oh, I'm not so sure. But you both got bullheaded." Annie chuckled. "Maybe, with some time, you'll both recognize some things about yourselves."

Rachel gave Annie a sour look. "He couldn't keep his hands off me."

"So? What guy in love can?"

Her eyes widening, Rachel stared at her roommate. "Love?"

"Sure, silly. It was written all over both of you."

Stunned, Rachel sat back, digesting that possibility. "He never said it to me."

"Probably afraid you'd accuse him of trying to get a kiss or, worse yet, get you in bed."

Mulling over Annie's statements, Rachel nodded. "Six weeks ago, I would have," she admitted tiredly, drained in every conceivable way. It was Chase's leaving at her request that had killed her spirit. And it was her fault.

"And now?" Annie prodded gently.

With a shrug, Rachel muttered, "I don't know anything anymore, Annie. Ever since that guy crashed into my life, I haven't been the same."

"Sounds like the love virus bit you good, girl."

Rachel managed a thin wisp of a smile, studying Annie in the poor lighting. "Love. Isn't that funny, I was assigning all his motives to sex, not love."

"Well, the two do go together," Annie said. She became serious. "Let me tell you a true story—about myself. I've never told anyone about it, but I think this is the right time and place. I fell in love a couple of years ago with Steve Holden, a pilot. I loved him, but I wouldn't go to bed with him. I was like you, saving myself for marriage and a husband." Annie's voice dropped into a painful whisper. "I loved Steve with all my heart. We'd been dating for six months. Oh, I'd kiss him, but pushed anything else away." Annie grimaced, unable to hold Rachel's shocked gaze. "One day," she forced out in a low whisper, "Steve's plane crashed."

Gripping Annie's hand, Rachel sat up. "I'm sorry," she said. "You never said anything about this before, Annie."

"Of course I didn't. Who wants to hear a sad story?" Annie patted her hand. "I told you because I don't want you holding on to some stupid notion about your virginity and letting life pass you by, Rachel. I'm so sorry I didn't go to bed with Steve. I'm sorry I'll never have those wonderful memories we could have shared. I'm not implying we should jump in bed with every guy that comes along. But when it's a serious relationship, with commitment...."

Moved, Rachel digested Annie's impassioned words. "Every time I'm around Chase, I—I want to, but I get torn. I thought every kiss meant going to bed with him, that was all. I never considered the possibility that he might be in love with me."

"Do what you want, Rachel, but Chase is crazy about you. The guy was like a lovesick puppy the few times I saw him visit."

"Ever since that last argument, I haven't slept well," Rachel admitted quietly. "I just keep rerunning the conversation. What if Chase was shot down? What if he died? Sometimes I want to talk to him so badly, I've even considered driving over to Taegu. I don't like how it ended between us. And—and if he is—was—in love with me, that would explain some of his need to hold me, kiss me...." Rachel looked over miserably at her friend. "What kind of game are we taught to play as women with men, Annie?"

"It's a mine field for both sexes," Annie reminded her gently. "Don't be too hard on yourself, Rachel. You're young to the ways of love. Have you ever fallen for a guy before?"

"You mean, having the kind of feelings I do for Chase?"

"Yes."

"Never."

"I thought so." Annie sighed. "I think you didn't realize you'd fallen in love with Chase. On the other hand, he was so head over heels with you, that all he could think about was showing you how much he loved you."

"Oh, no," Rachel whispered, closing her eyes tightly. "What if you're right?" She realized the terrible position she had placed Chase in, if that was so. If he had been bold enough to tell her he loved her, Rachel would have assumed it was a line to get her back into his arms.

"I think I am, Rachel. Really, I can't stand seeing you so glum all the time. I mean, when Chase left, a part of you died, too, Rachel."

Rachel opened her eyes, staring helplessly at Annie. "I've been such a fool. Is love always this painful?"

"It can be." She released Rachel's hand. "I think the nicest Christmas gift I can give you is talking about this. I've wanted to for a long time. I knew it wasn't any of my business, but you were hurting so much, I just couldn't stand it any longer. And take my word for it, love makes a fool out of everybody. Guaranteed." Annie brightened. "It's not too late, Rachel."

Rachel rubbed her face tiredly. "If I were Chase, I'd tell me to go fly a kite after all the paces I put him through."

Annie smiled wryly. "You'll never know unless you go to him and find out, will you?"

Rachel nodded, digesting the new possibilities. A flood of nausea struck her. How could she have been so dumb *and* blind? "I've done some terrible things to Chase."

"To yourself, too. But chalk it up to experience." Annie looked up, hearing orderlies bringing the first of the next batch of wounded men through the outer doors. "We've got more casualties. Look," she said hurriedly, rising, "you get over to Taegu as soon as you can. Don't hold back. Talk honestly and throw everything on the table. Understand?"

Shaken, Rachel stood, reaching for another set of surgical gloves and a mask. "Yes..."

The doors leading to the surgery theater were flung open, the first gurney wheeled through by the panting orderlies. The cold wind from outside rushed in with them, and out of habit Rachel glanced at the man covered with dark green woolen blankets. The fresh set of gloves dropped from her nerveless fingers.

"Chase!"

Annie whirled around at Rachel's anguished cry. Taking one look at the man on the gurney and one at her friend, she moved around the orderlies and gripped Rachel by the arm.

"Sit down," Annie ordered harshly, forcing Rachel back into the chair. Jerking her head to the right, Annie saw that Doug Thornton had completed surgery on his patient. He was the only available doctor. She told the orderlies, "Take Captain Trayhern to Dr. Thornton's table."

The orderly pulling the gurney nodded. "Yes, ma'am."

Rachel fought to get on her feet. "That's Chase. My God, my God—"

"No, you don't. You sit right there," Annie instructed tightly. "You aren't going to be the nurse on this case. I am. You can't possibly keep your emotions separate from what you'll have to do, Rachel." She looked around and spotted another orderly nearby. "David!"

Pvt. David Lesson came over, his thin face concerned. "Yes, Miss Johnson?"

"Take Miss McKenzie over to admin. Right now. Get her out of here and keep her away from surgery until I come for her. Understand?"

"Yes, ma'am."

Rachel moaned, trying to get free of Annie's grip. "Let me go!" she cried.

"David!"

The orderly leaped into action, putting his arm around Rachel's shoulders, physically propelling her out of surgery. Grimly Annie turned, grabbing a new pair of gloves, hurrying into the operating theater where Thornton was already beginning preparations for surgery on Chase Trayhern.

Rachel sat exhausted in the chair near the wood stove. Three hours had passed since Chase had been brought in unconscious. He was still in surgery. Cpt. Chuck Dancey, his wingman, had appeared fifteen minutes after Chase arrived and kept her company. Both waited tensely. He had told her that Chase had singlehandedly shot down three MiG jets before being blown out of the sky by the remaining six enemy aircraft.

Burying her face in her hands, Rachel felt tears squeeze between her fingers. David, the orderly, had immediately gone back to check Chase's medical status. The word from Dr. Thornton was "critical." Chase had a badly injured left leg and had lost a great deal of blood. There was grave doubt that Chase's leg could be saved. Dr. Bruce Bonham, a neurologist, was working with Thornton.

Dancey, a short, black-haired pilot, walked slowly around the perimeter of the tent, his face long and gray with worry. His hands were clasped behind him, his chin resting against his chest as he paced.

Rachel felt nothing but numbness. Every chance David got, he ran over to tell her what was going on in the surgery theater. Annie had been right: Rachel could not have functioned as a nurse, not under the these terrible circumstances. The door opened and quickly closed. David managed a sliver of a smile, his face mirroring his exhaustion.

"They've got him stabilized, Miss McKenzie," he announced triumphantly, glancing over at the pilot who joined them.

Her hand against her heart, Rachel rallied. "Thank God..."

"His blood pressure is holding. Finally. Doc Thornton said to tell you it's touch and go on his leg."

"How much damage?" Rachel whispered.

"Plenty," David confirmed. "There's not a lot of muscle left on his thigh, ma'am. And Dr. Bonham's afraid there will be permanent nerve damage. They're trying their best, but from the looks of it—" David grimaced "—well, you know."

Closing her eyes, Rachel slumped back in the chair. If Bruce couldn't locate all the torn nerves and repair them, Chase would have limited use of his leg. "What about gangrene? Was the wound dirty?" Rachel tried to steel herself against the possible answer.

"Miss McKenzie, there was an awful lot of debris in the wound. That helo flight from the front didn't help him. Doc Thornton said if gangrene sets in, Captain Trayhern's gonna lose that leg."

Dancey cursed softly, glaring over at the orderly. "Chase will fight this. The guy doesn't give up. He'll keep that leg, you wait and see."

"I hope you're right, Chuck," Rachel whispered faintly.

"The doc said it will be another two or three hours before they've got him fixed up, Miss McKenzie. He ordered you to go to bed and sleep. Miss Johnson said she'd come and get you when they've got the captain transferred to recovery."

Wearily Rachel got to her feet. Annie, as always, was practical. "I'll do that, David. Thanks. Could you show Captain Dancey to the men's quarters? He looks like he could use some rest, too."

Dancey nodded. "Yeah, I'd like to catch a cat-nap." He looked at Rachel with narrowed intensity. "Wake me up when he's in recovery, will you?"

"I'll have David come and get you, Chuck."

"Thanks."

Rachel stumbled toward the door, her mind fuzzy, her heart in constant pain. Annie's words rang in her head. The icy cold weather slapped her brutally, and Rachel sucked in a deep breath, the pain increasing in her chest. A gray ribbon lay along the horizon, har-binger of the dawn. The color mirrored how she felt inside. Trudging to her tent, Rachel had only one thought pounding through her: Chase had to live. He had to live to hear her tell him that she loved him.

Rachel sat next to Chase's bed, her fingers resting tensely on his gowned shoulder. It was eight in the morning, and the recovery ward was beginning to stir, the doctors making their rounds. Chase was pasty white, his mouth slack. Walnut-colored strands of hair swept across his wrinkled brow. Gently Rachel pushed his hair back into place. His flesh was cool even though recovery was kept warmer than normal for the patients. Two IVs hung on either side of his cot, the liquid dripping into the veins of his arms.

Numbly Rachel moved her fingers gently against his shoulder. Soon Chase would come out of the anes-thesia. And as he did, she was sure it would be rough on him. No one escaped the nausea and vomiting that occurred all too frequently after such a long and complex operation.

Doug Thornton dropped by on his rounds. He gave her a concerned look. "How you doing, Rachel?"

She shrugged. "Better than Chase, that's for sure."

"He rallied during surgery," Thornton told her, pulling back the covers and placing his stethoscope against Chase's chest, listening intently. A satisfied look crossed Thornton's face as he wrote some notes on the clipboard he carried. Bringing the covers up, Thornton muttered, "The man's got the constitution of a bull."

Feeling guilty because she thought she should be working, Rachel started to get up.

"Stay put," the doctor ordered her sternly. "We're trying to rest as many of our people as we can between these spurts of casualties coming in from the front. Just stay with him, hear?"

Rachel wanted to hug the doctor for his understanding. He was married and had three children back in South Carolina. "Thanks, Doug."

"You're off for the next twenty-four hours, so I don't care if you stay glued to his bedside or go back to your tent to sleep."

"I'm going to stay here until he's conscious." Doug's smile told Rachel everything. The doctor, who was forty-five, was giving her special privileges under the circumstances, and she was grateful. He walked off, going to visit his next patient. Rachel returned her attention to Chase and saw beads of sweat begin to form on his brow. She took a cloth and dipped it into a basin of warm water sitting next to the cot. *Live,* her heart told him. *I want you to live, Chase. You just have to . . .*

* * *

Chase moved his head, muttering something unintelligible. He saw the MiGs ganging up on him. He'd just dropped a load of bombs, climbing up and out of the Yongchong area, when they jumped him from behind a line of hills, coming directly out of the sun.

Chuck Dancey screamed a warning, and Chase powered the agile Mustang to a higher altitude, jinking violently to throw the first MiG off his tail. For the next five minutes, he fought for his life, taking down three enemy jets. Then, six other MiGs cornered him. A cannon shell fired from the nearest MiG struck just ahead of the cockpit, an explosion tearing through the Mustang.

Pain had ripped up his leg, digging deeply into his gut. Chase gasped, remembering that slicing pain and the jerk of the parachute seconds later, the icy cold of snow stinging his unprotected face. He remembered swinging like a pendulum through the gray sky, heading down toward the safety of the U.N. lines. As the ground came up to meet him, Chase remembered screaming out Rachel's name.

"Sh, Chase, I'm here. I'm here...." Rachel gripped his hand. Worriedly she sponged his face and neck as he fought off the anesthesia. He kept muttering her name and fragments of sentences. Hovering in the background was her fear that he no longer loved her— that he would reject her presence as soon as he became conscious.

Rachel's voice penetrated the fog Chase lay suspended within. He dragged his lashes upward. Seeing only a wall of white, he closed them again. Little by little, he became aware of a warm, small hand gripping his larger one. Weakly Chase squeezed back. *Rachel*. It had to be Rachel!

"Don't fight so hard," Rachel begged softly. She stood up, leaning over Chase, keeping her hand firmly on his shoulder to prevent him from moving around and possibly hurting himself. "I'm here, and I won't leave you, Chase."

Rachel saw him open his eyes, saw how dilated his pupils had become. She gave him a wobbly smile, her fingers stroking his roughened cheek. "Chase, can you see me? It's Rachel. You're safe, and you're going to live."

It took Chase several minutes to digest the message she repeated slowly over and over again. He clung to the sight of her face and her lips now pursed at the corners. He saw the anxiety in her forest-green eyes. Nausea stalked him, and he felt sick and hot, breaking out in a heavy sweat. Weak beyond belief, Chase struggled to keep his eyes open and on Rachel. It was impossible. Surrendering to the mélange of sensations, Chase gripped her hand, as if to lose hold of it would mean spiraling forever back into the darkness.

Rachel jerked awake, stiff from sitting in the straight-backed chair beside Chase's cot. Quickly she transferred her attention to him. Weak sunlight was filtering through the tent, giving more light to the ward as she sat up and checked on him. Her heart slammed violently in her breast. His eyes were open and less dilated, telling Rachel that the anesthesia was wearing off. Would he ask her to leave? In utter misery, Rachel had to admit she wouldn't blame him.

"Chase?" She placed her hand against his sweaty brow and forced a smile she didn't feel. All of her brisk nursing facade fell aside as he shifted his limited attention to her.

Frowning, Chase fought the wall of pain surging up through him. His vision was fuzzy, everything out of focus, but he recognized her voice and touch. "Rachel?" The word came out like sandpaper. His voice was raw and unsteady.

Swallowing against a barrage of feelings, Rachel stood and caressed his cheek. "Yes, it's me. How do you feel?" Right now Chase would be semicoherent, and speaking too fast would only serve to confuse him. Risking everything, she slid her fingers across his hand, holding it. Would Chase reject her?

Rachel was here, with him. His heart pounded hard, underscoring the sudden realization. God, he'd been lonely without her. His life had been hell since he'd lost Rachel's smile and her fiery, spirited nature. "I— like hell..." Chase closed his eyes, feeling her cool fingers against his hot flesh. Flashes of the fight with the MiGs haunted him. Tensing against a savage tidal wave of pain, Chase sucked air between his clenched teeth. His fingers tightened around Rachel's hand.

Biting back a cry as Chase's hand squeezed hers until the bones ground together, Rachel froze. The drug to halt his pain was wearing off. Checking the medication chart hanging at the end of his cot, Rachel saw it was time to give him another shot. She called to an orderly, asking him to get the necessary items.

Barely aware of the bite of the hypodermic needle, Chase rolled his head back and forth, the pain nearly unbearable. Rachel's voice entered his hazy awareness, only to fade away. *I love you, I love you.* Afraid he was dying, Chase tried to form the words on his lips, tried to force out how he felt. The pain crashed over him, and with a groan, Chase surrendered to the blackness.

Chapter Eleven

The third time Chase awoke, he had clarity. Sweat was dribbling into his eyes, and he lifted his hand to wipe it away. He was incredibly weak, barely able to lift his arm from the cot.

"Chase?"

He looked up and to the left. Rachel's face was drawn, shadows accentuating her beautiful bone structure. Exhaustion haunted her eyes. A light from the end of the tent made everything look ghostly. Chase surveyed his surroundings then moved his gaze back to Rachel. She looked so damned good.

"Where?"

Wringing out a cloth, Rachel got up, gently dabbing the sweat from Chase's tense face. "You're here at the MASH unit. You got shot down two days ago."

Her voice was as tremulous as he felt. Fragments slowly began to surface between the bearable waves of pain drifting up his leg. "Yeah. Two days ago?" His voice was little more than a croak, and he was dying of thirst. Rachel must have read his mind because she set the cloth aside and slid her arm beneath his shoulders.

"You've been through a six-hour operation and slept all day yesterday. Here, drink as much as you want." Rachel supported Chase's head against her neck and shoulder as he noisily slurped water from the glass. Her scent was welcome against the smells of anesthesia and alcohol that surrounded him.

"Thanks," he whispered. Unable to support himself any longer, Chase leaned against Rachel. "Do you know how many times I dreamed of you holding me? Hell of a way to get held, isn't it? I have to get shot down and wounded."

It was four in the morning, and the ward was quiet except for an occasional snore or moan from a patient. Rachel winced inwardly as she made Chase comfortable on the cot. "You have a terrible sense of humor, Captain, but am I ever glad to hear you teasing me again."

A vague smile pulled at the corner of Chase's compressed mouth. Rachel picked up his wrist to take his pulse. Her fingers were warm and his were cold. More memory tumbled back as Rachel walked to the end of the cot and picked up a clipboard. He watched as she duly recorded his pulse rate. In the gray shadowy world of the ward, she looked clean and wholesome, soothing the clutching fear inside him.

"Am I going to live?" he asked when she came back and sat down, facing him.

Tears suddenly sprang to Rachel's eyes as he slid his hand those few inches, placing his fingers across hers. "Yes. You had two of the best surgeons."

A ragged sigh pulled from Chase, his narrowed eyes on her. "My leg. I remember a lot of pain—thinking it felt like it was being torn off." Automatically he felt downward, reassured that it was still attached.

Taking his other hand, Rachel whispered, "It's all right, Chase, you have your leg." She tried to prepare herself for the eventuality that he no longer loved her. Rachel wanted to cry because she was a novice at love and didn't know how to handle the terrible rift she'd created with Chase. His eyes were dark with drugs and pain, and she could read nothing beyond that to give her any inkling of his real feelings for her. His teasing could be a cover-up for how he really felt.

Chase slowly flexed his fingers, feeling the softness of her hand on his. Rachel's tears glimmered like drops of dew down her cheeks. "I want the bottom line on my wound," he croaked. "What happened?"

Trying to muster a brave front for Chase's benefit, Rachel gave him a detailed explanation. "Dr. Thornton says the next forty-eight hours are critical."

"Critical? To what?"

Rachel lowered her lashes, holding his hand tightly. "To whether you keep your leg."

Chase stared at her, digesting her strained words. Immediately he rejected the idea. "No one's taking my leg. No one."

"It's not that simple, Chase—"

"Like hell it isn't!" he exploded softly.

"You're getting upset. I knew I shouldn't have told you."

"I never want you to lie to me."

She sat very still, seeing the anger and determination in his blue eyes. "What we share," she began in a low voice, "is built on misconceptions on my part, Chase, but never lies."

He flinched, turning his head away from her. The idea of losing his leg was too much to deal with. "I'm sorry...."

"Chase, no matter what happens, I—"

"I'm not," he gritted through his teeth, "going to lose my leg."

Rachel clung to his hand, watching the sweat form on his brow, his face naked with pain. She swallowed all her admissions, though they were begging to be said. Chase was fighting it with every breath he took. Leaning forward, she murmured, "What can I do to help you?"

Dragging in a deep, halting breath, Chase uttered, "Believe in me, Rachel." He met and held the gaze that so clearly broadcast her suffering for him. He loved her so damn much that the pain of knowing that outstripped the agony of his leg. She was fragile, he could see it in her eyes and in the tortured line of her beautiful mouth. Chase wanted to say so much, but the darkness was pulling at him, and he lapsed back into unconsciousness.

Chase pulled out of sleep, the pain awakening him. He had no idea what time it was, only that it was daylight. Rachel was gone, the chair beside his cot empty. Orderlies and nurses moved quietly up and down the aisle, attending to their duties. A doctor in a green smock came into view.

"Captain, I'm Dr. Doug Thornton." He held out his hand.

Chase shook his hand weakly. "You're the guy that saved my neck?"

Doug grinned and sat down, a clipboard resting on his thigh. "I am, and leg would be more like it. You're looking better. How are you feeling?"

"Like hell right now, but I'm not losing my leg, doc."

The doctor frowned. "Rachel must have told you the status of your injury."

Eyes narrowed, Chase nodded. "I asked her to cut to the bottom line." He made a weak jab at his leg, tightly bandaged beneath the blankets. "There's no way in hell I'm losing it. I know I'm in bad shape, but I'll do whatever it takes to keep it."

Doug scratched his thinning blond hair. "It's not that easy, Captain. I admire your fighting spirit, but I can't guarantee you'll keep the limb. Damage was maximum." He glanced down at the chart, noting the temperature and blood pressure readings that had been taken every two hours. "You're coming back strong, but I want to caution you on your optimism."

Glaring at the doctor, Chase bit back, "Not only will I keep this leg, doc, but I'll be back in the cockpit of a plane in six months."

Doug grinned and patted Chase's shoulder. "Okay, Captain. Let's take this one day at a time. I'm in your corner and rooting for you." He rose and placed the clipboard on the hook at the end of the cot.

"Where's Rachel?" Chase asked.

"Sleeping right now."

"Oh."

"That's quite a lady you've got, Captain. I hope you appreciate her. She slept in that chair, held your hand, gave you the necessary shots and took care of you. Right now, Rachel's under orders to rest." He smiled good-naturedly. "I don't need my best surgery nurse half-asleep at the operating table."

Chase was restless under a driving need to speak at length with her as soon as possible. "When can I see her, doc?"

Doug glanced at his watch. "It's 1400. Rachel is due in at midnight. She'll be the chief duty nurse until 0800 tomorrow morning."

"Thanks," Chase muttered, closing his eyes. Ten hours was too long to wait to see Rachel, to talk with her. Chase hungered to kiss her, to tell her how much he loved her. Clenching his fist, he focused tiredly on the image of her face. Midnight couldn't come too soon.

The ward was eerily quiet as Rachel padded softly down the main aisle. As chief duty nurse, she made rounds once an hour, checking on the twenty men who slept in the cots. With every step, her heart pounded a little harder at the base of her throat. Down on the right, Chase slept in his cot.

Slowing to a halt, Rachel took in Chase's darkly shadowed features. Relief flooded through her. Despite his pallor, she could see the determination to fight his injury mirrored in the set of his jaw and the line of his mouth. Chase might be trussed up with IVs and dressings, but he was battling back. Warmth spread through Rachel's breast as she walked to his bedside and sat down. As if sensing her arrival, Chase stirred. His lashes fluttered, then opened, revealing drowsy blue eyes.

Chase's heart exploded with an incredible sensation of joy as a soft, shy smile shadowed Rachel's lips.

It was her eyes, gloriously green and lustrous, that drew him out of his pain-filled sleep.

"How long—" he cleared his throat, frowning.

"I've been here less than a minute." Rachel tried to mask her tautly strung nerves, but the wobble in her voice gave her away. "Sure you don't have radar?"

Reaching out, Chase took a chance and opened his fingers in invitation. Rachel lifted her slender hand, hesitated momentarily, then placed it in his larger one. "So much strength and courage in such a small person," he whispered, his fingers closing around hers.

"In some ways, we're a lot alike," Rachel returned softly, leaning forward and blotting his brow with the cloth.

"Yeah?" Just hearing her voice, allowing it to wash through him, helped stabilize Chase's spinning agony-filled world. "How?"

Rachel held his ravaged gaze. "We're both stubborn, we speak our mind, and we have courage."

"Good traits." Chase squeezed her hand gently. "How are you doing?"

A small lump formed in Rachel's throat. "I'm doing okay—worrying about you, mostly."

"You look tired."

"You look wonderful."

He held her gaze, sparkling with undeniable warmth for him alone. Or was he misreading Rachel again? "Did you hear me muttering earlier?"

Rachel placed the cloth on the stand, continuing to hold his hand. "No. What were you saying?"

"That I wanted to talk to you, I had to see you."

She stroked his fingers gently, unable to hold his burning, intense gaze despite the fever in his eyes. "Chase...my God, I don't know where to begin,"

Rachel whispered, choking back a sob. Her fingers closed tightly over his hand, and she took nearly a minute before she could speak again. "I—I was wrong about so many things, Chase. About you. I was confused, and I made so many awful choices that affected us."

Chase saw the tears drift down her waxen cheeks, wishing he could sit up and smooth them away with his thumbs. "Look at me, Angel Eyes...."

It hurt to lift her head, and it hurt even more to hold his dark blue gaze. A sob made her tremble, and she felt his hand weakly squeeze hers. "I—I made some assumptions about you, Chase, that may not be true. And I based everything, my reactions, on them."

"What assumptions?" he coaxed, caught in the matrix of her tears, her utter vulnerability toward him.

"At the time we were caught behind enemy lines, I thought you were just like every other guy."

Chase managed a one-cornered grimace. "I was—at first."

"But," Rachel rasped, "that changed. I know when it did, looking back. When I led that patrol away from you and came back at the end of the day, things were different. Only, I was too shaken and worried to realize it. But, I know you did."

He closed his eyes. "Yeah, lying there in those rocks and brush for five hours wondering if you were alive, captured or dead played havoc on me. It forced me to get in touch with how I really felt about you."

Chewing on her lower lip, Rachel grew silent. "This is so hard, Chase... I'm finding out how naive I am when it comes to love. I never had a steady boyfriend before I met you. I had men who were friends, but nothing serious." She saw the tenderness in his eyes, and it gave her the courage to go on. "I hope I'm not going to embarrass both of us again by saying something stupid, but I thought—I mean, I—well," Rachel gave him a hopeless look. "Oh, Chase, I'm going to make a fool of myself again. But, did you fall in love with me at that time?"

Chase saw the fragility and indecision in Rachel's beautiful green eyes. His voice grew raw with feeling. "Didn't you hear me screaming in my sleep? Over and over again, I was calling for you, telling you not to leave me. That I loved you."

Rachel's breath snagged, and she stared thunderstruck at Chase. Had she heard right? Or were her spongy mind and shredded emotions playing some dreadful trick on her? And then the cold wash of reality hit her. Chase had used the word *love* in the past tense, not the present. Rachel didn't blame him for not loving her now. Her voice was barely above a hoarse whisper. "I don't blame you for how you must feel about me now. I misunderstood your advances. I thought you were trying to get me in bed without a commitment. That's why I reacted the way I did."

"I see." Chase grimaced. "Angel Eyes, we're both to blame, not just you." He forced a slight smile through the waves of pain. "I messed up first, by going after you purely on a physical level. Then, as I spent time with you, I fell in love with your spirit and fire. You never gave up, and you were just as stubborn as I was. I respected all those things about you. But, let's face it, I wasn't exactly a gentleman out there."

A tiny flicker of hope sprang to life in Rachel's heart as she absorbed his shadowy, bearded features into her. "I didn't realize you'd fallen in love with me, Chase."

"I finally figured that out." He squeezed her fingers. "I tried to make up for it when I got here, but by that time, the damage had been done. All I could do was deploy defensive strategy, and that didn't work, either."

"I didn't let it work."

"No, but I didn't blame you." Chase raised his other hand, resting his arm across his sweaty, wrinkled brow. "I really blew it when I gave you the silk robe and then kissed you. Hell, Rachel, I found myself up and across the room before I realized what had happened." He managed a thin smile. "When you smiled like that, I just melted inside. It was the first time I'd seen how you really felt about me. It was the proof I was looking for. And then, I tripped all over myself like a teenager and kissed you."

"It surprised me, too," she admitted.

"But did you like it?"

Rachel managed a grin, the hope burning stronger in her heart. "Yes."

"Good. That brings us back to you," he said, holding her tear-filled gaze. "How do you feel about me?"

She lowered her lashes, placing her other hand across his. "Annie helped me put things in perspective, Chase. I didn't realize it, but I was in love with you." There, the admission was finally out in the open. Rachel was afraid to lift her lashes to see what kind of impact the words had on Chase, expecting the worst.

"Was?" Chase goaded in a rasp. "What's this *was*? If you were then, why can't you be now? I know we've had some fights, but—"

Rachel smiled, meeting his desperate gaze. "I love you, Chase Trayhern, then and now."

Disgruntled, he relaxed and took a long, unsteady breath. "Whew . . . that was too close," he whispered. His voice deepened, holding her uncertain gaze. "Let's make this official: I love you, too. Then, and now and in the future. Okay?"

Rachel's heart contracted, and a shower of joy shimmered through her. The moments spun gently between them as he watched her from beneath hooded eyelids, monitoring her reaction.

"Look at me, Rachel."

Blinking back tears, she lifted her chin, holding Chase's dark, narrowed eyes. "I swore that if God let you live, I'd tell you how I really felt, Chase."

"After you told me never to come back, I didn't know what to do," Chase admitted quietly. "I figured the only chance I had left was to leave you alone and hope like hell that you would eventually sort things out. There was nothing I could say under the circumstances that would clear me of the impression you had of me."

"I know." Rachel gave a small sigh, feeling so much weight slide off her shoulders. "Let's never let this happen again, Chase. No matter what, we have to promise to talk—to stay at it until the issue's resolved."

Chase stared at her for a long time, digesting her admittance. He began to understand what kind of hell Rachel had gone through. "That's a promise. I figured once we were stateside, I'd find you and try to start over. I'd keep my hands to myself until after I married you."

A gasp escaped Rachel, and she pressed her hand against her breast, stunned. *Marriage?* "A-are you—"

"Yeah, I am. Will you be my wife?" Chase couldn't breathe, all his raw feelings boiling to the surface. He prayed that Rachel would say yes. She blanched, turning pale, and he grew afraid. Before she could speak, he blurted, "Look, I know I'm not whole like before. If—if I lose this leg—"

"No!" she cried softly, "you won't lose your leg. Don't even say it, Chase." Rachel laid her head against his shoulder, resting her arm across his chest. "I believe you'll beat the odds, darling."

Chase murmured her name, sliding his hand up across her back, tangling his fingers through her hair. "Listen to me, Rachel," he began thickly. "If I did lose my leg, I'd be a cripple the rest of my life. My career in the service would be over. I'd have to scrape for a living some other way. I wouldn't be able to provide you with the things you deserve, that our children deserve...."

She fought the sobs that wanted to tear from her, holding Chase tightly. Finally Rachel gathered her strewn emotions and sat up. With trembling fingers, she caressed Chase's damp cheek. "I'll love you with or without legs. And if the worst happens, you'll create a job for yourself. You're not the kind of man to give up and quit—no matter what the odds are." Giving him a broken smile, Rachel leaned down. For the first time, she shyly initiated a kiss between them.

Chase's mouth was cool compared to hers. Heat sang through Rachel as he responded, cherishing her, telling her in his wonderful silent language, just how much he really loved her. Although Chase was weak, there was nothing but strength in his kiss. Hungrily he captured her, nipping at her lower lip, soothing it with his tongue, worshipping her. His fingers tunneled through her hair, pressing her more tightly against his chest.

Breathing raggedly, Chase reluctantly released Rachel. Even in the grayness of the ward, he saw the rose flush in her cheeks as she drew away. He managed a lopsided grin.

"When you kissed me, the pain went away."

"Better than drugs, huh?" Rachel whispered, dazed by the power of the emotions he shared with her in those precious seconds.

"You never answered me. Will you marry me, Rachel?"

Rachel met and held his intense blue gaze. "Yes."

The last of the shadows that had haunted him since they'd split up, dissolved. Chase lay back, closing his eyes, savoring the happiness that made the pain disappear. Rachel was going to be his wife! "God, I love you," he quavered, holding her warm gaze.

"I know," she whispered, smiling brokenly. "If you hadn't possessed that Trayhern stubbornness, we'd never be here—together."

He smiled, proud of himself, of his tenacity. For once it had paid off—more than he ever could have imagined. Humbled, Chase captured her hand, holding her smoldering gaze. Rachel was hot and unbridled, not even aware how passionate she was. He closed his eyes. "I'm going to dream of a time in the near future when we can both be stateside—together."

Some of her euphoria dissolved. "Dr. Thornton said that you'll be here another week, providing you continue to progress."

"And then?" Chase had no idea where he would be sent to recover.

"You'll be flown into Travis Air Force Base near San Francisco. There's a military hospital nearby that has the best physical therapy program for wounds like yours."

"I'll be damned. San Francisco. Not bad duty, is it?"

She smiled and shook her head. "I swear, Chase, if you were handed mud, you'd find some way of selling it for a profit."

His grin was genuine. "You're right, honey. Will you be coming back with me?"

Her smile slipped. "No..."

A frown wove across his brow. "Why not?"

"I have to stay in Korea four more months. My tour isn't up until April of next year." It hurt to admit it, because a long separation was the last thing Rachel wanted. "I—I wish I could be transferred to that hospital to help you as the wound heals. But that won't be possible."

Chase lay quietly, thinking. Four months without Rachel would kill him. "I'm spoiled," he told her in a low voice. "Spoiled by getting to see you every day." His fingers tightened around her hand. "Dammit, Rachel, I don't want to be away from you that long."

Tears clogged her throat. "I know, darling...."

All his happiness backwashed. How in the hell was he going to survive without Rachel's laughter and sweet smile? At that moment, Chase began to realize just how deeply he loved Rachel, how much she had woven herself into the fabric of his life.

"You're going to need those four months to bring that leg back, Chase," Rachel explained in a strained tone. "You'll be going from one kind of pain to another. The physical therapy will be grueling. Believe me, you'll be busy and probably won't miss me at all."

He snorted. "There isn't a second that goes by that I don't think about you, Rachel." He moved his gaze upward. The tears in her eyes made Rachel even more beautiful. She was suffering as much as he was. "Do you know what air base you'll be flying into when you come home from this tour?"

"Travis." Rachel managed a small smile. "At least we can see each other when I get home."

"And you'll take leave?"

Nodding, she said, "All I can get. I want to be with you."

"What about your folks? Aren't they expecting to see you?"

She ran her fingers lightly across his hand. "I've been writing to them about you. I don't think they'll be too surprised if I take my leave in San Francisco in order to be with you."

"If we get married right away, the army has to discharge you," Chase said.

Rachel nodded. "That's right."

Chase lifted her hand, pressing a small kiss to it. As badly as he wanted to give her a sales pitch to marry him immediately after coming stateside and end her military career, he didn't. He'd learned the hard way that Rachel had a mind of her own, and Chase respected her for it.

"What do you want more than anything in this world, angel?"

Rachel closed her eyes. "To marry you."

His voice cracked. "What's the second most important thing to you?"

"To have your children." Rachel managed a shy smile. "You don't know how many times in the last few days I've lain awake thinking about us being a family."

"When you come stateside, we'll get married. It will end your military career, but you could be a civilian nurse if you wanted."

Rachel nodded. "I'd like that." She loved her career. Rachel was grateful Chase understood her needs. When the children came along, she would make a full-time career of motherhood, using her nursing knowledge and compassion for them.

Reaching up, Chase caressed her cheek. "Share your dreams with me," he whispered thickly. "Tell me what you're thinking."

Rachel began, her voice unsteady. "I'd like to have two boys and a girl. If the boys wanted to go into the military, I wouldn't mind. I see them being sensitive, like myself, and yet having your confidence and belief that they can do whatever they want."

"And our daughter? How do you see her?"

Rachel held his gaze, realizing there were tears in Chase's eyes. She pressed his hand against her cheek. "Exactly like me: headstrong, independent and capable. I never told you this, but my mother has red hair, even though I got black. I hope our daughter has her red hair, a banner to the world about what lies in her heart, her soul."

A warm feeling suffused Chase as he envisioned a red-haired daughter as feisty and spirited as Rachel. "What if she wanted to go into the military?"

"I wouldn't object. But I hope you'd allow our children to make up their own minds about carrying on the Trayhern tradition. I don't believe in browbeating a child into following in his father's footsteps."

Satisfaction sang through Chase. Rachel's cheek was warm and soft against the back of his hand. He ached to make slow, beautiful love to her. "I promise you, I won't push any of our kids into the service. They have to want it on their own." Then Chase whispered hoarsely, "You'll be a wonderful mother."

"I want to be a wonderful wife, too." Rachel closed her eyes, nuzzling into his large hand.

"You will be," he said, choking back the tears. "We've come this far together, Rachel. We'll go the rest of the way—together."

A ragged whisper of pain escaped Rachel. Turning her head, she pressed a small kiss into Chase's palm. "As much as I want to stay here and talk about our future, I've got to complete my rounds." She rose, sliding her hand to his shoulder. "Get some sleep. I'll see you tomorrow morning."

The light and dark lovingly embraced Rachel. Chase murmured her name, pulling her down so that he could kiss her just one more time. She came without hesitation, her lips meeting, melting against him. There was such softness and sweetness in Rachel as Chase molded his mouth to hers. It would only be a matter of days, perhaps a week, and he'd be transferred. As Chase reluctantly broke their kiss, he looked up into eyes that were lustrous with invitation. One that he wanted a lifetime to pursue.

"Rachel?" Doug Thornton knocked on the door to her tent.

"Come in, Doug." She had just come off duty and had removed her boots to give her tired, aching feet a well-deserved rest.

Doug shut the door, pushing back the parka hood. Outside, it was snowing again. "I know you want to catch some sleep, but I was over at Colonel Rhodes's office and heard that Chase will be transferred out of here tomorrow morning."

Her eyes widening, Rachel felt as if someone had hit her in the chest with a fist. "So soon?" It was more of a cry than a statement.

With a grimace, Doug nodded. "He's been here a week, Rachel. And his leg has stabilized to the point where he won't lose it." He added with a shake of his head, "I don't know how, but it has."

Chase was going to be torn away from her. Rachel sat on her cot, her hands in her lap. Each day, she had stolen precious moments away from surgery to visit him. They couldn't kiss or show how they felt toward each other during the day, but that didn't matter. They were getting the time to talk, explore and find out even more about one another. She had volunteered for night duty in order to be with Chase. In the hours of darkness, he had taught her the meaning of love through the simple act of kissing. Now she wanted more. So much more.

"Rachel?" Doug tipped his head to the side, grinning. "Where'd you go?"

"Sorry," she muttered. "Does Chase know yet?"

"No. I happened to be in the radio room when the orders came through for him. He's going by chopper to Taegu, and a transport will fly him to Japan. From there, he'll eventually get to San Francisco. In another month, he'll be ready to start therapy on that leg."

Incredible agony filled Rachel's heart. The feelings were so overwhelming, it was hard to think. This past week had been wonderful, a promise of things to come. "Thanks," she said, shaken, "for telling me, Doug."

"Got the duty tonight?"

"Yes."

"Good. Give that guy a proper goodbye." Doug pulled the hood back over his head and opened the door, leaving.

Rachel sat there a long time. She had four months without Chase stretching ahead of her. Tears welled up in her eyes and fell down her cheeks. Rachel would cry now, not later. She didn't want Chase to see her sad. She would try and make the parting as painless as possible for him.

Chase waited impatiently. The watch on his wrist read 12:10 a.m. Where was Rachel? Usually she appeared promptly at midnight. He sat propped up in the bed, his injured leg throbbing.

The doors at the end of recovery swung open. Rachel appeared in her olive fatigues, a stethoscope around her neck, clipboard in hand. Chase absorbed her shadowy features as she quietly moved from bed to bed, checking on each patient. Her black hair gleamed in the dull light, emphasizing her paleness. As she drew closer, Chase saw no life in her eyes and sensed something was wrong. Normally Rachel's eyes shone with welcome and happiness, which never ceased to lift his glum spirits. Being forced to stay in bed twenty-four hours a day was boring as hell.

Rachel forced a smile as she approached Chase's cot. "You're looking chipper tonight," she said in greeting. Taking the board from the end of his bed, she came over and popped the thermometer into his mouth before he could say anything. His eyes spoke for him, and Rachel trembled inwardly. The need to fulfill herself as a woman in his arms was almost tangible, a driving force so powerful that it left Rachel feeling weak in its path.

Chase watched as she expertly fitted the cuff around his left arm to take his blood pressure. "Why are you so pale?"

She slanted him a warning glance. "Chase, don't talk with the thermometer in your mouth. You know when you do, it just has to stay in there that much longer for an accurate reading."

His nostrils flared, and he watched her. Rachel was smiling, but it didn't reach her eyes. Each time her fingers touched his arm, they sent a wave of desire through Chase.

"I'm okay," she told him in a low voice that only he could hear. At this time of night, the other men were sleeping. Taking off the cuff and jotting down the findings, Rachel pulled the thermometer out of his mouth, reading it.

"Normal."

"Red-blooded American male, too."

She grinned and put the thermometer into a glass filled with alcohol. Sitting down, Rachel rested the clipboard on her lap. "No one knows that better than me."

"You're not well. What's going on?"

Rachel felt sadness overwhelm her. She tried to keep up her buoyant facade, but it wasn't working. "Have they told you yet?"

Chase picked up her hand, holding it gently. "What?"

Taking a deep breath, Rachel informed him about the transfer orders. Automatically Chase's hand tightened around hers. "I didn't want them hauling you out of here tomorrow morning before I could say goodbye."

Chase raised her hand, kissing each of her fingers. Her eyes grew languid as he turned it over, running his tongue across her palm, biting the soft pad gently and then smoothing it with a stroke of his tongue. Rachel's lips parted, her lashes lowering in reaction.

"I want to love you so damn badly," Chase said in a roughened tone.

"I know..." Rachel pulled her hand from his, her palm tingling wildly, heat pooling and collecting between her thighs as it always did when Chase touched her.

"Tomorrow morning?" He frowned and reached under his pillow.

"Yes, at 0800." Rachel tilted her head, watching him dig beneath the four pillows. "What are you looking for?"

"Nothing. Close your eyes, Miss McKenzie. I was planning on giving this to you next week, but the army, in all its lousy timing, has decided to kick me out of here sooner than I'd anticipated."

She obediently closed her eyes. "Chase, what are you up to? Two days ago, Chuck Dancey slipped you a bottle of whiskey and by the end of the day, half the guys in here were drunker than skunks. What did he do? Slip you another bottle?''

Grinning, Chase finally located a box, dragging it out of its hiding place. ''No, Miss McKenzie. Your starched-and-laced Maine background is showing again. So what if I passed the bottle around so each guy could have a swig or two? It sure as hell kills that antiseptic smell we have to lie in twenty-four hours a day.''

A laugh bubbled up in Rachel, chasing her sadness away for just a moment. ''You're incorrigible, Chase. I've said it before.''

''Okay, Angel Eyes, give me your hands.''

Rachel held out her hands. She felt Chase place something in them. ''Now open your eyes,'' he commanded. Rachel eyed the box. Frowning, she looked over at him. Chase was expectant, barely able to swallow the now-familiar catlike smile that lurked at the corners of his mouth whenever he was up to something.

''What is this?'' she demanded, examining the box closely.

''Open it and find out.''

Rachel gave him a dirty look. ''Annie said you gave one of our nurses a box like this the other day and it had a huge black rubber spider in it.''

Chuckling, Chase said, ''Well . . . the boys needed a little laugh, Rachel. The nurse that opened it screamed and threw the box sky-high. It hit the ceiling of the tent.'' He lifted his eyes upward, impressed. ''That's a long way.''

''Yes, and Susan hasn't been the same since. She hates spiders, Chase. That was a rotten trick to pull on her.''

"Ah, she's always such a sourpuss, honey. We just wanted to see if she had any emotion besides her standard all-business frown." Chase chuckled with satisfaction. "She does."

Rachel held his smiling eyes. "Chase Trayhern, I feel sorry for the nurses and doctors who are going to take care of you in San Francisco. You'll drive them crazy."

He agreed, motioning to the box she held. "Go on, open it. There's something in there to remind you of me."

"Sure. It's probably that rubber spider."

His eyes rounded. "Now, would I do that to you?"

Rachel wanted to reach out and embrace Chase. He looked like a precocious little boy, and she wanted to ruffle his hair with her fingers. "None of the nurses know what you've plotted or planned for them, Captain." She studied the cardboard box. "Give me one good reason why I should trust you enough to open this and probably get the wits scared out of me."

Chase sobered. "Because you love me."

A shiver of need coursed through Rachel. "Okay," she whispered, "I'll open it because I do love you." Cautiously she lifted the lid. Inside, surrounded by white tissue paper, was a smaller box. Taking it out, Rachel sprang the tiny gold latch and opened it. Although it was shadowy in the ward, Rachel saw the weak light strike a diamond ring set in gold. She gasped.

Chase watched her expression go from wariness to utter shock and then tenderness. "It's an engagement ring. Bob Shore, one of my squad mates, was going to Japan on leave, so I gave him the money and told him to find the most beautiful ring he could." Anxiously

NOW 4 titles every month!
See 45¢ Coupon on Back
Even if you've never read a historical romance before, you will discover the same great stories and favorite authors you've come to expect from Harlequin and Silhouette like Patricia Potter, Lucy Elliott, Ruth Langan and Heather Graham Pozzessere.
Enter the world of Harlequin and share the adventure.

Journey with Harlequin into the past and discover stories of cowboys and captains, pirates and princes in the romantic tradition of Harlequin.

Chase watched as she lightly touched the half-karat diamond. "I'm sorry I couldn't get it myself, but it's the thought that counts, honey."

Rachel had promised herself not to cry, but tears welled up in her eyes as she reverently held the box containing the ring. "It's so beautiful," she quavered.

Reaching over, Chase took the box, prying the ring from its pad. "You're beautiful. Give me your left hand, Angel Eyes. Come on...."

Sniffing, Rachel held out her left hand. Chase slipped the ring onto her finger. "There," he said with a growl of satisfaction, "this makes it legal." And then he smiled up at her tear-stained face. "See? I was serious about us getting married."

Rachel's heart broke as she drowned in Chase's solemn blue eyes. She had planned to be upbeat and positive over their separation and was failing miserably. Instead, it was Chase who was stronger and keeping their parting joyful. With a trembling hand, Rachel wiped away the tears.

"It's lovely, Chase." She watched the light ignite fire through the diamond.

"And you thought it was a rubber spider." Chase grinned.

Managing a choked laugh, Rachel continued to stare in shock at the ring on her finger. "No, it wasn't a spider."

"Now you can write your folks and tell them you're 'legally' engaged."

She leaned forward, framing Chase's face between her hands. "I love you," she whispered.

He settled his arms around her shoulders. "Prove it to me," he baited, feeling her moist breath against his face. "Show me, Angel Eyes. Give me a kiss that will last me four months. God, that's such a long time apart from you."

"I know," Rachel quavered, kissing each corner of his mouth, feeling his returning heat, his strength. Chase pulled her hard against him, his mouth capturing hers, beginning a wild, hungry assault that dissolved reality, hurling her into a world of bubbling liquid heat and light. The breath was torn from her as his mouth claimed hers in savage adoration. Rachel felt herself becoming sunlight, absorbed into Chase, carried on a river of fire that arced and raced throughout her. In those unshackled seconds, nothing existed but the man she loved with a growing fierceness that left her breathless and wanting more. Much more.

Chapter Twelve

"Captain Trayhern, I've got bad news for you."

Chase glared across the Travis Air Force Base operations desk at the enlisted man who worked in aircraft scheduling. "What?" he ground out.

"Sir, that transport carrying the medical personnel from Japan has been delayed by winds aloft. They aren't going to land for another hour." The clerk, dressed in a starched and pressed khaki uniform, gave him a sympathetic look. "I'm sorry, sir. I know you've been waiting a long time."

With a curt nod, Chase thanked him, limping away from the desk with the aid of a cane. He hated the cane, but it was better than hobbling around on crutches, which he'd thrown away last month.

Unhappy over the delay in Rachel's flight, his leg aching, he went over to the lounge filled with plastic-backed chairs and sat down. Military personnel were constantly moving in and out the doors leading to the landing apron where aircraft were parked. Most were wounded soldiers returning from Korea. Others, like himself, waited patiently for loved ones to arrive from overseas.

He stretched out his injured leg, scowling at it. Lately he'd been a bear about everything. Four months without Rachel had worn on him. He missed her more than he could ever tell her. One hour. One lousy hour longer before he'd have her in his arms, warm, alive and smiling. Chase rubbed his face tiredly. He hadn't slept well at the hospital this past week in anticipation of Rachel's arrival.

He slid his hand inside his Air Force blouse, pulling her last letter from his breast pocket. Holding the stationery to his nose, he inhaled the fragrance. Rachel always put a drop of perfume on the letters, and he'd appreciated the feminine touch.

Glancing out the double glass doors, Chase watched as a wife and two children waited anxiously on the steps, calling to a man walking wearily from a transport plane, his face slack with exhaustion. Chase saw the man's eyes light up with life as his wife ran down the steps, throwing herself into his waiting arms. He swallowed hard, unable to watch the poignant reunion. How would Rachel react to him? How was he going to behave? His hands shook as he carefully unfolded the long, thick letter.

Rachel wrote to him every day. He'd receive five or ten of her letters at a time, because getting mail out of Korea was inconsistent at best. Still, Chase had lived for those times when the postal orderly stopped at his bed and delivered a bundle of letters to him. It made up for those long, interminable days when he didn't receive any.

Her handwriting was pretty, the letters curved and flourished. *Like her,* he thought, lifting his chin, staring sightlessly through the crowd of civilian families milling around in the terminal, eagerly awaiting returning fathers, husbands and brothers. All the noise, the laughter and talk faded from Chase as he focused on Rachel's last letter.

The past four months had been hell on her, too, if her letters were any indication of how much she missed him. Chase memorized all her letters, running them through his mind and his heart. When pain from his healing leg kept him awake at night, he would narrow his world, his feelings, to just Rachel. Memories of her brought relief from the agony he suffered twenty-four hours a day.

Outside the windows, the sun had broken through the low-hanging stratus clouds that were as much a part of San Francisco as the Golden Gate Bridge was. Cargo transport planes trundled like overweight behemoths along the taxi strips, taking off or landing. There were always ambulances on the apron, waiting for the medical transports to disgorge their wounded occupants and carry them off to the military hospitals.

Chase remembered that time, frowning. The first week without Rachel had been pure, unadulterated hell. Chase glanced at his watch. How could a minute take so long to go by? And yet, in combat, a minute was a different kind of eternity. Still, these were the longest moments of his life, right now. He was unable to sit any longer, having been in bed too many months without much exercise. Resting wasn't his forte. Even though physical therapy was a special kind of hell, Chase looked forward to getting out of bed and leaving the ward for an hour or two each day. He'd return from therapy weak and exhausted.

Chase replaced the letter in his breast pocket and slowly got to his feet. The cane he carried in his left hand would be thrown away—soon. None of the nurses thought he'd recover so quickly. The doctors at the military hospital were pessimists at best. He didn't have much respect for them. Chase limped over to the row of unending windows, staying clear of the constant stream of traffic at the doors. The clouds were lifting and separating, letting thick slats of sunlight shaft downward to highlight the busy air base. It was spring, and the grass was a vivid green, surrounding the city of concrete hangars.

As he stood waiting, Chase wondered what Rachel was thinking, how she was feeling. Was she as excited as he was? Scared? Chase felt like an unraveling ball of emotions. He closed his eyes, wanting so badly just to feel her in his arms again.

Rachel pressed her hand against her heart, which was pounding like a kettledrum in her breast. The cargo plane had just landed at Travis. Inside the murky grayness of the fuselage, specially rigged cots contained many patients. She and five other nurses, all returning from their tour of Korea, had cared for the injured soldiers en route. Peeking out a window, she could see the tower and operations building in the distance. Was Chase waiting for her inside that large glass enclosure? Had he gotten her letter detailing the time and place she would arrive?

Rachel heard the plane's four engines change speed, the aircraft creaking and groaning as it trundled across the runway toward the operations building, known as Ops. She saw row upon row of waiting ambulances. She was the senior medical officer on board. Before she could go to Ops, she had to oversee the disembarkation of the patients. Rachel closed her eyes, taking a ragged breath. *Chase...* In her heart and mind, she could picture him. What did he look like now? How well was he walking? Was it true that he was already using a cane?

Rachel smiled, picturing Chase throwing his crutches into a wastebasket. That would be like him. His letters were life to her. He wrote every day, something that had surprised her. Men usually weren't letter writers. Her love for him had mushroomed over the months. It was as if Chase sensed that she needed the lifeline of his words and thoughts. Over the course of four months, the letters they had exchanged had made up for the brief period they'd known each other. Any communication trouble they'd had before was gone.

Every letter contained something new and fascinating about Chase—how he felt, what he believed or how he saw the world and himself. There were times that Rachel had sat in her tent, reading and rereading his letters. Sometimes she cried. Sometimes she broke into helpless gales of laughter over Chase's latest pranks on the hospital personnel. She was sure the nurses on his ward would be glad to see him go— sooner, rather than later. A smile tugged at her lips, and Rachel savored Chase's boyish good humor. He was a kid playing grown-up. And she loved him fiercely for that.

The plane drew to a halt, the brakes shrieking. The door was opened by a flight crewman, and the moist sixty-degree weather flowed into the fuselage, replacing the stale antiseptic atmosphere. Rachel unfastened her seat belt and got up, moving forward. For the next hour, it would be all business. And then, she would be free—free to see Chase.

Standing at the opening, Rachel looked across the concrete apron that separated her from Ops. It sat a quarter of a mile away, but it might as well have been an ocean of distance to her. She squinted against the sun, the wind lifting and playing with strands of her hair. A mass of civilians crowded the steps, waiting for their loved ones to be brought from the plane to the ambulances. Disappointment threaded through Rachel because she couldn't locate Chase. Perhaps he hadn't received her letter in time. Turning, Rachel tried to prepare herself emotionally for the fact that the doctors might not have allowed Chase to leave the hospital grounds to meet her.

Trying to put aside her own anxiety, Rachel rallied for the sake of the men. Even if Chase wasn't at Travis, she would find a way to get to him. Nothing was going to stop her. Nothing.

Glumly Chase stared out the windows. Ops was quiet once again, all the families of the injured having gone out to meet them at the ambulances. He'd spotted a red-haired nurse, a blonde and a brunette, who had directed the orderlies to ferry the patients off the plane and take them to the ambulance area. But at no time had he seen Rachel.

Turning away, Chase saw the last patient enter the ambulance. All three nurses walked from the plane toward Ops. Rachel hadn't been on the plane. He'd already questioned the scheduling clerk, but until the pilot left the plane with papers identifying everyone on board, Chase wouldn't know anything further.

His joy turned to pain, and he felt his heart exploding with grief. He'd waited so long for this day. Somehow, Rachel hadn't gotten on the plane. Maybe she was still back in Japan or worse, Korea. There could have been all kinds of travel snafus preventing her from arriving at Travis. Limping slowly toward the lounge to retrieve a cup of coffee and wait for the pilot, Chase knew there was nothing else to be done. But dammit, waiting was hard. Shoving his hand into his pocket, he felt around for the folded confirmation slip from the Mark Anthony Hotel where he'd made reservations for them. All his plans were destroyed.

"Chase!"

He jerked to a halt, his eyes widening. Rachel's voice. *No, impossible!* He twisted his head to the right. His mouth dropped open and his heart took one long, hard leap in his chest. Rachel stood poised just inside Ops' glass doors, her hair in disarray, her green eyes huge and beautiful with welcome.

"Rachel..." he whispered, turning around.

Rachel raced across the polished tiled expanse, her arms open, her hair flying across her shoulders. Chase stood, disbelief etched in his rugged features. As she closed the distance between them, Rachel saw tears in his blue eyes. Choking out his name, she slowed and threw her arms around his neck.

"Chase..." she quavered, pressing the length of her body against him, burying her face against his wool uniform.

"Oh, God, you're here...." Chase whispered raggedly, gathering her into his arms, holding her tightly—holding her forever. Chase plunged his face into her clean-smelling hair, groaning, taking her full weight. She felt so good against him, warm and pliant. His cane clattered to the floor as he lifted both hands to frame her joyous face. Tears streaked her flushed cheeks, but this time, they were tears of joy.

"I love you," he said simply, capturing her smiling mouth, drinking deeply of her sweetness, her liquid warmth. Seconds spiraled into forever as Chase hungrily kissed Rachel, tasting her lips, the corners of her mouth and finally, worshipping the inner softness of her. He felt her moan, her fingers digging frantically into his shoulders. They were both trembling.

Laughing breathlessly, Rachel touched Chase's face. "You're here, you're real...."

"Yeah, I am. God, you look more beautiful than ever," he whispered hoarsely, threading her silky hair through his fingers. "So beautiful..."

Rachel stood wrapped in Chase's arms, staring deeply into his eyes, absorbing his love, his emotions. "I'm sorry for the delay, but I had to unload all the patients before I could leave the plane," she said, her voice barely audible. "I tried to get the pilot to radio Ops to tell you I was here, but he cited regulations."

Chase's hands tightened on her shoulders, his eyes flashing with anger. "The bastard."

She grinned. "He's obviously not in love, or he'd have understood and made the call."

Chase stared down at her, unable to keep his hands off her. As always, Rachel's olive fatigues couldn't hide her womanliness from him. "You're here, that's all that counts," he said roughly.

Reaching up on tiptoe, Rachel kissed him repeatedly. They were little kisses all over his face, reminding Chase of a highly excited, squirming puppy.

Laughing, Chase groaned and held her hard against him. "You feel so good," he whispered. "You don't know how many times a night I dreamed of this moment, of feeling your softness, your heart against me...."

His words, low and gritty, created an ever-widening ache through her. Rachel nodded, content to be held, her head pressed to his chest and her arms around his waist. "I won't even tell you about my dreams," she admitted breathlessly.

Chase bent over, catching her amused green eyes. "Torrid, by any chance?" He saw her blush and laughed heartily. God, it felt good to laugh again. He was alive! Alive!

"I'm taking the Fifth on that one, Captain Trayhern." His smile drove through her like lightning illuminating the sky.

"Where's your duffel bag? We'll pick it up and leave. I've got a car parked out front and we've got reservations for the finest hotel in San Francisco."

Her heart picked up in beat. "One of the flight crewmen took all the duffel bags to Baggage Claim. A hotel?"

Chase nodded, his arm around her shoulders, keeping her close. "How does that sound?" As badly as Chase wanted to love her, he wasn't going to try to stampede Rachel into it. He saw momentary darkness in her eyes and added, "Listen, I love you. I'm not going to force you into anything, Rachel. If you want two rooms, I'll get us two rooms."

She rested her head wearily against his shoulder. The fifteen-hour flight had left her exhausted. "That's not it, Chase," she said softly.

"Then what is it?" he demanded, watching her worriedly.

A slight, deprecating smile pulled at Rachel's mouth. Lifting her lashes, she met his intense azure eyes. "I—well, I just felt scared for a moment, that was all. One room is fine."

Touched beyond words, Chase simply held her. It took a minute before he found his voice again. Caressing her hair, he managed an unsteady smile. "There is nothing I'm going to do that will ever cause you to be scared, honey. I love you too much to cause that look ever to come back to your eyes." Leaning down, he placed a tender kiss on Rachel's lips. "Trust me?"

His mouth was strong, cherishing, and Rachel smiled. "With my life, darling."

Giving her one last kiss, Chase leaned down and retrieved his cane. "Let's get your duffel bag and get the hell out of here. I don't know about you, but I'm starved for you, some good food and sheets that don't smell like the hospital."

"Chase..." Rachel breathed, turning around in the center of the suite, "this is a beautiful room!"

Having tipped the bellboy, Chase closed the door. Rachel stood in her heavy combat boots, a look of wonder on her face as she examined the sumptuous suite. He limped into the main room. An Oriental rug graced the floor, and the antique Queen Anne furniture highlighted the opulent room.

"Far cry from a tent in the middle of Korea, isn't it?" he asked dryly.

Rachel shook her head, giving him a wide-eyed look. "I never knew places this beautiful existed." She approached him, sliding her arms around his waist. Chase was unbearably handsome in uniform, proud and confident.

Leaning down, Chase caressed her smiling lips. "What do you want to do first?" he breathed.

Tiny ripples of expectation feathered through Rachel as she tasted the strength of his mouth. "A shower?" Her voice was unsteady, filled with longing.

"Together?"

She smiled shyly. "I never thought of that...."

"I have." Chase forced himself to stop kissing her, because he knew his own control was rapidly disintegrating.

"You've got a lot more experience in this sort of thing," Rachel accused, meeting his amused gaze. She watched as Chase dropped the cane into a chair and slowly unbuttoned his blouse. The shirt beneath it was starched and pressed to perfection, revealing the breadth of his chest. A pulse leaped at the base of her throat as she dragged her green eyes upward to meet his. Rachel drowned in the darkening blueness of them, snared within the heated look he shared with her.

"My experience is worth nothing if we can't share it together," he said huskily. Chase stood, watching the play of emotions across Rachel's face. He read yearning there, coupled with shyness and nervousness. Reaching out, he traced her cheek. "I want to show you how much I love you, Rachel. In all ways," he whispered hoarsely. "I've missed you, our conversations, our funny moments and our serious moments."

"Chase..." she murmured, and closed her eyes, his fingers brushing her flesh, creating a fire of urgency within her.

Picking up her hand, Chase drew her toward the large tiled bathroom. "Come on, Angel Eyes."

All her fear, her apprehension, vanished in the beauty of the moment that surrounded them. The lovemaking in the cave in Korea had been urgent and blindly hungry. Rachel hadn't thought of her nakedness, or his, then. Now she did. To her, it was like the first time all over again, in a different way. Chase turned on the shower and closed the bathroom door. Rachel stood on the thick rug within the rectangular bathroom, allowing Chase to unbutton the fatigues she wore. Drowning in the piercing blue of his eyes, she was surrounded with his love, and the need to return that love to him dissolved her fear. As each article of clothing dropped away, it became a symbol to Rachel of shedding her old way of living. Today she was with the man who had captured her heart and soul within his trembling hands as he reverently undressed her.

Reaching up, Rachel began to unbutton Chase's shirt, smiling into his eyes. The softened line of his mouth told her everything as she pushed the shirt off his broad shoulders, exposing his powerful chest, dark and thick with hair. She longed to press her fingertips against the tensile strength of his magnificent body.

Chase read those thoughts in her eyes. "Go ahead, touch me," he whispered hoarsely, settling his hands on her shoulders. "Like you did in Korea. I never

forgot the first time your fingers moved across me...."
A ragged groan came from Chase as her fingers glided
across his chest, tangling gently in the mat of hair,
sending prickles of pleasure through him.

The steam from the shower built within the room.
Mist-laden curls of heat flowed across the top of the
shower stall, silent fingers reminding Rachel that her
own hands caressed Chase's taut, hard flesh. As he
eased the straps of her bra from her shoulders, her
breath caught. It wasn't out of fear, but from the sensual movement of his hands exposing her breasts to
him.

"They're just as beautiful as before," Chase gritted out, gently cupping them in his hands. Looking
into Rachel's eyes, he saw their depths were dazed with
pleasure as he caressed her breasts' silky roundness,
watching the nipples harden into small pink rosebuds
begging to be lavished with attention. A ragged sigh
came from Rachel as Chase skimmed her nipples
lightly with his thumbs. She swayed toward him, her
fingers digging deeply into his upper arms.

"So hot, so willing," he breathed, capturing her
against his naked chest. A thin barrier of material remained between them. Rachel's mouth was liquid
warm with welcome, her kiss eager and hungry,
matching his need. As they stood in each other's arms,
drowning in the lava heat, Chase worked at slowly
discarding the rest of her lingerie. Her fingers trembled as she pulled the boxer shorts down his narrow
hips. In moments, they stood naked.

Chase moved his hand down Rachel's long, slender
back, fingers splayed, capturing her hips, drawing her
slowly against him. He groaned, feeling her rounded
belly against his hardness, feeling her tremble vio-

lently. He deepened the kiss that bound them. She felt
so good, her flesh pliant, yielding to his exploration.
Chase wanted to part her long, wonderfully curved
thighs and thrust deeply into her, burning to consum-
mate their coupling.

Shaking with barely controlled hunger, Chase drew
Rachel into the shower, sliding the glass door shut, the
steam swirling and curving sinuously between and
around them. Her eyes were half-closed, emerald with
fire, her lips pouty with the strength of their previous
kiss.

Water struck Rachel's back, rivulets streaming
down like hundreds of trailing fingers across her, in-
citing the fire already burning hotly within her. She
raised her hands, her fingers curving across Chase's
broad chest, watching satisfaction come to his eyes,
hearing his groan reverberate through the mist that
cloaked them. Now she understood Annie's words of
wisdom. There was far more to love than a kiss, a letter or a look. As Rachel skimmed her hands across his
shoulders and down his taut arms, she was enveloped
in the rightness of loving Chase.

Rachel's hair curled slightly, framing her flushed
face. Chase smiled, curving his hands downward from
her sculpted collarbone, across her smooth arms to
cup her breasts. Her lips parted, silently asking him to
touch her again. He saw the pleading in her eyes.
Bending his head, he drew the first wet bud into his
mouth, tasting her, tasting the sweetness of life from
her loving body. A cry tore from Rachel as he suckled
her, and Chase placed his hand behind her, drawing
her hotly against him. Heat and water mingled and slid
between them, creating more friction as he hungrily
sampled the other breast, feeling her fingers dig deeply

into his shoulders in convulsive movements tele-
graphing her pleasure.

All the lonely days and nights melded torridly together as Chase focused again on her pouty lips,
molding his mouth to Rachel in fiery celebration.
Sliding his hand down along the smooth roundness of
her belly, he sought and found the juncture of her
thighs. Whispering against her lips, he asked her to
trust him, and she did, allowing him entrance to that
moistness that brought tears of gratitude to his eyes.
She was more than ready to receive him. In one
movement, Chase lifted her against him, wildly aware
of her breasts sliding against his chest. Her thighs
parted as he gently brought her down upon him.
Rachel's arms tightened against his neck, and he heard
her gasp and then tense. He held her immobile, the
warm water trickling down upon them, the steam rising, playing and creating clouds of swirling heat.

Rachel felt his maleness press against her. The sensation was one of pressure, not pain. She longed to
complete herself with Chase, easing herself down upon
him. He whispered her name and moved within her. A
cry escaped Rachel, but it was one of triumph as she
arched her back, claiming Chase, claiming the one-
ness she had hungered for as much as he had. Each
slow movement of his hips excited her, sent more
throbbing fire curling within her and she moaned,
pressing herself against him in need.

Satisfaction soared through Chase as he moved her
languidly against him, hearing her cries of welcome.
Each stroke, each small movement drove him closer
and closer to the edge of exploding. He felt Rachel
tense, realizing that she was experiencing a climax.
Her little cry of surprise and joy was absorbed by the

steam. She lifted her face, lips parted, eyes closed and her body taut against him. Seconds later, he gave her the gift of himself. She was limp in his arms afterward as he gently withdrew from her hot, liquid core. Gently he settled Rachel on her feet, and she pressed her head against his wet chest. They rested weakly against each other, embraced by the life-giving warm water.

All Chase could do was stroke Rachel's sleek back and hips, cherishing her, placing small, loving kisses on her damp hair, temple and cheek. Gradually she regained her strength, giving him a tremulous smile filled with wonder and joy. Rachel leaned upward, kissing Chase tenderly, telling him in her newfound language that she wanted nothing but him for the rest of her life.

Chase soaped Rachel's back, running his fingers provocatively across her, spanning her belly. He brought her back against him, resting his head against her shoulder and neck.

"How many kids did you say you wanted?" he asked her thickly. Her belly was gently rounded, hips wide enough to deliver a strapping son, Chase thought, a fierce love welling up through him.

"Three," Rachel whispered, leaning her head on Chase and closing her eyes. She slid her fingers across his hands resting on her belly. "Two handsome, strong sons and one beautiful daughter."

Nibbling playfully on her delicate earlobe, Chase caressed her neck with a series of kisses. "Which do you want first?" he teased huskily.

"A boy." Rachel sighed, submitting to the delicious fire spreading hotly in the path of his mouth. "A girl should always have an older brother to look up to, don't you think?''

Chase met her emerald look beneath the black lashes framed with tiny beads of water. A very male smile pulled at his mouth. "Maybe every boy needs a big sister to look up to?"

As his hands moved provocatively upward, cradling her breasts, Rachel closed her eyes. "You've finally changed."

With a chuckle, Chase finished washing her. "I had to. You're the one that convinced me women can be just as independent and different as men are."

Turning around in his arms, Rachel lifted her chin, smiling into his laughter-filled eyes. "I love you, Chase Trayhern."

With a sigh, he covered her lips with a long, heated kiss. "Enough to marry me?"

His mouth was strong, capable, and Rachel relished his power at making her feel thoroughly feminine. "Of course..."

"Tonight?"

Her eyes widened considerably and she drew back. "Tonight?"

"Yeah? Like two hours from now?"

She gave him a wary look. "What are you up to now, Chase?"

Chase tried to give her a boyish grin, but Rachel's pretending to be miffed didn't work. Instead, he laughed, sliding his arms around her small waist, lifting her up against him, kissing her repeatedly.

Giggling, her hair in limp, ebony ropes around her face, Rachel held Chase. "You had this all planned. All of it!"

"I did," Chase admitted, licking the water streaming between her small breasts. "When you didn't come off that transport, I thought all my grand plans were scuttled."

Chase allowed Rachel to slide downward, the sensation creating a startling need for him all over again. Water softened the hard planes of his face and she shook her head. "What else have you got up your sleeve?"

"I've got a minister coming up in two hours, we'll be married, have a sumptuous dinner and go on our honeymoon."

Bewildered by his strategy, Rachel simply shook her head.

Alarmed, Chase blurted, "You don't want to get married?"

"Yes, I do."

"Then why did you shake your head? You don't want to eat? Or go on a honeymoon?"

His concern was touching, and Rachel took the soap, lathering his shoulders and magnificent chest. "I'm just amazed at that steel-trap mind of yours, Chase Trayhern, that's all."

Relief flooded his features. "Then... you want to get married, eat and honeymoon?"

Fingers sliding tantalizingly across his taut muscles, Rachel saw the effect she had on Chase. "I do...but not necessarily in that order...." She leaned upward, pressing a long, inviting kiss against his mouth. A shiver of expectation feathered through her when Chase growled, claiming her lips, his tongue tracing the inner curves of her mouth. Heaven was on earth, Rachel hazily decided, meeting and molding against his powerful male body.

Their children, Rachel realized, would be special in so many wonderful ways. They would inherit Chase's confidence and tenacity. From her, they would garner sensitivity and faith. Together, they would give the children of their future, courage, a hallmark they both possessed. With a sigh, Rachel succumbed to Chase's sweet, fiery assault, melting into his arms, wanting nothing more of the future. She had found her mate for life. A life that would be hard and demanding because Chase would always be part of the military. But they had the courage it would take to face it—together.

Epilogue

"And that night we spent at the hotel guaranteed you," Rachel said, giving Morgan a tender look, and sharing it with his wife, Laura.

Chase nodded, squeezing Rachel's shoulder tenderly. "Nine months to the day, she had you, son."

Morgan grinned bashfully, looking over at his brother and sister with their spouses. "I was the ten-pound sack of potatoes from what I hear."

Rachel rolled her eyes, looking up at Chase. "That you were! I blamed Chase during the forty hours I was in labor." Morgan resembled Chase most strongly of their two sons. Noah and Aly took after her.

"Yes," Chase added blandly, "and my ears have never been the same."

The family broke into laughter, and Chase's grin

broadened. "You even taught me some new cuss words."

"Chase Trayhern!" Rachel jabbed him lightly in the ribs. "That is a bald-faced contortion of the truth and you know it!"

Aly leaned forward, fondly looking at the last of the photographs in her album. "Mom, Dad, this has been the best Christmas we've ever had." She shook her head, running her fingers across the thick photo album. "The time it must have taken for you to do this for each of us..."

Rachel loved her daughter fiercely. Aly was a spitting image of her, in almost every way, just as she had promised Chase so long ago. "Honey, it was a labor of love."

"And we enjoyed going back over the memories," Chase added with feeling.

"Still," Noah added, glancing at his wife, Kit, who was holding their two squirming children in her lap, "it was a monumental task. Thanks."

Rachel's gaze moved lovingly around the circle of family that surrounded them. Melody climbed off Kit's lap, running over to her. Matthew, who was barely two, squirmed out of Kit's hold, too, following his older sister. Chase leaned down, picking up his red-haired grandson and tucking him tenderly into the crook of his arm.

"Your father and I want to thank all of you for coming, for sharing this holiday with us," Rachel said, a catch in her voice. Tears blurred her vision, and Melody reached up, touching the drifting tear curving down her cheek. Giving the little girl a kiss on the brow, Rachel added, "Now, you can begin photo albums for your own children."

Kit nodded, giving Noah a wry look. "I don't think anyone else in the family has to worry about having enough kids for the next generation of the Trayhern dynasty." She gently patted her belly, giving Rachel and Chase a soft smile. "I'm three months along with our third baby."

Rachel heard cries of surprise and saw the joy in everyone's faces over Kit's unexpected announcement. Noah and Kit were so happy together. Their love of children was obvious, as it was for each other.

Morgan cleared his throat, getting everyone's attention. "Well, I don't want to brag or anything, but—" he looked down significantly at Laura, her cheeks flushed a rosy pink "—do you want to tell them, sweetheart?"

Laura shyly looked up, her slender, artistic hands lying lovingly across her stomach. "Morgan..."

He grinned, pride in his eyes. "Laura's pregnant."

"Wonderful!" Aly cried, clapping her hands in delight. "How soon?"

Laura smiled up at her husband. "You can't keep any secrets, can you?"

Morgan's grin broadened, and he gripped her hand. "Not on something like this. Mom, Dad, Laura's going to have our first baby in June of next year. That was going to be our Christmas announcement to everyone. How about that?"

Chase observed that there were no dry eyes in the house. Morgan had gone through so much hell that he deserved this kind of incredible happiness. "I hope your child will give you as much joy as you did us, Morgan," he said, meaning it.

Morgan grew somber, remembering all the entire family had been put through because of him. "Thanks, Dad, that means a lot to me."

"Well," Aly said, grinning, "I don't have any pregnancy announcements, but Clay and I are going to be transferred next month." She grinned over to her parents. "Guess where?"

Rachel gasped. "Here? To Florida?"

"Yup," Aly said, satisfaction in her voice. "We'll be on special assignment with the Coast Guard down at Miami, flying high altitude, locating drug boats in the Caribbean."

"It's a three-year assignment," Clay added, smiling at his happy wife. "So, I imagine you'll be seeing us on a pretty regular basis. It's not too far between here and Clearwater."

Chase patted Rachel's shoulder. The news was all good. He knew how much she missed their children, how much she loved each of them. "I'd say this Christmas gathering has been the best ever. We've all come through some hard, trying and dark times."

"Together," Rachel whispered, Melody helping her continue to wipe the tears from her cheeks. "It was the love within the family that brought us all through it."

Chase gazed down at his Rachel, loving her more, if that was possible, than he did when he met her on that fateful day so long ago. In his eyes, she hadn't aged, the spirit of life in her eyes never dimming with the years. Leaning down, he pressed a kiss to her cheek.

"I love you," he whispered, catching her glance filled with incredible tenderness for him alone. "Forever..."

* * * * *

BEGINNING IN FEBRUARY FROM

SILHOUETTE

Western Lovers

An exciting new series by Elizabeth Lowell
Three fabulous love stories
Three sexy, tough, tantalizing heroes

In February, *Man of the Month* Tennessee Blackthorne in *OUTLAW*
In March,   Cash McQueen in *GRANITE MAN*
In April,   Nevada Blackthorne in *WARRIOR*

WESTERN LOVERS—Men as tough and untamed as the land they call home.

Only in *Silhouette Desire!*

DOU-1A

SILHOUETTE·INTIMATE·MOMENTS®

NORA ROBERTS
Night Shadow

People all over the city of Urbana were asking, Who was that masked man?

Assistant district attorney Deborah O'Roarke was the first to learn his secret identity . . . and her life would never be the same.

The stories of the lives and loves of the O'Roarke sisters began in January 1991 with NIGHT SHIFT, Silhouette Intimate Moments #365. And if you want to know more about Deborah and the man behind the mask, look for NIGHT SHADOW, Silhouette Intimate Moments #373, available in March at your favorite retail outlet.

NITE-1

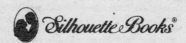 *Silhouette Books*®

MAN FROM THE NORTH COUNTRY
by Laurie Paige

What does Cupid have planned for the Aquarius man? Find out in February in MAN FROM THE NORTH COUNTRY by Laurie Paige—the second book in our WRITTEN IN THE STARS series!

Brittney Chapel tried explaining the sensible side of marriage to confirmed bachelor Daniel Montclair, but the gorgeous grizzly bear of a man from the north country wouldn't respond to reason. What was a woman to do with an unruly Aquarian? Tame him!

Spend the most romantic month of the year with MAN FROM THE NORTH COUNTRY by Laurie Paige in February... only from Silhouette Romance.

Silhouette Books®

FEBSTAR